B P Walter was born and raised in Essex. After spending his childhood and teenage years reading compulsively, he worked in bookshops then went to the University of Southampton to study Film and English followed by an MA in Film & Cultural Management. He is an alumni of the Faber Academy and currently works in social media coordination at Waterstones in London.

You can follow B P Walter on Twitter @BarnabyWalter

B P WALTER

A VERSION
OF THE TRUTH

This novel is entirely a work of fiction.
The names, characters and incidents portrayed in it are
the work of the author's imagination. Any resemblance to
actual persons, living or dead, events or localities is
entirely coincidental.

AVON

A division of HarperCollins*Publishers*
1 London Bridge Street,
London SE1 9GF

www.harpercollins.co.uk

A Paperback Original 2019

1

Copyright © B P Walter 2019

B P Walter asserts the moral right to
be identified as the author of this work

A catalogue record for this book is
available from the British Library

ISBN-13: 978-0-00-830961-9
TPB ISBN: 978-0-00-832341-7

Typeset in Bembo by
Palimpsest Book Production Ltd, Falkirk, Stirlingshire

Printed and bound in Great Britain by
CPI Group (UK) Ltd, Croydon CR0 4YY

MIX
Paper from
responsible sources
FSC™ C007454

This book is produced from independently certified FSC™ paper
to ensure responsible forest management.

For more information visit: www.harpercollins.co.uk/green

To my parents

Prologue

Knightsbridge, London, 2018

I'm reaching for a Mulberry purse when I feel someone standing close behind me. Too close. I edge to the side and turn round to see a small, blonde-haired woman standing there.

'Hello, Julianne,' she says. She smiles at me warmly.

I glance around. There's nobody else near us. She's a bit younger than me, probably late thirties, and is wearing a big, fluffy, blue coat, even though it's the height of summer outside. She starts to walk closer still and I take a step back.

'Hi,' I say, smiling back, worried she is someone I should know, although I don't recognise her at all. 'I'm so sorry, do I . . . ?' I feel her studying me, looking me up and down, almost like she's sussing me out.

'My name's Myanna. I'm an investigative journalist for the TV production company Exploration Media UK. I was wondering if I could have a quick word with you?'

I stare at her. 'How do you know my name? What's this regarding?' I'm still holding the purse and sense a shop assistant looking over at us. I feel like I've been caught in the act, doing something wrong.

'It's about your husband, James Knight. I need to talk to you. I was thinking we could go and get a coffee somewhere. Or maybe you could come into my office for a chat?'

My husband. Something about my husband. My mind is racing. Why does this woman know my name? And my husband's name?

'Please, Julianne. We really need to talk.'

The back of my neck is feeling hot and suddenly I want to get out of the shop, away from her.

'This is all very strange,' I say, and laugh a bit awkwardly. I take another look around to see if anyone else is listening, but we're still very much alone, apart from the shop assistant, who is now tidying the centre clothes display.

'Tell you what, take my card,' the woman says, reaching into her bag and then holding her hand out towards me. 'I don't want to force you into anything, but I would really like us to meet. I think you might know what this is about. So, when you're ready, just give me a call.' Her voice softens. 'And I'm sorry if I startled you. I'm on your side, Julianne.'

With that, she is gone, and I'm left standing in the Harrods accessories section, her card clasped between my fingers, wondering why it feels like the ground is moving beneath me.

Chapter 1

Julianne

Knightsbridge, London, 2019

I lay my hands on the kitchen work surface and let my head fall a bit, just enough so the strands of my hair stay clear of the water in the sink. The sense of exhaustion throbs through me. Christmas should be an enjoyable time, but this year it feels like a stress on the calendar. I do love it, I really do, all the lights on the trees and the cold, although it never gets as cold as my childhood in Chicago. I've always thought that when English people moan about the weather they should be transported to the Windy City in the middle of winter. Then they'd really feel cold. Some part of me misses it; the layering up as if you're about to go on some huge expedition up a mountain when you're actually just going to the library or the shops.

I hear movement behind me by the door of the kitchen. 'Do you fancy a top-up of wine?' I call out to my husband. 'My mother will be arriving soon, so you'd better get in quickly before she drinks us out of house and home.'

I take a pan of vegetables off the AGA as I talk, the billowing steam coating my face in a sheen of moisture.

'Mum?'

My son's voice takes me by surprise. He's looking at the floor and something about his face makes me stop. Has he been crying? His eyes look red. Not red enough for me to rush to him and ask him what's wrong, but just slightly tinged at the corners. He may be approaching his eighteenth birthday, but it's amazing what little details can wind back the years and remind you that, not so long ago, your tall man-in-training was just a small, frightened child. Maybe he's unwell, or his hay fever has been flaring up again. Unlikely in December, though.

'Oh, sorry, honey. I thought you were Dad. You can have some wine, too. One glass.' I wink at him and smile. I'm well aware his classmates are probably knocking back beer, wine, vodka and God knows what else every night in the run-up to Christmas. Not my Stephen, though. He's not one of those seventeen-year-olds.

'I'm cool with a Coke.' He walks to the fridge and gets himself a can. He pours it in silence and then turns back to face me.

'Mum,' he says again, then hesitates.

I keep my smile going, but feel a slight coldness in

my stomach. That simple word can be said in a whole galaxy of different ways. With love when they say goodnight, with anger when you tell them they have to do their homework, with annoyance when you probe too far into their personal lives or ask about who they're dating. And then there are the times when they say 'Mum' in a way that makes your blood freeze in your veins. It's immediately clear: something is very wrong. My mind starts to run wild, offering me a slide show of different horror stories, each more dismaying than the last. Maybe he wants to drop out of doing his exams? Is he being bullied? Has he got himself mixed up in something awful or criminal?

'Stephen, honey, what is it?' I say. I want to go to him and hug him but have learnt from experience it's best not to crowd a teenager when they are about to tell you a piece of information that's clearly causing them concern. In their overtaxed brains, flight is often an attractive solution to dealing with a problem. It's best to stand well clear until the danger of this has passed.

Stephen moves his head, looking at the floor, as if he's trying to gather his words but failing to get them in order. I try to be patient but fail. 'Is it to do with your exams after Christmas?' I see his face tighten as a result and curse myself for starting the interrogation too soon.

'It's . . . it's nothing to do with that.' He shakes his head, like he's trying to brush his own thoughts away. I continue to stare, trying to keep my imagination at bay and remain calm.

'Boyfriend trouble? Is it a problem with Will, then?

Have you two had a fight?' He winces, though I'm not sure if this is because I'm wrong in my presumption or because of my use of the word 'fight'. He's always been quite brutal about my 'Americanisms', as he calls them.

'No, nothing to do with him either. It's about . . . it's about . . . Dad.'

This catches me by surprise.

'What do you mean?' I say, letting out a small, odd-sounding laugh. 'What's Dad done? Has he upset you about something? I know he goes a bit crazy with the pressure and all his talk about Oxford, but that's only because he wants the—'

'The best for me, I know.' He cuts me off. His eyes are staring somewhere above my shoulder, still not meeting my gaze. 'I told you, it isn't anything about exams.'

'Then I don't see what he's done to upset you.'

'It . . . it isn't like that. Forget it. I'm sorry, it was stupid to bring it up now. Especially when you're doing all this for tonight and have your dinner party on Monday . . .'

'It's only Grandma coming to dinner, not a CIA operation,' I say, playing down my own stresses. 'And "dinner party" might be a bit of an overstatement – it's just Ally and Louise and Ernest.' The mere thought of the three of them descending upon us for our usual Christmas gathering makes me feel instantly tired, but I don't let it show. 'Just tell me. I'm sure it's nothing we can't fix. Has he said something about me? Something I've done wrong? Have I upset him? God knows it can be easy to, sometimes.'

'No, nothing like that.'

I feel myself getting exasperated. 'Darling, you keep saying that but don't actually say what it is about. How can I help if I don't know what it is? Are you in trouble with the law? I'm going to keep guessing until you tell me.'

'I'm sorry, I'm being stupid, it's really nothing. Do you need any help with the plates and stuff?' He gestures at the kitchen table.

'No, it's all under control,' I say distractedly, wishing it were true and trying not to think how many more things need to be done before my mother arrives. Now he looks me in the eye and I see fear. It's cold and stark and horrible, the look a mother hates to see in the eyes of her child. I move a few steps forward and take his shoulders in my hands, feel his warmth and the firm muscles beneath his Abercrombie sweater. 'Tell me.' I say it calmly but firmly and he opens his mouth to speak.

'Could you . . . could you quickly come upstairs for a minute?'

My concerns about the unprepared food fall away quickly. 'Of course,' I say. 'Lead the way.'

As soon as we are upstairs, he leads me into his room and gestures at me to close the door. 'Tell me now, what's wrong.' I walk to the other side of the room and sit down on his desk chair, facing him.

'I shouldn't have said anything,' he mutters. He keeps glancing at the door as if it's going to burst open at any moment.

The sentence frustrates me. How can he expect me to accept that as an answer?

'Honey, Dad can't hear us. I'm fairly sure he's downstairs in the library, avoiding me in case I give him a job to do. We're alone. And I'm not leaving until you tell me.' I'm talking firmly now. Firm, but kind.

He finally looks me in the eye, takes a deep breath, apparently trying to choose his words carefully, and says: 'I found something. Something a bit strange.'

'Found what?' My mind starts diving wildly to various different things he could have found. What does his father keep secret? Does he have a gun? That possibility is so unlikely it almost makes me laugh. Maybe evidence of an affair. That one sends a cold chill crawling across my skin.

'It's . . . it's a bit hard to explain. They're files. Files I found on Dropbox. In his folder.'

This takes me by surprise. 'What? What do you mean? Why were you looking through his Dropbox folder?'

He sighs and rubs his eyes. This is clearly torture for him. I just want to hug him, but I'm scared of interrupting his explanation, so I sit still.

'It's . . . I think it's something bad. Like, really bad.'

That cold chill is back. I really don't like where this is going. A dark, menacing mass is forming in my head, as if it's been let out of a deep, sickening recess of my mind.

'What kind of thing are we talking about here?'

He stares at me and, for the first time this evening, I see resolve in his eyes. He's going to tell me everything.

'I think I'd better just show you.'

I nod, preparing for the worst.

'Okay. Let me see.'

Chapter 2

Julianne

Knightsbridge, London, 2019

I can feel myself getting colder, an ice cube making its way down my neck, across my back, burning its icy stain into my blood.

'I really don't want to rush you, but I don't think we have much time.' I try to sound kind, rather than impatient, but waiting for Stephen to snap into action is making me tenser by the second.

His eyes are starting to overspill and I reach out to put a hand on his shoulder.

'Please, Stephen, I need you to show me. Right now. It may not be what you think it is. You may have got the wrong idea.'

He just shakes his head.

'Is that a 'no' as in you won't explain, or 'no' as in you won't show me, or 'no' as in you haven't got the wrong idea?' My smooth tone is breaking at the seams, my impatience to discover if the worst is true tearing me apart inside.

'No, as in I don't know. I'm not sure. I just know it's been eating me up for two days now and I need to talk to you about it.' After a pause, he goes to a bag by his bed and takes the device out of its leather case. I sit down on his desk chair while he perches on the bed and starts tapping away on the tablet, his face bathed in the blue-white glow of the screen.

'And you don't think this could be anything to do with his work?' I say, partly to fill the silence.

'I don't know, that's why I wanted to show you.'

I nod and wait. Overall, James keeps his work to himself, a lot of it bound up in such rigorous confidentiality it's hard for him sometimes to even vaguely explain what project he's working on. My mother once joked that he was like a spy – a bit of a James Bond – but I assured her the job of a head analyst and coordinator at a data services company is one full of spreadsheets, desk work and boardroom meetings rather than anything very exciting.

Stephen is offering me the iPad. I take hold of it and glance at the screen, a mass of files in front of me. From the ends of the file names, I can see they're PDF documents. There's something in this that comforts me. At the back of my mind, I think there was a part of me that expected to see .mov or .mp4. But these aren't videos.

12

That's a good thing, surely? I scan down the list and then turn towards Stephen.

'And these were in his Dropbox file?' I ask.

'In *our* Dropbox. The family one. The one we use to transfer photos and things and where I used to put my homework back when you wanted to check it over before submission. It's Dad's section of it. I clicked on it by mistake.'

This makes me feel ever so slightly better. If James had anything to hide, surely he'd be a little more savvy about protecting it than to upload it all to the family Dropbox account, the place I store family holiday snaps and copies of dull household documents like the TV insurance details?

'Tap on one of the files listed here.' His voice sounds strained, as if he's trying to calm himself.

I look over at him. 'If you're really that worried, I can look at these later? We don't have to do this now.' As I say this, though, I know there's no chance of me happily going back downstairs to carry on with the cooking. I need to know what this is about.

'No, I'm fine,' he says, and moves to the edge of the bed, crouching forward, his elbows resting on his knees. He looks like he's about to take a particularly gruelling exam.

I focus back on the iPad and, as instructed, tap on the first in the list of files. They're all unnamed, save for a list of seemingly random numbers and the file type. A document appears on the screen and I turn the device to view it in portrait mode.

A company logo is the only thing on the page. **Clover Shore Construction** is all it says, with a small clover leaf at the end of it. Underneath, in all-caps Times New Roman font, it says: **BUSINESS PROPOSAL**.

I flick the page with my hand and it changes, this time bringing up what looks like some kind of CV or personal profile, with a photo at the top of the page, followed by a name, date of birth and separate categories filled with bullet points. I look at the photo. It's of a young woman. She isn't looking into the camera; her eyes seem vacant, staring off into the distance. There's something about her expression that I find quietly alarming. It's as though she's drunk or stoned and doesn't quite know she's having her photo taken. Although it's a colour photo, her skin is pallid and grey, her dark hair untidy and her face drawn in and gaunt-looking.

'Who is this?' I say out loud, though more to myself than to Stephen.

'Read the information. It's pretty specific.'

I take a look and see what he means.

Name: Ashley Brooks
Date of Birth: 12 March 1989
Occupation: Officially unemployed,
    ex-stripper, occasional sex worker
Area: Ilford, East London
Reference: Daffodil

'I've never heard of an Ashley Brooks,' I say. 'This is . . . this is very strange.'

'It gets more detailed as it goes on,' Stephen says.

I continue to read.

14

Lifestyle details:
- Ashley is dependent on a variety of legal and illegal substances, including heroin and cocaine. Best knowledge indicates she's been using since she was eighteen.
- She's rarely seen out of her flat. When she is, it's usually to buy alcohol from the independent off-licence near her council flat in Ilford. She has been seen shouting expletives at random passers-by and crying in public.
- She doesn't own a car, nor has she been observed using public transport within the last six months.
- She lives alone. Occasionally young men are seen delivering packages to her door – believed to be illicit substances. Sometimes they go inside, but usually do the transactions on the doorstep.

Crime:
- She's been twice observed having sex in public, once in the car park of the Billington Estate where she lives, and on another occasion was issued with a caution by police after being observed performing oral sex on a young man at a bus stop late at night.
- She was arrested and charged with possession of a Class B drug in April 2012. She did not serve prison time.
- She was arrested for drunk and disorderly

**behaviour near her flat in September 2016.
She was released without charge.**

I look up from the iPad at Stephen. He's still looking at the floor.

'How would anyone know all this if it didn't come from the police or lawyers or somewhere?'

He shrugs. 'I don't know. That's what makes it so strange.'

I look back down at the screen.

Support network:
- **Best knowledge suggests Ms Brooks has not been in contact with her mother or father for many years. Her mother is currently serving time in HMP Bronzefield in Surrey for GBH and the attempted murder of a man she was previously living with. Her daughter has never visited her.**
- **It is not believed Ms Brooks has any close friends or acquaintances outside the group of men who deliver her drugs.**
- **She does not have a consistent romantic interest or sexual partner.**
- **She has no siblings.**

Risk:
- **Ms Brooks is considered a low-risk potential investment.**
- **Trial runs, completed by our staff, have been highly successful, embarked upon by men**

posing as tax officials, social services workers and gas-meter inspectors. These have been undertaken using both single and multiple participants. She has reported none of these incidents and her behaviour has not changed other than a potential increase in drug purchases. We believe it is highly unlikely any reports to police would be made after future appointments of this nature.

- **During a trial run, a blood sample was taken. Ms Brooks tested negative for HIV or hepatitis as of August 2019. In spite of this, use of contraception is always strongly advised.**

I finish the page and stare back at Stephen. 'I really don't know what to say about this,' I tell him. It's the truth. I'm completely baffled and appalled. This Ms Brooks seems to have had important information meticulously detailed. Everything gathered together, from her lifestyle and sex life to her criminal record. And all of it points to a very vulnerable, unwell young woman.

'I don't know what this is, but I think . . . I think we best . . .'

'Best what?' asks Stephen, looking up at me, moving his eyes, apparently reluctantly, away from the floor.

'I don't know. It just seems so likely this is part of your dad's work. I know it's not pretty, but maybe they gather information for the police or some law enforcement agency . . .'

'I don't think he's allowed to bring it home.'

17

He's got me there. But then again, what do I know? Neither of us knows that much about the way James works in his current position at data-gathering company Varvello Analytics. The thing nagging at me, quietly but firmly at the back of my head, is that this is in our personal Dropbox. Not his work account. Not even his *own* personal account. If they were work documents, surely he would have had to transfer the files and pass-word-protect them?

There's another thing troubling me. 'When you said to me that it was something bad . . . I sort of expected . . . I don't know . . . something involving porn . . . or maybe . . . God, this sounds ridiculous . . . evidence of an affair . . .'

'I'm sorry.'

I touch his arm, 'No, no, it's okay,' I say, trying to sound comforting. 'How many of these have you looked at?'

'All of them.'

'And they're all like this? The same sort of thing?'

He nods.

I don't know what to say to this at first. Then something falls into my head – a strange sensation, almost like déjà vu. That we've been here before. 'You know a few years back, when you had all that stuff on your computer. All those images of naked women that kept opening every time you clicked on something . . .'

Stephen looks up sharply and cuts me off, 'That was a virus.'

'Yes, I know.' I hold up a hand to offer reassurance, but he looks offended.

'Are you saying you think this has something to do with me?'

'No, I'm just trying to make sense of it. And it reminded me of it, that's all. Could this be the same thing? A virus your dad has downloaded, maybe when he was buying something or downloading music? And he got a load of someone else's content by mistake?'

Stephen shakes his head, 'He downloads music from iTunes. I can't imagine him buying anything from anywhere . . . well . . . dodgy. And anyway, why would the files turn up on our family Dropbox, in his folder?'

'I . . . no . . . it doesn't make sense. I just don't understand how . . .'

I stop talking. Both Stephen and I have heard it. Someone is coming up the stairs. And there's only one other person in the house. We look at each other, as if we're two children about to be caught doing something we shouldn't. I stay very still and hear the sound of my husband going into our shared bedroom, then the noise of a drawer opening and closing. He must just be looking for something or changing his sweater. The noise of him coming back out onto the landing causes Stephen's eyes to widen in alarm, but I shake my head. It's okay. The sound of his feet is growing distant and, after a few seconds, the creak of the stairs signals his retreat back down to the hallway.

I let out a breath I only now realise I've been holding the whole time, and turn back to the screen. Do I carry on after our close shave? Or give him back his iPad, tell myself it's going to be fine and just talk to James later, ask him to explain, get everything out in the open? After nearly a minute of us sitting in silence, Stephen hunched over, watching me, I go back to the iPad and click on the second file.

It's almost identical in layout to the first, except the photo is of a different woman – a young black girl. She's smiling, holding a drink up to the camera. I cast my eye down her details.

Name: Carly Gale
Date of Birth: 1 April 1991
Occupation: Sex worker, former shop assis-
    tant, now officially unemployed
Area: Clapham, South-West London
Reference: Daisy

Another sex worker, I think, a chill moving down the back of my neck. I read through the rest of her details. She used to be employed in a clothes shop in Central London but after making an allegation of sexual assault against her manager left her job and hasn't been employed since. She, too, has no support network to speak of. The phrase 'trial run' once again catches my eye. What does this refer to? Was this some kind of brothel agency? Was my husband seeing prostitutes?

- **No attempts to contact police have been made since the second trial run in February 2019. Ms Gale tested negative for HIV and hepatitis as of this second trial run.**

20

Participants are still strongly advised to use protection.

These aren't prostitutes. This information is telling a far more sinister story. One I can't get my head around right now, especially not with my teenage son watching me. The screen blurs suddenly and I think something's gone wrong with the iPad, then realise it's my eyes. Without me realising, they've filled with tears that now begin to stream down my face.

'Mum?' Stephen says.

'I'm all right.' I quickly brush them away. Then I hear the doorbell.

'Julianne?'

Stephen's face drains of colour as soon as he hears his father's voice. I instantly hit the lock button on the iPad, like a child caught with their hands in the cookie jar. *Fuck*, I think to myself.

'Julianne?' I can tell he's at the door to the kitchen, probably confused as to where I've got to. 'Where are you?' he calls up the stairs now.

'We need to go back downstairs.' I go to hand him back the iPad, then a thought strikes me.

'Hang on just one minute.' Without thinking too much about what I'm doing, I open the tablet again, navigate back to the folder of files and take a screenshot, capturing the full file path information.

'What are you doing?' Stephen asks.

'Don't worry about it now.' I rush what I'm doing, clicking the home button and locating the Facebook

21

Messenger tab on the menu screen, finding myself on the list of Stephen's chats. I send the screenshot to myself.

'We'll talk about all of this later. We will. Just . . . just try not to think about it . . . There'll be an explanation.' I'm talking fast, trying to stifle the panic I can feel building within me. I give him back the tablet as I make for the door.

'Okay,' he says.

'Julianne?' James's voice is louder this time. 'Sorry, Diane, I'll find out where she's got to.'

In spite of my panic, there's a familiar feeling of irritation bristling within me. Can't he deal with his mother-in-law on his own for five minutes? Why do I always have to play the host?

'I'm coming!' I shout back, trying to sound normal. Walking the short distance across the landing and down the stairs feels like I'm doing the last leg of a double marathon. I keep thinking I'm going to stumble and fall, but I hold on tight to the handrail and press on, determined. Determined not to believe the worst. Determined to shake the horrible feeling that something, finally, is threatening to shake the foundations of what we've built together. Determined to remain convinced he'll explain everything, clearly and calmly, and all of this will go away. He'll tell me the documents are something he accidentally got sent. Or important documents from his work that somehow ended up in the wrong folder. He'll tell me how sorry he is that I had to worry about all this, especially at Christmas, and that I should put it all out of my mind and forget about it. I think of the relief I will feel when I hear those words.

Chapter 3

Holly

Oxford, 1990

Oxford wasn't for the likes of me, that's what my father told me. He even repeated it as we were driving up towards the halls of residence. 'We're simple folk, you, me and your mum. Don't forget these types have had it all. Don't forget you're different.'

I hopped out of the car first to speak to one of the stewards showing us where to park, asking the best way to negotiate the trailer through the tiny lane that snaked around Hawksmith Hall – my new home away from home. I'd been worried Dad would bring the trailer ever since he and Mum had started working out the logistics of taking me and my stuff up there on my first day. I knew he had a customer in a village just outside of Oxford – I'd almost missed my interview when he'd insisted on having his 'business meeting' first. Business meeting. More like ripping off an overenthusiastic collector. He had been working in the antiques business for about ten years, ever since the chemical factory had made him redundant. Old furniture, great big chests, mirrors, tables, all sorts really, anything you could use to furnish a home. He'd bought loads of books on the subject of antiques dealing. I'd been surprised there were that many, but apparently it was an area of interest for a lot of 'retired people'. That was how he always put it: 'retired'. Never 'laid off' or 'redundant'.

Once we finally got ourselves sorted in the car park and the trailer was safely out of the way next to a wall of bushes, I ventured in and up the stairs, carrying a bag in one hand and my key in the other. My parents followed behind me, lugging the heavier bags. I'd told them I would come back to get them but they were as keen as I was to see where I'd be staying. 'Very nice,' my mum kept saying as we climbed the stone steps to the first floor. 'Thank God you got that grant, Holly,' she said in a whisper, which still carried audibly through the corridor. 'It's good you get to experience a place like this.'

'Mum, please,' I murmured. I didn't mind people knowing I hadn't been born with a silver spoon in my mouth, but it wasn't something I wanted broadcasting as I walked through the door. Besides, there must be a lot of people here who didn't come from privilege. This was the 1990s. Class was something we were leaving behind, wasn't it?

The room was spacious, if not exactly homely. It looked rather grand, as if someone had converted part of a cathedral into a living space. The bed was a single, but more than adequate, and the floor had a large, deep-red rug in the centre. In the far corner were a desk and chair. I placed the bag I was holding on the bed and turned to my parents, taking in their reactions.

'Very nice,' Mum kept saying. 'Very, very nice.'

'You'll be comfy here,' said Dad, as if he'd parked me in a B&B. I think he was rather overwhelmed by the whole thing. In fact, I knew he was by the way he kept looking around and then quickly focusing on the floor, as if someone might notice him staring.

'Can you guys stay here while I get the last few bags from the car?' I said, slightly worried about leaving them. They might wander.

'Of course, love, but we can come and help.'

'No, Dad, it's fine,' I said, backing out of the door. 'I'll be back in a minute.'

I left before they could protest any further and walked the short distance back to the car. When I got there, I saw three girls standing by it, looking at something. As I got closer, I could see they were peering over into the car and laughing. I felt rather nervous as I approached, worried they'd try to speak to me, and when they saw me they took a step back. One of them looked a bit embarrassed, as if she'd been caught out, but the other two had looks on their faces that weren't quite as nice.

'Is this yours?' one of them asked.

I eyed her suspiciously and replied that, yes, it was and

asked if there was a problem. One of the other girls laughed, while the one I was speaking to just looked back at the old car, partly splashed with mud, the boot slightly dented from a minor back-end collision a year ago. I saw her eyes flick to the trailer, the old, ripped covering my dad used to cover up whatever was being transported bundled in the back, and then they fell back on me. She didn't say anything. Just looked me up and down one last time and walked away, the other two following her like sheep. I waited until they'd disappeared out of sight around the side of the building before opening the car. There were more bags left than I'd realised and I tutted to myself at the thought of having to come back again for the rest. I didn't really want to admit how they'd made me feel in our half a minute of meeting, but the sense of unease I'd had ever since getting the letter of acceptance from Oxford had suddenly become a lot stronger.

Back in my room, my parents helped me unpack for a bit, but I could tell Dad was itching to head off to meet his antiques contact. Mum, on the other hand, had settled herself on the bed and was unballing my socks from the bag and folding them neatly. At one point a girl knocked on our door asking if we knew the way to somewhere called Gallery Heights as she'd been looking around for ages. I tried to answer quickly, but my dad got in first: 'We're not locals, love. Never been here in my life. Apart from when I was a teenager. Not at the university – God, no – but as a lad when I was working for the railways . . .'

'Dad.' I cut in to rescue the girl, who was looking at

him as if he were a strange animal in a zoo. I turned to face her. 'I'm sorry, I've only just arrived and I don't really know the way around myself.'

The girl nodded. 'Oh, no problem,' she said stiffly, then vanished from the doorway.

After another awkward twenty minutes of unpacking and questions from Mum on where I'd be keeping my knickers and 'lady things', we all traipsed back down to the car to get my last two bags.

'Full of books, I bet,' Dad said, shaking his head, lifting one of the bags out. 'Well, I suppose you proved they had some worth, getting into this place. Never understand how you have the patience, love.' I'd heard this speech more times than I wanted to remember and didn't respond now. All through my childhood I'd been treated like some weird outcast, as if spending one's weekends buried in a novel were a sign of derangement. Mum frequently made comments about how I'd never really made an effort with 'more traditional things', like make-up and nice clothes. When I'd told her there wasn't much point, as we couldn't afford expensive make-up and nice clothes, she'd told me I was ungrateful. Maybe I was. Or maybe I was just angry at not being allowed the thing I alone enjoyed without being made to feel bad about it whenever someone else came into the room.

'You guys can get going. I'm fine from here, honestly.'

Mum looked doubtful. 'Are you sure?'

I nodded and tried to give her an encouraging smile. 'Yes, very sure.'

She hugged me and then so did Dad, a little more

awkwardly, and then they got in their car and drove off, Mum giving a little wave out of the window as she went.

It only took just over an hour to get the unpacking finished and organised neatly into drawers and the rather generous cupboard standing up against one of the stone walls. Its dark, mahogany doors made me think back to a similar kind of thing my grandfather had when I was a little girl. I used to play hide and seek with him, well aware he wouldn't ever find me. He knew where I was, of course, but he let me win.

I sat down on the bed and scuffed my shoes on the rug. What now? I thought I should go and meet some other people. I knew there would be a gathering of some sort down in the common room, and we'd be given older students as sort of parents so we had a first port of call if we ever needed to talk to someone who knew the university back to front. I was about to get up when there was a knock on the door.

'Come in,' I called, then, realising it was on the latch, said, 'Oh, hold on a moment.' I ran to the door, hurriedly flattening down my hair as I did so in case I looked like a crazy blonde haystack. I unlocked the door and opened it to find a beaming girl's face greeting me.

'Hi,' she said, very loudly – too loudly, I thought, considering I was standing right in front of her. 'How's it all going? Have you got unpacked yet? Absolute nightmare, isn't it? I've only got through one and a half bags.'

She strode past me and stood, hands on her waist, looking about.

'Oh my gosh, how tidy you are! We are going to be such friends, I know it. They say opposites attract and I am hands down the messiest person you've ever come across. Honestly, it's scary.'

Her low, rather plummy voice was both reassuring in its confidence and intimidating in its speed. I smiled politely and thought I'd better take things back to simpler, more introductory areas of conversation. 'Hi, I'm Holly.'

'Oh, of course you are, of course you are. So sorry. What a lovely name, too. Holly. Holly.' She said it out loud twice, as if trying it on for size, then nodded. 'Good, good. I'm Aphrodite. My mum did classics. Obsessed with Greece. Bit of a freak. You can call me Ally, though. Everyone does. What kind of fucking sadist names their own child Aphrodite, eh?'

'Umm, one obsessed with Greece, I suppose,' I said feebly, hoping it sounded like a light-hearted response rather than an insult towards her mother.

'You've got it in one. Totally bonkers, all of my family are. Though they think I'm stark raving mad for wanting to come here.'

I raised my eyebrows at this. Her accent was very upper class, but maybe that was just affected. Maybe she actually did come from a relatively normal family like mine. 'Are you the first in your family to go to uni?' I asked.

She looked at me as if I'd suddenly spoken to her in Japanese. 'No, of course not. But they all went to sodding Cambridge. I'm the rebel who went to Oxford . . . well, Ernest and I. My brother, Ernest. We're twins, but he is light years more intelligent than I am. Thinks I talk like a commoner.'

I laughed nervously, worrying what he'd think of my accent if he thought she sounded common.

'He's already here. In the year above. Started early. You'll meet him. Everyone does at some point. Rampant shagger, my darling brother. He'd have his eye on you. Blonde hair, blue eyes, slim figure and a vagina. You're ticking all the boxes so far, so watch out.' She let out a low rumble of laughter. I was reminded of a gym teacher we had when I was seven. Miss Marks, I think her name was. Her laugh seemed to reverberate around the school hall, although this girl, Ally, seemed to carry off her low voice with sophistication rather than awkwardness. She was substantially taller than me, also blonde, though a darker tone, especially at the roots, and seemed to be able to command the room around her, even though I was the only audience she had.

'So, have you met your mummy yet?'

For a second I wasn't sure what she was talking about, then I understood. 'Oh, the older student?'

'Yes, the one to show you around, make sure you're not crying yourself to sleep at night, that sort of thing.'

I shook my head. 'No, I haven't.'

'Oh, that's not good. They should have met you when you arrived. And your daddy. Or have they axed daddies? I'm not sure. Let's go and find you one.' She made it sound like we were going off to get an ice cream. I wasn't even certain I wanted a 'mummy'. I'd always been pretty good at finding my own way through things, but I didn't

30

want to look standoffish. Ally grabbed my hand and led me out of my room.

'Don't bother locking your door, nobody does around here. There's a general rule: if you've locked your door, you're having sex. Or a total essay-breakdown. My brother has those from time to time.' She was leading me through the corridors, apparently confident in where she was going. 'Ah! Here we are.' A small gathering of students was in front of us, some of them looking lost, others holding clipboards. One of the clipboard girls smiled at Ally and said hello and the others nodded. Apparently everyone knew her. 'Got an orphan here for you, Catherine; her name is Holly,' Ally barked at her.

'Oh God, have you been left without a parent, too?' The girl called Catherine was looking down her clipboard. 'I'm so sorry about this, there's been such a mix-up with numbers. The person who helps organise all this is from the maths department, but you wouldn't know it. Let's see . . .' She chewed on her pencil while I just smiled politely, trying not to look too demanding.

'I don't need anyone, honestly,' I said quietly, but Catherine didn't seem to hear.

'Holly Rowe? Is that right? . . . Hmm, you're supposed to be with Caitlin, but I don't know where she's . . . ah, here she is now.'

Another girl had appeared, as if from nowhere. Short, round and looking extremely cheerful, I couldn't help but feel heartened by her presence. Here was someone I didn't have to be intimidated by, I thought, then instantly despised myself for the value judgement. Was it a value judgement?

I decided to ponder that later and offered my hand. 'Hi, I'm Holly,' I said, then realised I'd interrupted Catherine, who was halfway through asking Caitlin why she hadn't been there to greet me on my arrival.

'I'm so sorry,' Caitlin said in a warm, kind-sounding voice with a slight northern slant. She shook my outstretched hand, still grinning. 'I was double-booked, so to speak – given another girl in a different block, which is strange as I thought I'd made it clear . . .'

'Well, I'm glad all this has been sorted,' said Catherine curtly, then promptly left our little group and went to speak to another student on the other side of the hallway.

'She's a bit of a force of nature, Catherine,' Ally said. 'I think she hates me, but is too proud to show it. Probably because she fucked my brother and he didn't get back in touch.' I saw Caitlin blush at this. Ally turned to her and said, 'You know what, I'm super-fine to take care of Holly if you wanted to get back to your other charge.'

I began saying that I didn't need taking care of but Caitlin got in first. 'I don't think that would be allowed. You're a first year and the whole point is . . .'

'Oh, nonsense. I've been here heaps of times. My brother, Ernest, is a second-year here.'

Caitlin's eyes widened a little. 'You're Ernest Kelman's sister?'

'Guilty as charged!' Ally said brightly, then laughed loudly.

'So that means your . . . your dad is . . .'

Ally rolled her eyes, as if to say *here we go again*. 'Yes, dearest Daddy, also known as Clive Kelman, Tory MP. One

32

of Auntie Maggie's closest chums. Major prick in private, though don't tell the *Telegraph* I said that.'

'I . . . I won't,' Caitlin said, looking a little starstruck. I wasn't sure if I was supposed to look equally impressed, but politics had never been a strong interest of mine and the name didn't mean anything. Still, the fact that her dad was an MP was interesting, regardless, if rather daunting. If the first person I'd met was the daughter of an MP, I didn't like to think about the backgrounds of my other fellow students. Who would I meet next? The offspring of judges? Film stars? Minor royalty?

We headed back down the corridor towards my room, Caitlin's concerns obliterated by Ally's familial connections. She'd rushed off, giving me a small wave and an encouraging smile. We had almost reached my room when Ally stopped and approached one of the other doors. The sound of voices was emanating from it. Male voices. She seemed to be listening intently.

'What is it?' I said, looking at her and then at the door. 'Whose room is that?'

'It's my room,' she replied in a loud whisper.

'Has someone broken in?' I said, louder than I meant to, then cringed at how melodramatic it sounded.

'Someone has certainly entered uninvited. I was just trying to work out who was with him. Oh dear, as if I didn't know . . .'

I wanted to ask who she was referring to, but before I could she'd flung open the door forcefully and marched inside. I wasn't sure if I was meant to follow, but was too intrigued to wait, so walked in after her.

'Well. This is a pretty sight, isn't it?' Her hands were on her hips again.

Two boys were lying on her bed, laughing. One had a cigarette in his hand, the other a hardback book. There was something odd about the way they were lying together, side by side, on the single bed, their legs up against each other. I'd never seen boys behave like this, as if they had some deep-rooted familiarity. Both were extremely good-looking. One was blond, slim, with a distinct jawline, and was obviously Ally's brother. The other was larger, though from muscle rather than fat, with dark hair and a face that wouldn't have looked out of place on a movie poster. In fact, he could almost have passed for a younger Tom Cruise.

'Sis!' The blond one pulled himself up into a sitting position. Tom Cruise stayed horizontal, his eyes settling on us.

'Don't call me sis,' she snapped.

'Very well, Aphrodite.'

They both laughed.

'Don't give me that. Why are you on my bed?'

The blond boy adopted a look of great offence and clutched a hand to his white-shirted chest. 'You wound me, sis. I thought you said to come and visit you whenever I liked.'

'I said nothing of the kind.' Ally now turned her cold eyes on the other boy. 'James, I expected better of you.'

'He led me astray,' the boy said in a low, resonant tone. For some reason his voice sent a ripple down my shoulders. I shivered slightly and his eyes flicked over to me.

'Are you cold?' he said, smiling, as if he somehow knew he was having an effect on me.

'I'm fine, thanks,' I said.

'Introduce us to your friend, sis,' the blond boy said, drawing on the cigarette.

Ally turned to me. 'Holly, this is my prat of a brother, Ernest.'

I wasn't sure if I should offer my hand, but he didn't seem inclined to get off the bed any time soon, so I just waved. He smiled in return. A nice smile, making his otherwise hard face seem friendlier.

'The other layabout is James, my brother's best friend and occasional shag-buddy.'

Ernest's smile became more of a smirk. 'Still dining out on that joke, sis? Wasn't funny the first time.'

'Makes me laugh,' she said.

The other boy was also smiling. 'Not entirely a lie, though,' he said, nudging Ernest with his elbow. He winked at me and I felt myself blushing.

'Too much info,' Ally said, tersely.

James pulled himself upright and stepped off the bed. He held out a hand to me and I took it. 'James Knight. Very nice to meet you . . . Holly, was it?'

'Yes,' I said, trying to hold his gaze but finding it diffi-cult. It felt as though his dark eyes were staring right past my face, reading my thoughts. It was an uncomfortable sensation, but electric somehow, and part of me didn't want it to stop.

'Well, isn't that nice.' He pulled his hand back. 'Ernest and I need to leave his sister in peace now. But I suspect we'll be seeing a lot more of you soon. A friend of Ally's is a friend of ours.' He said it as if it were a strict rule he was fully committed to. I just nodded, hoping I didn't appear as uncomfortable as I felt. Eventually he said, 'Come on, Ern. Let's take our leave.'

Ernest got up off the bed, flattening his shirt down and patting his sister on the shoulder as he passed her.

'Thanks for the secondhand cancer,' she said, waving a hand in the air to clear the smoke. Once the door was closed she sat down on her bed with a sigh.

'So that was Ernest.'

I smiled, standing awkwardly in front of her.

'And James, of course. James is all right.'

'Yes,' I said, and realised I was smiling. 'He certainly seemed to be.'

She glanced at me and laughed. 'Oh, sure he's gorgeous. Less of a womaniser than my brother, though. More choosy.'

I wondered if she was implying he was out of my league. I thought about asking if he was single, then worried that would sound too forward, as if I was actively interested. Which I was, I realised, with a lurch in the stomach. *If only*, I thought, then pulled myself together. It felt silly to imagine such things, having barely set foot in the place or met anyone new. I was tragically out of my depth – even a passing stranger on the street would have been able to tell as much, been able to spot my lack of experience, my awkward approach to socialising. In the future, I would wonder what it was I did during that afternoon that led to me being singled out from the rest, chosen, made to feel both special and alone. And, after a lot of introspection and clawing back over the past, I still don't really have the answer. I was just being me. No mask, no pretence. Being myself. That's what you're supposed to do when you meet people for the first time. That's one of the main rules. Isn't it?

Chapter 4

Julianne

Knightsbridge, 2019

James is staring at me from the bottom of the stairs. 'Where have you been?' he asks.

'I was . . . just talking to Stephen.' It's the truth at least, but I avoid his eyes as I say it. My mother is currently doing her best to avoid mine. She does this – it's one of the little games she plays. Starves people of attention, makes them crave it, then turns the spotlight on to full beam and makes you want to shrink from view. At the moment she's moving her scarf from one peg to another.

'I don't want it getting all crumpled and covered in stuff when people go in and out the door,' she says by way of an explanation to the wall, making it sound like we regularly have a pack of mud-covered dogs going in and out of the house.

'Hello, Mom. And there's nobody else coming, so your scarf will be safe regardless of where it is.'

She lets out a 'Hmmm', her way of saying *I'm not convinced*, then finally leaves her scarf alone and turns to look at me. 'Julianne, dearest, how have you been? You look . . . haggard.'

If anyone else had said this I'd be offended, but from my mother it's only to be expected. 'It's only been two weeks since I last saw you. I can't have changed that much.'

She shakes her head and looks at me as if staring at someone who's just been told they're terminal. 'It just saddens me to see you run yourself so ragged. You're probably doing too much again. Where's that housekeeper of yours? What does she actually *do*? I swear she has a holiday every other day.'

'It's Cassie's day off. Her first this week. And she isn't always on holiday.' I hear the closing of a door upstairs and jump slightly. Stephen must have gone back to his own room. My slight movement doesn't escape my mother's ever-observant eye.

'Goodness, you're twitchy. Maybe you should sit down.'

'No, Mom, I need to go and finish the food.'

'I can do that,' James says, probably considering it the lesser of the two evils when compared with making small talk. He disappears off to the kitchen, leaving my mother smiling and shaking her head a little.

'James is such a dear,' she says.

I stare back blankly at her. My husband always gets the

compliments, the praise, the terms of endearment. It's probably because of all the money he's given her over the years. Helping her buy a new property when we were married. The steady money she's become used to, going out of our joint account and into hers every month. He's her saviour, in many respects.

'I don't know what the world's coming to when the man of the house has to tend to the cooking.' She drops her gaze as she says this and continues to shake her head, as if slightly sad.

On some days I fight back. I pick her up on her sexism, her little digs, her many prejudices, her dated worldview. But today I haven't got the energy. I just look at her, standing there in her crisp tailored blazer, as if she's about to attend a boardroom meeting. She's never set foot in a boardroom in her life, but dresses every day like she's ready to negotiate a corporate merger or try to poach a big new client from a rival legal firm. 'Dress for success' is what she always used to teach me as a child. I can see her now, eyeing up my plain, dark-green, John Lewis own-brand cardigan, her lips curving down slightly at the sides. She doesn't approve.

'Come on into the lounge, Mom.'

I walk in ahead of her and immediately go to the drinks table. 'Do you want anything?'

'If you're referring to a drink, Julianne, I will have a small sherry.'

I sigh as I pour the liquid into a glass and turn round to hand it to her. She's appraising the Christmas tree, stepping back, slowly and deliberately, as one would in an art gallery when trying to take in a painting as a whole. She nods. 'Very nice,' she says. 'Very . . . homely.'

'Well, this is a home, so I guess something went right,' I say.

'I suppose.'

I don't know what she means by that, but I'm not about to interrogate it right now. I sit down on one of the sofas before she does. After the tree, she continues her tour around the lounge, slowly turning, taking it all in, as if she hadn't already seen everything hundreds of times before. She stops at the TV.

'I did always tell you, Julianne, an excessively large television can seem a little . . . how shall I put it . . . ?'

I can feel myself getting more tense by the second. 'I don't know, Mom, probably in your usual kind and generous way.'

She glances over at me, an eyebrow raised. 'No need to get snippy, Julianne. Maybe you should have a drink yourself. Take the edge off.'

I continue to stare back at her and she turns away from the television. 'I just fear a large television suggests that it has too much of an important place in your life.'

'Or that we don't all want to be squinting at some old twenty-two-incher as if this was still the 1990s. We've had that for over a year, Mom, and it's not that much bigger than your new set. You've never had a problem with it before. You spent most of last Christmas glued to old musicals on it. In fact, I even think I remember you remarking how good that Blu-Ray boxset of yours looked on it compared to your previous old antique.'

She makes a tutting sound and shakes her head some more. 'It was only an observation, Julianne. You don't have to take everything as a personal attack.' She moves over to the single sofa seat opposite me and sits down on the edge, straight-backed and looking less than comfortable. 'Where is my favourite grandson?'

'Your *only* grandson is upstairs finishing something. He'll be down for dinner soon.'

'Finishing something? Not schoolwork, four days before Christmas?'

'It's a big year for him, Mom. A levels, you know.'

'No, I don't know,' she says, picking a nonexistent bit of fluff from her sleeve. 'I don't know how these schools work over here, and I never get much sense from you or James when I ask. I find the whole thing a bit incomprehensible compared to the American system.'

'Mom, even that's probably changed since you were there.'

'Well, how would I know? Twenty-five years on, this whole place still feels like a mystery to me. I can barely understand the young people now. Some uncouth young man served me in Waitrose the other day and slurred his words so much I had to ask him five times to repeat himself.'

'Maybe you're going deaf.'

'I certainly am not. Then he had the cheek to ask if I was over here for a holiday. I said to him I'd lived in this hellhole longer than he'd been alive.'

'Richmond isn't a hellhole, Mom.'

'Well, it's all right for you, living here, in the centre of

43

things. Not banished to the suburbs with the waifs and strays.'

This is too much for me. I can't be doing this right now. I'm struggling to remain calm, the mounting level of unease causing a dull nausea to ebb and flow around my body. I stand up and try my best not to shout. 'Waifs and strays? Do you know what kind of a life you have compared to some people out there?'

As soon as I've said this, my mind darts to those documents. Those young women – the desperate state of their lives intricately detailed. I shiver involuntarily, but my mother doesn't notice. She bats away my comment. 'Oh, you don't need to have a go at me, Julianne. Not this early in the evening. I'm aware I'm not one of those refugees you see crawling across Europe. I make do with what I have and I don't complain.'

In another mood I might have found the sheer awfulness of what she's just said funny, but today it riles me all the more. 'Jesus Christ, can you hear yourself, Mom?'

She looks at me again, an expression of puzzlement and mild alarm stretching across her preserved skin. 'Julianne, you seem to be quite emotional tonight. Would it be better if I left?'

I'm about to tell her, yes, it would be goddamn marvellous if she could just turn around and leave, but before I can say anything, James walks back in suddenly and my stomach lurches slightly. Diane smiles at him and picks up her sherry from the coffee table.

'Not arguing, are we?' he says, his eyes wandering in my direction.

'Not at all,' Diane says smoothly, laying a hand on James's shoulder as she leaves the room. 'Julianne's just expressing the stresses of the season. Christmas is always much harder on the women. But the girls in this family have always been headstrong. At least, they always have been in the past . . .'

She disappears in the direction of the dining room and I realise I'm standing in the middle of the room, my hands clenched into fists.

'Dinner's practically ready. You coming?' James says.

'Sure. Can't wait for round two.'

He smiles at me encouragingly. 'Try to go easy on her. It's Christmas.'

'Maybe one day she could just go a bit easier on me.'

He chuckles as if I've said something amusing, then goes out into the hallway and shouts up the stairs to Stephen. There's no reply.

'He's just finishing up some work,' I say and try to steer James towards the dining room, but he holds still.

'He should have come down to greet his grandma.' He looks faintly annoyed. When I don't answer he looks back at me. I don't say anything.

'Julianne? Hello?'

I realise I've been staring blankly at him. 'Er . . . sorry,' I muster.

James is clearly puzzled. He turns back to the stairs, and for a second I think he's going to march up them to find Stephen, but then he shrugs and walks away.

'He'll be down soon,' I say, hoping I'm right.

Chapter 5

Holly

Oxford, 1990

The first month went by in a bit of a blur. There was a lot of enforced socialising, with societies and study groups and after-seminar catch-ups, where the really eager people, a group I had accidentally fallen into, stayed behind and went over what had been discussed in class. There were study sessions with tutors, too, sometimes one-to-one, but usually with a study partner. My partner was a small, red-haired boy named Peter. Like many people there, he was polite and generally friendly to me, while remaining a little distant. It took me a few weeks to realise he was part of 'The Ally Club', as I had come to call them.

Ever since the first night, Ally and I had been friends, though our meet-ups mostly consisted of watching television on her bed, her curled up in a big plush throw or baggy jumper and me seated a little awkwardly at the end. She was obsessed with the soap *Neighbours* ('It's about *Australians*') and watched it religiously, recording every episode onto a video cassette during the day and then watching them, usually with me, on the evenings she wasn't out. I was never sure where she went on these nights and she never volunteered the information, so I didn't feel I could ask in case it sounded like I was hankering after an invite. I suspected she was spending time with her brother, or friends on her French and Philosophy course, but tried not to dwell on it. Thinking about Ally's friends meant thinking about Ernest, and thinking about Ernest meant thinking about James. I'd had crushes on boys before; quite strong, all-encompassing crushes that never went anywhere, but always ended in me feeling down and discontented with my looks. I had never really thought of myself as vain, but I was far from confident in my appearance, even if my mum did insist on referring to me occasionally as her 'little blonde beauty'. I didn't want James to become a crush. He wasn't my type, he was out of my league, and there was something about him that irritated me. That calm, entirely self-assured way he had been lying on his friend's sister's bed. Insolent, maybe? I wasn't sure, but I was certain life would be simpler staying out of his way.

I first came to realise Ally had a sort of group when I was coming back from the cinema with Becky and

Rachael, two girls from my Victorian Literature class. I hadn't really made much of an effort to get to know them in the first few weeks, but I was flattered when they asked me if I wanted to go with them, and it was a film I'd been wanting to see, a gangster movie called *Goodfellas*. It was the type of movie my mother would have been appalled at but my father would have secretly enjoyed, before agreeing sternly with my mother that such violence was 'quite unnecessary'. Becky and Rachael also seemed to find the violence unnecessary and spent most of the way home talking about how nasty the whole thing was. I'd really enjoyed it and was tempted to ask why they had gone to see a crime thriller with an 18 certificate if they both felt, to quote Becky, 'sick at the sight of blood'. As we were passing our college library, Rachael said she just needed to dive in to return a book before it closed. It was early November and bitterly cold, so we sheltered in the hallway of the library, which wasn't much warmer, while Rachael went up to the desk.

It was then I heard Ally's laugh, quite unmistakable, that hearty, low rumble, building to a crescendo of enthusiastic mirth. I peered inside and saw the librarian at the desk glance irritably to her left at a group of students seated around a circular table near one of the bookshelves. There she was, sitting with her brother, one arm around the back of his chair. James was there too, and my stomach lurched as I took in his navy-blue jumper, pulled tightly over a light-pink Oxford shirt. Though close-fitting, his clothes didn't seem to restrain him and he moved with a sense of casual fluidity as he bent down to take a book out of his bag and add it to the pile of tomes on their table. They seemed to be in the midst of a study session. Then there was Peter, smaller than both the others, who seemed absorbed in his reading, his hands up around his head as if he was trying to block out the surrounding chatter, a mop of ginger hair falling over his forehead.

'Friends of yours?'

Becky had come to stand next to me. I realised I must have been staring and took a step back from the inner warmth of the library into the cold hallway. 'No,' I said, quickly, unsure why I felt suddenly pressured into giving an explanation. 'Well, sort of . . . the girl, Ally, she's in the room next to me.'

Becky nodded and said, 'I know, I've seen her a few times. Her brother is rather handsome, isn't he?'

I glanced back at Ernest Kelman, at his stylishly cut blond hair and bright-white shirt, looking almost identical to when I'd seen him last, lying casually next to James on his sister's bed.

'Yes, he is rather. Not my type, though.'

Becky laughed. 'I know what you mean. There's something a bit "Hooray Henry" about him, isn't there? Wouldn't say no to his friend, though.' She raised her eyebrows and I realised she was looking at James, who was now away from the table, scanning the nearby book-shelves. It pained me to admit it to myself but I couldn't help but feel a tinge of irritation when she said this, as if James's attractiveness was to be appreciated by me and me alone. I gave a non-committal nod and turned my back to them, smiling at Rachael as she returned to meet us, tightening the scarf around her neck before we resumed our walk back to our respective halls.

Chapter 6

Holly

Oxford, 1990

'Virginia Woolf is overrated.' I heard myself say it, but I couldn't quite believe it had come out of my mouth. I frequently participated in my study sessions with Peter and Dr Lawrence, but never in a such a blunt, potentially controversial way. I could feel Peter's eyes staring at me. Dr Lawrence, meanwhile, smiled knowingly.

'Maybe you could expand on that interesting analysis, Holly.' He had a way of saying things that made me half-wonder if he was taking the piss, but his interjections were full of encouragement and a clear passion for his subject.

'Well, she wraps everything up in these airy-fairy metaphors instead of actually saying what she should be saying:

53

life is tough, you'll never find a sense of belonging and, to be frank, the hunt for it isn't worth the effort, even if you actually do find it.' I paused and realised my voice had been getting steadily louder.

Dr Lawrence nodded. 'Do go on.'

'Well, that's it, I think,' I finished, lamely, and glanced at Peter. 'Do you have anything to add?'

I wasn't quite sure where my newfound confidence had come from, but I had started to enjoy it.

'Umm, well . . .' Peter was taken aback, and I noticed Dr Lawrence seemed mildly amused by the effect my words had had on him.

'Let's take a step back, shall we?' he said, coming to Peter's rescue. 'Let's think about the idea of symbolism in *To the Lighthouse*. Do either of you have any initial thoughts on that before we probe it further with some examples within the text?'

After the study session, Peter spoke to me. I had been struggling with my bag; the cover of *Mrs Dalloway* had become torn when I'd inadvertently shoved my dictionary in on top of it in a hurry. I was hoping Peter would just pack up and leave as he usually did, but today he lingered.

'You seemed more alive today.'

It was an odd thing to say and it caused me to turn and look at him with more attention than I had in a while. 'Er . . . thanks. Does that mean I look dead most of the time?'

He laughed, though the laugh wasn't convincing, like a grunt. It was a strangely masculine sound, closer to something I'd imagine hearing from Ernest or James. I continued to stare at him, waiting for a proper answer, but it didn't arrive. Finally he said, 'I think we – I mean, I think you – should spend more time with us. With me, James, Ernest, Ally. I think you'd like it.'

'I'd like it?'

'Yes. You're friends with Ally, aren't you? You live practically on top of each other.'

This wasn't exactly true. Despite having adjacent rooms, Ally's social life meant our time together was usually spent brushing our teeth in the morning before lectures or chatting on the way out of the showers. Time snatched away from the day here and there and the odd episode of *Neighbours* – hardly the basis of a close friendship. For Peter's benefit, however, I nodded.

'We talk about things. Books mainly. Music, sometimes. Cinema, if James is holding court. He loves films. Always tries to battle against Ernest's snobbery towards them.'

'Ernest doesn't like films?'

'Oh, I don't think it's to do with not *liking* them, exactly. It's more he feels they can't be interrogated in as rigorous a way as, say, Kant or Hume, or the great novelists like Dickens and Austen.'

'I think that's crap.'

Peter laughed. 'It may well be, but that's Ernest for you. Not one to budge on his opinions, even if the opposite is clearly true. James likes films, though. I think you'll get on with him. So long as you don't mind your entertainment a little on the dark side.'

I thought of Becky and Rachael complaining about

the violence in *Goodfellas*, whereas I had been left relatively unmoved.

'I can do dark,' I said, trying to sound confident. A confidence I hadn't really earned. How did I know I could 'do dark'? Something shifted within me uncomfortably, like I was just reaching out and touching a barely visible line I'd never really known was there. New horizons. Uncharted territory. I was intrigued.

'Then you'll probably get on with him rather well.'

When I got back to my room, I found Ally waiting for me at my door. I was disconcerted by this. Had Peter had time to contact her during my short walk over from Dr Lawrence's office and tell her what a fool I'd made of myself during the seminar? She was smiling, though, in her usual, enthusiastic way, and her eyes seemed to glow with excitement. 'We're going to the Wimpy.'

At first I thought I'd misheard and just stared stupidly at her. She rolled her eyes, as if she could guess what I was thinking.

'Oh, I know, I know. You're probably thinking it's not quite our style. I'm not completely unaware of the image Ernest and I must give off. We do go to fast-food chains on occasion. It's not just caviar at The Ritz every day, you know.'

I found my voice again. 'I know that. Sorry, I wasn't . . . I didn't mean . . .'

More smiles. More eye rolling. 'Relax. So do you want to come?'

I couldn't imagine anything weirder. Sitting on those

dingy, scruffy chairs at those grease-stained tables with the always immaculate-looking Ernest and James while Ally laughed in her rumbling Sloane Square tones at whatever witty aside James had made about Proust. But I nodded and told her it would be lovely. She didn't seem convinced, but she smiled sweetly and then grabbed my arm. 'Come on, let's go and get ready.'

Getting ready involved Ally trying on multiple cardigans of various colours and weaves while she mused and puzzled about the temperature outside, the velocity of the wind and the cardigan's usefulness if she was going to be wearing a coat over it in any case. I passed the time by browsing Ally's book collection. There were some of the usual suspects there. Dickens and Austen. A couple of Brontës. But there were some surprises, too. I tried to quiz her on her apparent love for Kingsley Amis, but got a snort of derision as a response: 'That old misogynist! Can't stand the man. I should really throw them out, if I'm honest, but it's a little bit awkward.' I asked her why it was awkward and she just tossed her head to dislodge a gold strand of hair that had got stuck between her eyes and said casually, 'Oh, he's a family friend.'

I found myself in a strange, scratchy mood, as if I wasn't quite sure what was going on. There was something about the randomness of the invite to the Wimpy that unnerved me slightly and I kept flicking between deciding not to go and feeling quietly excited they'd decided to let me into their little gang. When I found myself thinking this latter thought I mentally kicked myself. We weren't back in school. The idea of having cliques and gangs was supposed to go away when you were past the age of seventeen, surely?

Apparently not, it seemed, as we set out on the short walk to the boys' dorms. I could see other little packs making their way across the courtyard; small huddles of friends who had decided they belonged together. Whether through sports, studies, societies or just common interests, these people had decided they worked better as a team. We're sociable animals by nature, of course, but the politics of friendship seemed to be emphasised here to a disproportionate degree; worse, perhaps, than when I was at school. The horrendous weather, which, combined with the spires and churches on the skyline, made it seem as if we'd slipped into a Hammer horror movie, meant Ally and I had to hold our coats hard to our chests for fear of them blowing open. The rain hadn't started, but we both knew it wouldn't be long, dreading the moment we would have to open our umbrellas and fight to keep them from being turned inside out with every gust that came our way.

When we reached the boys' halls, I felt my stomach drop inside me, a feeling that only got worse as Ally marched down the corridor that led to their rooms. The thought of being in such close proximity to where they lived, where they slept, where they undressed – where James undressed – made me squirm slightly. Ally didn't bother to knock, just barged into what I gathered was Ernest's room. The place was shockingly messy, even messier than Ally's. Clothes littered the floor – white shirts, mostly, which seemed to be Ernest's trademark apparel, along with jumpers, underwear and stacks of books, many of which seemed to be written by obscure European philosophers and various other authors I had never heard of. On the desk was an extensive array of orange Penguin paperbacks and on the shelves were hardbacks from the Everyman's Library series. It seemed that when he'd moved in there had been some effort to establish order, though these foundations had been tested over time.

'See anything you like?' said Ernest, who'd noticed me looking at the books. His face hadn't quite spread out into a full sneer, but I was suspicious of the smile dancing around his lips.

'Maybe,' I said, then turned to Ally. 'Is James's room close? Are we meeting him and Peter at the restaurant?'

Ally was about to speak, but Ernest's laughter cut her off. 'Three things. First, I don't think "restaurant" is usually a term employed in relation to the Wimpy, unless one is using it very loosely. Second, Peter has lost some book he desperately needs and is having a strop in the way only Peter knows how. He will indeed be meeting us there, if he finds his missing tome. And third, you might want to take a look at Sleeping Beauty in the bed over there. Better still, maybe you could give him a nudge for me. I've been trying to get him up for the past hour.'

I looked over at the bed and there was indeed, amidst an excessive amount of pillows, a human-size mass under the sheets, with the duvet pulled up so high that only a glimpse of brown hair could be seen nestled among the folds. I felt a jolt of something uncomfortable in my spine as I realised it was James, sleeping silently. I could see the rise and fall of his breathing, ever so slightly, in the shape of his shoulders.

'Oh, for God's sake, I thought you guys would be ready. I'm fucking starving.' Ally stomped across to the bed and tore back the duvet. For one mortifying moment I found myself partly dreading, partly hoping, that he would be unclothed – perhaps even naked – under the covers, but he wasn't. He was wearing pyjama bottoms and a navy-blue Oxford hoody.

'Wake up.' He recoiled from her harsh bark, moving closer to the wall, burrowing his head deeper into the mound of pillows. She got on the bed and began poking his back. 'I want a bloody burger, and your idle behaviour isn't going to stop me from getting it.'

Ernest was grinning, with his hands on his hips, watching his sister drag his friend from his bed. 'We had a bit of a wild night last night,' he said. 'It takes poor James a little longer than most to recover. Delicate creature, he is.'

James was now sitting on the bed, rubbing his eyes. 'I should go have a shower.'

'No time for that. Didn't you hear me? Me. Food. Want. Now. You look fine, anyway.'

'Probably better than most of their clientele,' Ernest drawled, rolling his eyes and smirking, though I kept my face neutral, refusing to be complicit in his casual snobbery.

'Your trousers are around the floor somewhere, if you can find them,' he said, but James shook his head and murmured something about jeans before wandering off out of Ernest's room, presumably to his own to get some fresh attire.

It took about fifteen minutes for James to get ready. I spent most of it awkwardly perched on Ernest's bed while Ally made complaints about her stomach and how she could feel the muscles contracting in protest due to extreme hunger. Ernest showed no sympathy and made a crude comment about James having a wank in the shower. Ally tutted at this and accused him of being vulgar. 'Oh, he likes to knock one out in the mornings. Does it like clockwork.' Ally reminded him that it was 5.30 p.m., which didn't count as 'the morning', regardless of what time one woke up.

When he finally arrived, James did look a little more kempt, with his hair in a less-ruffled state and wearing a pair of dark-blue jeans. He'd swapped the hoody for a chunky burgundy jumper, which made him look like one of those dreamy-looking boys I'd seen once in a Ralph Lauren advertisement – boys who, I'd told myself at the time, weren't real and had been crafted in an evil man-lab somewhere to make girls feel lightheaded and other boys feel jealous, resentful or sexually confused.

'At bloody last,' Ally huffed, and we all left Ernest's room.

Conversation was attempted and then aborted as we walked around the corner to the fringes of the city centre. It was impossible to hear one's own words, let alone those of anyone else, when the wind was screeching like a tortured farm animal and battering us from either side. The much-feared rain eventually arrived just as the warm, welcoming glow of the Wimpy came within sight, causing us to dash madly down the street and in through its little door before we got soaked to the skin.

The restaurant was almost empty, save for a woman and little boy in a dark corner at the end of the restaurant. She glanced around at me as we arrived, then turned back to the child, apparently trying to coax him into finishing the last of his chips.

'Could we get a table for four, please? I'm afraid we haven't booked. Is that a problem?' This ridiculous question came from Ernest, who could barely contain his mirth at his own joke as he spoke to the bored-looking Asian lady behind the counter.

'No,' she said flatly. 'Please sit where you like.'

'You can be a bit of a dickhead, Ern,' said James, though Ernest just beamed in response to this as if he considered it a compliment.

Peter was still nowhere to be seen, so we settled at the table nearest the window, away from the woman and child, and Ally began dishing out menus, grabbing extra ones from the tables nearby. I took the slightly sticky laminated sheet in my hand and looked through the options. Though I hadn't been in a Wimpy for years, I wasn't surprised to see only minimal changes had been made to the array of burgers, strangely plastic-looking sausages and other fried food. When the waitress came to take our order, I was slightly disconcerted when everyone ordered exactly the same thing: a cheeseburger and fries with a strawberry milkshake, as if it was some kind of set menu I wasn't aware of. I almost changed my own choice so as not to be the odd one out, but stuck to my guns and ordered a burger with no cheese but tomato sauce, fries and a Coke.

Although I had been afraid of awkward silences, conversation came quite naturally, with Ally conducting everyone like an orchestra, asking me questions about my course in a way that enabled me to have a part in whatever they wanted to discuss. It turned out that, as with me, literature was their primary topic of conversation, as Peter had suggested. And I could see why he'd recommended I join in with them more after our discussion on *To the Lighthouse*; the group were apparently going through a bit of a Woolf phase. *Mrs Dalloway* seemed to be the focus today, with Ally declaring it 'utter, pretentious claptrap', while James and Ernest objected to her criticisms and said she 'just didn't get it'.

'There's no need to denigrate one of the greatest authors of the twentieth century simply because you have a short attention span.' Ernest had a wicked smile on his face, knowing full well what would wind his sister up.

Ally almost spat her milkshake out of her nostrils. 'I do not have a short attention span.' She shifted in her seat irritably. 'Where's the food? They don't usually take this long.'

'I think you've just proved my point.'

'Hunger has nothing to do with attention spans.'

'And yet you used it to change the subject.'

Ally glared at him. 'Peter's still not here.'

'Well spotted,' said Ernest, peering over James's shoulder at the rain-soaked night outside. 'Perhaps he took one look at the weather and decided we weren't worth it. Or he's crying in one of the stacks of the library, having a little private funeral for the remnants of his essay.'

I took in Ernest's fluid movements, his laughter, his playful barbs aimed at his sister. Some girls would like that type of thing, I thought as I watched him. But turning my attention to James, I felt a deep swell inside me, like a force rebelling against any attempts to tame it, and knew I wasn't one of those girls. The quiet, serious type was my thing – a 'thing' I'd never really known I had until I met him for the first time. My lack of experience with boys was probably plain to see for people like Ally and Ernest who, by all accounts, enjoyed their respective sex lives in an unfussy, matter-of-fact kind of way. And when the topic of conversation turned, as it was always going to do, to the subject of sex, I found myself wanting to crawl under a rock somewhere. Or a table.

'The problem is, she's just never had it done to her,' Ernest said, describing a girl he had gone home with a few nights before. 'When I told her the name of it, she made this shrieking noise, as if she was repulsed.'

'It does sound like some kind of infection, doesn't it?' said Ally, grimacing. 'Cunnilingus. Cunn-i-ling-gus.'

'It does if you say it like that.' James grinned. Like me, he'd barely spoken throughout the whole dinner, just silently consumed his burger and chips, though leaving the two halves of the bun neatly on the side of his plate, having eaten the contents with a knife and fork. Ally rounded on him.

'Ahh, so you have an opinion on this, do you?'

'Not necessarily.'

'Practise it much?'

James didn't answer, instead picking up one of the fries that had fallen off Ernest's plate and starting to move it around his own, mopping up a minuscule amount of tomato sauce from the edges.

'His silence speaks volumes,' said Ernest and winked at me.

'Oh yes, sorry, I forgot. My brother doesn't have a vagina, so of course James would have no interest in going down on one. A cock, on the other hand . . .'

'Here we go.' Ernest rolled his eyes. 'I knew the *Mrs Dalloway* talks wouldn't last long. Come on, let's hear it, sis.' He turned to me. 'In case you haven't already noticed, my sister likes nothing better than to imply James and I are sodomising the night away together. Just jealousy, I'd say. Plain and simple. She can't bear the thought that I converse with and laugh with and breathe the same air as another individual other than herself.'

I wasn't sure whether to laugh or not, so I glanced at Ally, who had a look of triumph in her eye.

'Sodomising the night away? Interesting turn of phrase, dearest brother. I don't remember anyone saying anything about sodomy. Interesting that your mind should jump so quickly to penetrative sex. I was merely implying oral, but if you want to plunge straight in at the deep end, be my guest.' She shot me a wicked smile, raising her eyebrows, enjoying the game. Her references to gay sex startled me somewhat. I wasn't naïve – I knew some men did such things – but throughout my teens my parents had always implied men who had sex with men were disease-ridden

AIDS sufferers who would soon perish as a result of their aberrant desires. This bothered me throughout the rest of our meal and, after Ally had got bored and all the fries had been eaten, the quick trudge in the drizzle back to our respective dorms. Ally seemed to be treating it all as a bit of a laugh, though I wasn't entirely sure if her comments were manifestations of her own prejudices towards gay men, or if they were actually based on a glimmer of truth, and she just enjoyed torturing the two boys with this knowledge. Presumably the boys had slept together last night, if James had been in Ernest's bed for most of the day. Perhaps their friendship wasn't purely platonic. But Ally had also implied Ernest was a prolific 'shagger' of ladies, and that I was (or at least appeared to be, on the outside) just his type. I'd heard some people liked both genders, but to me this seemed even farther removed from my everyday life than homosexuals pure and simple. The idea of not being restricted by gender frightened me slightly, though I didn't quite know why. It had a rather thrilling, anarchic quality to it, as if the constraints on gender that dominated the lives of the many didn't apply to them. They were free.

Ally and I got back to our halls first and she waved goodbye to the two boys without properly looking at them. I was surprised at the abrupt ending to the evening. It was still only 7.15. Hardly a wild night out for a bunch of students. Maybe they were all going to congregate later on when I was safely back in my room. They might swap notes on how well they thought I'd done. I was cross I hadn't had more time to really assert myself or make my presence seem worthwhile. Instead of an active participant, I'd become a passive spectator, watching Ally trade quips with her brother about his sexual preferences. My mind was dwelling on this in such detail that I didn't realise, as we were walking towards our rooms, that Ally was in the full flow of conversation.

'. . . I just thought it would be nice for you to see us all together. We're not exactly a frightening bunch. I know Ern can be a bit, well, spikey occasionally, but that's just his insecurities showing through. He collects them, don't you know? Like some people collect stamps or rare novels, he collects insecurities. Intellect is the main one. It's like he's absolutely terrified one day everyone — teachers, professors, friends, the world — will discover he's actually just 'rather bright' rather than 'insanely brilliant'. There's a big difference between the two, of course, and Ernest is traumatised by the knowledge that if anyone dug too deeply they'd probably place him in the former category.'

She unlocked her door and walked in still talking, presuming I would follow.

'Anyway, I don't know why he's worried. He'll get what he's always wanted — a seat in the Commons. Daddy's practically got it all sorted for him. He'll have no trouble winning a place.'

I made a vague sound, somewhere between affirmation and 'do go on'.

'Yes, well, he'll just need to get a first, of course. Daddy's rather firm about that. And it's not a question of how clever he is; it's more about whether he actually does what he's told. Studies the things he's supposed to study, not the nonsense he's more interested in.'

'Surely he should focus on his interests?' I said, unsure why I was standing up for him.

'Hmm, you sound like my mother.' Ally rolled her eyes and collapsed onto her bed, causing the springs in the mattress to twang noisily.

Being likened to someone so close, at least biologically, to Ally must, I decided, be a positive thing, so I smiled and peered around awkwardly at the untidy room.

'Oh, please, Holly, sit down. You're making me tense just standing there.' She gave one of her bark-like laughs.

I started to think about what it would be like to lie down next to Ally in the same way Ernest and James did. Our bodies touching, the strands of our hair intermingling. The thought didn't repulse me, but at the same time I felt there were other people I'd rather do that with. Wondering whether this might be the harbinger of a lesbian experimentation phase – a rather candid art teacher at my school had once implied all girls went through something of this nature at university – I opted to sit in a restrained fashion at the edge of Ally's bed, careful not to let my body touch hers.

'Let's talk about sex, Holly.'

Ally's words sent a jolt of concern through me. I didn't believe in mind-reading, but it was amazing how sometimes people could hit the mark. I must have jumped, because she laid a hand on my arm and said, 'Don't flinch. Oh goodness, anyone would think I'd offered you heroin.' She was smiling and looked relaxed, so I nodded.

'Holly, you seem, well, I hate to say this, but . . . quite innocent.'

'I am innocent,' I said. Then, worried this might sound a little strange, I added, 'I mean, I've had limited experience.'

Another laugh. 'That's not so unusual. You're only eighteen.'

'Nineteen in five months,' I murmured.

'Does it bother you, being a virgin?'

Though she was clearly trying to be kind, it sounded as if she was actually asking, *Do you mind being disabled?*

'I . . . I don't really know.' I tried to choose my words carefully, but I felt my heart beating a loud, relentless chant in my chest and was keen to drown out the noise of it. 'I've done some stuff. But not everything. There was a party once. And then another time at a picnic. But I had hayfever and needed an antihistamine.' I doubted this added detail was necessary, but it seemed like a legitimate mitigating factor. Who'd want to have sex while being plagued by three-minute-long sneezing fits and streaming eyes?

'Oh, poor you. That must have been awkward. Did you not have any male friends you could, you know, experiment with? A few of Ernest's school chums came in handy for me. So to speak.' She winked.

'I did have friends who were boys. I was very close to one of them: George. We did everything together, for a bit.' Ally's eyes widened, and I rushed to clarify. 'Everything school-wise. Nothing like *that*. That would have been weird.'

'Would it? Sometimes friends can be good. Stops it

69

getting too romantic. It's like a barrier, a prearranged stop sign that helps you both stay on the same page. Although my first time – well, first sexual experience – was a sort of date, at the opera of all places. *Tosca*. I was fifteen. We were in a box watching the performance and my mother was keen for me to sit next to this boy called Archibald. Well, he liked to be called Archie but his parents thought that common. So, anyway, Archibald is an aristrocrat, which explains my mother's reason for wanting us to be close. We were just getting to the torture scene when I felt his hand creeping up my thigh. We were slightly to the side, hidden – or at least I hope we were – from the view of my parents and his parents. I didn't stop him. He kept on and I felt my knickers getting wet. He slid in so easily. God, it felt good. I came incredibly quickly, much faster than I had ever done by myself. I had to keep silent, though. To this day I've been rather proud of how I did that. A little concentration and the odd well-placed yawn go a long way.'

I felt slightly dazed by this level of oversharing, completely at a loss as to how to respond. If that had been me (which was unlikely, since my parents were always commenting on how pricey tickets to the local am–dram performances were), I think I'd probably have been too shocked and embarrassed to ever tell anyone. But Ally said it so coolly, in her no-nonsense, matter-of-fact way. I was quietly in awe of her.

'James would probably fuck you, you know. If I asked him to. Do you want me to mention it?'

I gasped. 'What?'

Ally laughed again, and this time I felt a prickle of annoyance. Was she playing with me? Trying to make me feel uncomfortable?

'Oh, come on, Holly. You've got to lose the big V at some point. It might as well be to a man you clearly have the major hots for. So many girls fancy James. Many would kill – literally kill – for the chance. I swear some have got close to murder in the past. He's left a trail of broken hearts in his wake. And broken hearts can be a dangerous thing. I'm sure you've read enough tragic love stories to know that.'

I was feeling very awkward now. 'I think . . . I think I should go back to my room now.' I made no immediate move to go, but Ally looked alarmed.

'Oh goodness, I've upset you.'

'You haven't. I'm just not used to talking about this stuff.'

Ally surveyed me, as if thinking deeply about something. 'Yes, I can see that.'

We sat in silence for a few seconds, her looking at me while twisting one of her locks of blonde hair around an index finger.

'Bedtime,' I said, and gave Ally a smile in case she thought I was offended. 'I know it's early but . . .'

'It's time.' She nodded, returned the smile, and sat up on her bed. She gave me a hug at the door. There was something strange about the hug that I couldn't quite work out. A mixture of comfort and acceptance. I felt I had passed a test in some way. Proved I was interesting enough to warrant her attention, perhaps? Or maybe the opposite. That I was innocuous and plain and wouldn't change their equilibrium too much, so hey, they might as well have this boring poor girl as a friend. Or maybe I was just overthinking it. I said goodnight to Ally and went next door to my room.

Chapter 7

Julianne

Knightsbridge, 2019

Dinner isn't going well. If I were being honest with myself, I would admit I'd made a pasta bake partly to piss my mother off a little, as I knew she'd regard it as unsophisticated. But as I carved a chunk of the slightly overcooked congealed mass out of the bowl and a flap of solid cheese flopped onto her plate, I wished I'd gone with oysters.

'My, you've certainly been busy,' Diane says, moving a few tough bits of pasta to the side with her fork. 'Every room looks as festive as could be. Must have taken you a lot of time and energy.'

'A bit,' I say, then turn round as I hear a noise behind me.

'Ah, it's my favourite grandson.' She stands up to embrace Stephen as he walks into the room.

'We started because we didn't know if you were coming,' James says in a voice that makes it clear he doesn't approve.

'I explained you were busy finishing up some work,' I cut in quickly.

'I'm sorry, yes, French coursework.'

'They work you too hard,' Mom says, pinching Stephen's cheek. 'Both the teachers and your parents.' As she sits back down and Stephen goes to take the chair next to his father, a ripple of sadness runs through me. She never thought I was being worked too hard when I was up until one in the morning writing essay after essay, doing more than all my friends, desperately trying to get into one of the world's most prestigious universities in a country I didn't know. She didn't tell me to have a break or suggest I should take Christmas off. No matter what I did, it was never enough. If I so much as watched a single episode of a soap opera or read a magazine, I was made to feel like I was shirking. Little comments would be made at the dinner table, suggesting television 'was all I cared about these days' or that she should donate some of my school-books to Goodwill 'because I hardly ever opened them any more'. I'd sit there with the tears close behind my eyes, trying to ignore her. Some things never change.

'Stephen needs to work hard,' James says. 'He's aiming for the best. Of course, if he'd gone to Eton like we originally planned, things might be more certain.'

When I married him, I'd been quietly confident we wouldn't turn into one of those couples who make digs

at each other across the dinner table – bring up old disa-
greements to wound the other. My parents did that
throughout my childhood. And now, here's James, making
a little jibe about my problem with Eton. It's deliberate.
And it hurts.

'Oh, I couldn't agree more,' Diane says. 'There's a reason
it's world-famous. But it's amazing what he's done to pull
himself above the rest at that new-fangled place he's at.'

I almost choke on my food. 'Westminster is *older* than
Eton, Mom. As if that matters. Especially to you.'

She looks affronted. 'Of course my grandson's education
matters to me. And I did think the decision was made a
little rashly. After all, James does know about these things.'

'Well, it was all years ago now,' James says. 'And nobody
doubts Westminster is a great school.' He gives me one
of his warm smiles, probably worried he's upset me. I
automatically send one back his way without thinking.
Usually he's pretty good at presenting a united front
when my mother's here. I just wish he was doing better
today.

'You do realise you're all talking about me like I'm not
here.' Stephen's looking sullenly into his food.

James lets out a laugh. 'I'm sorry, you're right. You must
excuse us. It must be tiresome to have your old folks
wittering on about you.'

'Less of the old!' I say, trying to sound more cheerful
than I feel. James gives me a chuckle in response but
Stephen and his grandmother remain stonily silent. I even
see Diane raise one of her perfectly plucked eyebrows a
little, as if to say, *Well, you're not exactly young.* She then

turns to talk to Stephen and asks, 'What are you planning to do with your Christmas holiday?'

He looks disconcerted by the question, as if it's a trap he might fall into. Taking a fleeting look at his father, he proceeds to give a mumbled list of his homework assignments, social arrangements with his school friends, and how he plans to stay at his boyfriend's house in the gap between Boxing Day and New Year.

'How is William?' James asks. 'We haven't seen him for weeks. Busy revising, is he? He's determined to get into Oxford, Diane. Such a hard worker.'

'Just like Stephen is,' I say, coming to his defence before his father's digs become too blatant.

'Well, I imagine Stephen's a dead cert for Oxford, too. First my daughter, then my grandson, both off to the best university in the world. I'm so proud just at the thought of it.'

That niggle in my head is back again. The sense of resentment that only now, decades later, can my mother suggest she is 'proud' I got in to Oxford. On the day I found out I'd won a place, she'd acted like it was merely another big task she could tick off her to-do list. Daughter into Oxford: check.

'I think,' I say, choosing my words carefully, 'that Stephen is keen to go to the college that suits his skills the best and offers the course he most likes. He won't be going anywhere just because Will is.'

My mother looks so horrified it's almost comical. 'Julianne, are you telling me you're actively trying to dissuade the boy from attending the greatest—'

'Oh, spare me the greatest university in the world talk, Mom. There are plenty of other great universities.'

I can see James moving food around his plate with sharp stabs of his fork. I've pissed him off now.

Stephen looks around at us. 'You're all doing it again. I'm still here you know.'

Nobody laughs this time. My mom is looking around her as if trying to suss out where in the argument she could fit in. 'I'm sensing some tension,' she says eventually.

'How observant of you,' I reply, not looking at her.

'I'm sorry, Diane,' James says. 'We can't be much fun tonight. Julianne is clearly stressed with Christmas and everything . . .'

'Am I?' I say, looking at him. 'You've decided that, have you?'

'. . . and Stephen,' he says, ignoring me. 'I think he must be getting worried about his mountains of coursework.'

Stephen shakes his head. 'I'm not that worried.'

'Then why, may I ask, have you been sitting at this table like a grumpy teenager all evening?'

James is doing his strict-parent voice now. I've never understood why Stephen takes it so seriously and rarely answers back when his father gets angry. To me, it sounds like someone in a play, just pretending, speaking the lines they think they should say without being totally sure how they should be saying them. He's never been the loud, forthright one – that's partly the reason I fell for him, back when I was just nineteen. He was more the quiet, brooding type, exerting a quiet confidence rather than a forceful one. The more show-offy bursts of emotion he'd left to his friends, Ally and Ernest.

Stephen doesn't immediately respond to his father, but carries on staring at his food. I'm growing steadily more worried about him. While I'm desperate to talk to James about what I've just seen on his computer, I would very much prefer Stephen not to be present and, if possible, minimise his part in the whole thing. The thought of my mother being within hearing distance is mortifying.

'I've . . . I've just got a lot to think about,' Stephen says, and then carries on eating his food.

Silence resumes for the rest of the meal.

After dinner, my mother is keen to gravitate towards the lounge pretty quickly, and it becomes clear, as she locates the Christmas bumper issue of the *Radio Times*, that there's a showing of *The Best Exotic Marigold Hotel* she's keen to see. She often stays to watch something with us on TV after dinner, but it's rarely longer than an hour and a full-length feature film is certainly not the norm. 'It's rather long,' I say, looking at the listing in the magazine, noticing that, with commercials, it will run for two and a half hours.

'Oh, it's a glorious film,' James says, settling down in his usual spot on the one-seater. Back when we first bought the house, he and I used to snuggle together on the sofa, sometimes with toddler Stephen between us. As the years had gone by, however, it'd become just Stephen and I sitting together at each end of the long sofa, and James on his own at the other side of the room. Thinking about it now, I wonder when that happened. When did he first make the move to sit alone? I can't place the moment in my head. The change just seems to have slipped into my life without my noticing it.

'I've been wanting to see it for ages, ever since Susana at the swimming club told me how much she and her husband love it. It's become one of their favourites, apparently. I was worried I was going to miss it when you invited me round to dinner; then I thought it might be nice for us to watch it together.'

A flash of panic courses through me. I'm not sure I have the energy to watch something right now. I need to clear my head. Get things sorted. Talk to my husband. As I turn towards the television screen, my mind flicks back once again to that clinically cold list of details about those young women, their haunting faces, their lack of family or friends or proper employment. I know people live like that. I know not everyone is as lucky as I am. But who would want to collect all that information and pool it into one horrible document?

'You don't mind, do you, Julianne? I'd hate to miss it.'

My mother's voice snaps me back to the present. She's brandishing the TV remote at me. I'm tempted to remind her of the state-of-the-art Sky Q facilities she has at home and how, if she was so desperate to see this particular film, she could have easily recorded it. Instead, I resign myself to another few hours of her company and try to get myself in the frame of mind to watch Judi Dench and Bill Nighy smile and joke their way across India, knowing it's the last thing I want to do.

Chapter 8

Holly

Oxford, 1990

My dad once told me that friends come and go and you never really know which ones mean the most until they abandon you. Strong words for a father to tell his seven-year-old child, but that was my father for you: inappropriate and unaware. My mother overheard him and came to tell me that Daddy had actually had a bit of a mix-up and forgotten to mention that most people grow up to have a great group of friends they can have a fun time with. Dad stood back as Mum set about correcting his statement, looking slightly puzzled. When my mum walked back into the kitchen – we had been standing in the corridor, me swinging precariously from one of the lower banisters –

he had sighed deeply and then just said, 'Maybe I was wrong. I'm sure you'll work all this out for yourself, little Holly.'

Although I probably wouldn't say this conversation caused me to be a loner throughout the rest of my childhood and most of my teenage years, it was probably a contributing factor. I always found I could never quite trust someone enough, whether it was Stephanie and George in art class, who liked to chat endlessly about popstars and trashy movies, or Greg, the first boy I thought that, in another world, I could have dated. None of them managed to install a framework of trust within me. There was no pattern of reliability; not because they continually let me down – more because I never gave them much of a chance not to.

When Ally suggested she thought I should spend more time with her, Ernest, James and Peter, I saw this as proof my mother had been right, but also, at the same time, a challenge to the gods of fate to see if my father would be right as well. I did test them privately on this, when I used the communal telephone in the hallway. Mum got one version of the story: I had met a lovely group of people, very posh but not bad posh, and I was having a good time discussing my interests with them, most of which they shared, and we had nice outings and food together ('The Wimpy! I know, so strange, but really fun') and I thought there might be something of a romance blossoming between one of the boys, James, and me. That last bit was pure exaggeration. My feelings for James had grown more intense by the day, to the point where I had started to pull out a couple of strands of my hair to take away my nerves each time I went somewhere I knew he would be. Not enough for there to be bald spots on my head. Just one or two. I found it helped. But I didn't tell Mum that part.

Dad, on the other hand, received a different version of Holly's Time at Oxford University. He was told that I'd sort of befriended a group of posh people I didn't think he would like. I didn't like them much either, but I was focusing mostly on my studies and they were good for me to sound ideas off. No, I wouldn't be bringing any of them home over the Christmas holidays, he didn't have to worry about that. Boyfriend? No, there wasn't anything much like that on the horizon. Maybe a boy I liked, but it wasn't anything worth mentioning.

Some people might have found the way I approached occasional phone calls home to my parents odd, but it worked for me. Each conversation was crafted so it lasted long enough to make the call worth the money but not so long as to bore any of the parties involved. The details that would most impress Mum were emphasised and the parts that would least appeal to Dad were played down or excised completely. All in all, I did a pretty good job of giving each of them what they wanted.

So when I found myself going on my third outing as part of 'The Ally Club', as I continued to call it in my head, I found I was judging conversations and how people reacted to me through the dual perspective of my parents. Or, rather, through my own filtering mechanism, deciding how I would relay the event to each of them if I were to call them when I returned home (which I wouldn't be doing, since I had phoned them only four days previously).

We were going to Blackwells, in Broad Street. I knew it was a famous bookshop – I had been there with my parents when we'd looked round the university and read the little plaque on the wall saying it had been opened in 1879 – but I still nodded and seemed interested when Ernest told me this. He was frequently doing this; treating me as if I needed the world explaining to me (and not even just the posh aspects of the world; sometimes things as mundane, though curiously unmanly, as how best to get stains off clothes). I usually just smiled and nodded and said the right things. I'd always been good at doing that. And that's why I quite enjoyed occasionally doing the complete opposite and challenging what people said. A lot of pleasure could be derived from being the mouse that roared.

Ally and I had arranged to get a milkshake from a small café before meeting the boys at the bookshop. The purpose of the visit was to stock up on reading material for the Christmas holidays. Over their school breaks, Ernest and James had always held a competition: which of the two could read the most pieces of literature. They had devised a points-based scoring system, too. Five points per book under six hundred pages. Ten points per book over six hundred. Two points would be deducted if the book had been written after the turn of the century, with the exception of those that had won either the Booker or the Pulitzer, or were by authors who had won the

Nobel Prize for Literature. Five points would also be deducted from the total amount if the participant failed to include a 'reasonable spread' of genres, periods of writing and nationalities. Ally gave me a thorough explanation of all this on our way to buy the milkshakes and while we drank them. 'Apparently the teachers at Eton egged them on, rather. Kept recommending books they should add to their lists. They like competition, Etonians. They'd turn everything into a game if they could. God, they even turn masturbating into a competitive sport.'

I realised I'd pulled a face at the word 'masturbating' but Ally seemed spurred on by it. I got the feeling she'd come to like shocking me. 'Oh yes, apparently they all stand around in a circle with a biscuit on a table in the middle. Then they pump away at themselves and the first person to spill his seed, so to speak, is the winner. The last person is, well . . .'

'Well, what?'

'The loser.'

I grimaced. 'And what happens to the biscuit?' I said, thinking I could probably guess the answer.

'The loser has to eat it.'

'That doesn't sound very appetising.'

Ally chuckled. 'I don't think it's meant to be. Just a bit of fun, I'm sure.'

'Can't you get AIDS that way?'

She tilted her head to one side and took a sip of her milkshake, apparently considering this. 'I don't think so. I'm not sure, to be honest. I doubt it. Otherwise I think most MPs would be on their deathbeds!'

She laughed loudly at her own joke.

'So, do you know which books they'll be picking this time?' I said, keen to get the conversation away from boys consuming their own, and others', semen.

'Well, they have a bit of trouble now, since they've read so much already, so there's naturally a bit of double-dipping. They haven't really found a way to control that side of things, so they just try to make sure their lists are made up of a healthy majority of titles they haven't read before, and the ones they have they aren't supposed to have read for a good few years.'

The book lover in me liked the sound of this, although I knew I wouldn't be able to compete with Ernest and James in a million years. They both seemed to swallow literature, or inhale it like a long drag on a cigarette, relishing it as they went. I read for pleasure, first and foremost, whereas they seemed to see it primarily as a form of self-nourishment.

'Do you ever join in?' I asked.

'Christ, no. I wouldn't be able to keep up. It would be a humiliation.'

Come to think of it, I couldn't remember the last time I'd seen Ally with a book, or even properly studying. Perhaps she was one of those people who just sailed through coursework and exams without ever really having to try. There had been a couple of girls in my school like that. I'd envied them greatly.

We tried to enter Blackwells, but didn't get very far. A young bookseller, in the midst of neatly arranging copies of a Stephen King novel on a small table, looked up and told us we'd need to finish our milkshakes before we came any further. Ally rolled her eyes at him and for a minute I wondered if she'd ignore him and just march in, but to my relief she stepped back outside. A few minutes later, having discarded our empty milkshake cups in a wastepaper basket the bookseller had helpfully offered us, we walked purposefully, with me following Ally's lead, through the store towards the back. It was a vast shop, and went further back than I remembered. We found the section marked 'Classics' pretty quickly. I noticed it was divided up into 'English Literature', 'World Classics' and 'Modern Classics'. Each one was full of a vast array of volumes, most of them sporting the black or light-turquoise spines that characterised a sizeable chunk of Penguin's publishing output. There were hefty, more academic volumes of famous novels mixed in too, no doubt containing annotations, guides to the text, essays, lists of further reading and various other extras. I was about to start perusing the shelves properly when Ally tugged at my arm.

'Come on, round here.'

She steered me around the corner of one of the shelves towards a small alcove with a table and set of armchairs. Ernest and James sat side by side on one of them, the former lounging back, his head buried in an extremely large book which I recognised as *The Count of Monte Cristo*. James, on the other hand, was leaning forward, running an index finger down what appeared to be a long list, written in a leather-bound exercise book.

'Ding dong merrily, my little Christmas readers!' Ally

said loudly. I glanced around, slightly embarrassed, but there wasn't another person in sight and the alcove was well-hidden from view of the main part of the shop.

'It isn't Christmas. It's October, sis.'

Ernest didn't even bother to lower the book as he spoke. James's reaction was friendlier. 'But she is indeed right that we are here with Christmas in mind.' He nodded towards the empty sofa in front of him and then looked back at us. 'Sit down, you two. You can join in the fun.' Not for the first time, his eyes lingered on me slightly longer than Ally. I could feel myself reddening, so sat down quickly on the sofa, with Ally following suit slightly less gracefully.

'My mother likes to put up our Christmas tree in November,' I said. I didn't know why; I just needed to start speaking. 'A fake one, I mean. It's plastic. Then she swaps it for a real one in December.'

I baffled myself with my own words and the boys seemed a little surprised, with Ernest arching one of his neat eyebrows slightly. Ally, however, wasn't fazed, or at least came to my rescue.

'Oh, that does sound sensible. And plastic trees can look rather good these days, can't they? I see them in shops sometimes.'

I got the feeling the boys were trying to hide their mirth and being careful not to look at each other. I couldn't really blame them.

'So, what have you got so far?' Ally asked, pulling a stack of books in front of her. 'God, these are all a bit . . . well, trendy. *Last Exit to Brooklyn*? Really? Ginsberg,

Burroughs, Henry Miller. Going to be a cheerful Christmas.'

'That's James's pile.' Ernest rolled his eyes, glancing at the slim volumes in Ally's hands. 'Plus, they're relatively short. He'll need to read a lot of them.'

James kept his eyes on his exercise book, now making notes, allowing a small smile to creep across his face.

'What about you? How are you going to raise the game?' I asked, meeting Ernest's gaze, then worried it sounded like I was defending James (which, if I was honest with myself, I sort of was). It didn't escape him. The glint in his eye made that clear. He leaned forward and pushed a stack of books in my direction. 'Only seven so far. Slightly ashamed to say I've never read any of these, so am going to put that right this year.'

I pulled the stack of books towards me and went through them one by one. *The Mayor of Casterbridge* by Thomas Hardy, *The Monk* by Matthew Lewis, *The Way of All Flesh* by Samuel Butler, *Evelina* by Frances Burney, *The House of Mirth* by Edith Wharton, *The Scarlet Letter* by Nathaniel Hawthorne, *Tess of the D'Urbervilles* by Thomas Hardy.

'*Tess*? You must have read *Tess*?' I say, holding up the book.

He smirked, 'Okay, guilty. I have, but a long time ago. I was about nine or ten.'

I raised my eyebrows. 'Really?'

'Precocious child,' Ally said, shaking her head. 'We couldn't take the books from him. He clutched them too hard. Would cry and scream and wail so that nothing could be done.'

'Oh, nonsense,' Ernest said to her sharply, while continuing to smile at me. 'Go on then, Holly. Which books should be in my pile?'

I considered for a moment. 'I'd add some Joseph Conrad, Truman Capote, Émile Zola. Also, if you haven't already, try some Hermann Hesse, too. And maybe, if you could bear it, some Agatha Christie. Plus a few ghost stories. You always need ghost stories at Christmas.'

Ernest tilted his head on one side, apparently impressed. 'Nice. Curious range. Perhaps you could go and pick me out some.'

I felt a glimmer of irritation at this. Who did he think he was, ordering me to go and find books for him? Ally apparently had the same thought.

'You lazy sod. Pay no attention to him, Holly.'

I was about to do as Ally suggested when James piped up.

'I'll come with you. You can suggest some of your favourites to me, too.'

Before I knew what I was doing, I had agreed and risen from the sofa.

'Sure!' I cringed as I said it and quickly looked at Ally and Ernest to see if they'd noticed my overenthusiasm. They had of course. They were doing their best not to show it, but the slight curl to Ernest's smile was all I needed to see.

James stood up, too, and navigated his way around the table and stacks of books, walking straight past me. He clearly expected me to follow, so I did, turning the corner into the dense and completely deserted classics section. He knelt down to a lower shelf, apparently looking for a particular volume. I waited, watching his chinos tighten around his waist, the line of his underwear starting to show. He eventually pulled out an extremely thick paperback book and held it up to me.

'You should read this,' he said simply, offering it to me. I stared at it for a good few seconds. 'Can you take it?' he said. 'It's hurting my arm.' His small smile was back, dancing somewhere around the corners of his mouth. It was like the whole of him glinted occasionally when that smile hovered near the surface. I took the book, trying not to drop it when it became clear to me how heavy it actually was.

'God,' I exclaimed as I held on to it. 'I'm not sure I'm brave enough for something this size.'

He smiled more fully now and got back up, smoothing down his crumpled cream Oxford shirt. 'That's what I thought when Ernest first gave it to me, back when I was at school. But it's worth it. Trust me, it really is.'

I glanced down at the cover. It depicted a sad or even slightly frightened-looking girl sitting at a desk writing what appeared to be a very lengthy letter. Samuel Richardson. *Clarissa*. I'd heard of Richardson, of course, but hadn't ever read him, though I thought I might have bought an old copy of his (much shorter) novel *Pamela* at a car boot sale a couple of years ago. I lifted the book up and down in my hand, feeling its weight fighting against my fingers. You could have killed a small child with it.

'I'm worried I might die before I get to the end.'

He laughed. 'Well, better start soon then.'

I glanced down at the price. It was £7.99. Very expensive for a paperback, though I reasoned there was at least the same amount of content crammed within it as one would get with three novels costing £3.99. Put like that, it was rather good value. During my outings with the Ally gang, the money difference hadn't really been an issue. I'd been worried at first that we'd be zooming off in expensive cars to grand hotels and dining like the infamous Bullingdon Club did. Thankfully their tastes seemed a little more modest. I also suspected that Peter, who had grown more and more absent from our outings as term went on, didn't have as much cash as his friends. I had tried not to read too much into Peter's increasing absences from our social occasions, though I couldn't help but feel there was a correlation between the group's adoption of me and his no-shows. He'd even missed a couple of tuition seminars, much to Dr Lawrence's irritation.

'Do you like the sound of it?'

James's voice jolted me out of my thoughts about Peter. He was staring at me, looking almost hopeful, as if some of his confidence had been stripped away. I felt as if, by recommending the book to me, he had exposed part of himself; shown me a glimmer of what was inside him.

'Yes,' I said hurriedly, 'I do. I'm going to get it. It will take me a while, though. I'm not that quick a reader.'

'It's worth taking your time with,' he said, then winked at me. It felt as if I'd just been doused in freezing-cold water and I looked down quickly in case he noticed it in my face.

He cast an eye down the corridor of shelves, out into the main part of the bookshop.

'Our Christmas celebrations are never really much of a big deal, so I'll have plenty of time to read over the holidays,' I said, flicking through the pages of the novel, trying to sound more casual than I felt. I glanced back up at him and was about to carry on talking when I sensed he wasn't really paying attention. He was still looking over my shoulder, as if something had caught his attention and he was having trouble drawing his gaze away.

'I'm sorry, Holly, would you excuse me for a second?' he said suddenly, then skirted round me and walked purposefully away. I felt a little abandoned, even though I was only metres away from where the others were sitting. On my way round the corner, back towards the alcove, I glanced towards the book-laden tables in the main part of the shop to try and see what he'd been looking at, but I couldn't spot him.

'What did he show you?' asked Ally, when I arrived back and sat down on the sofa. 'God, it wasn't poetry, was it? I spotted him reading some Keats in the library once. Very unfashionable. I think he fancies himself a tormented, romantic soul.'

I wanted to ask what romance in particular he was tormented about, but didn't dare.

'Oh gosh, he didn't press that on you, did he?' Ernest nodded at the book in my hands.

I gave a small nod. 'He did. I'm going to read it over Christmas.'

Ernest gave a low laugh. 'He is for ever begging me to share his love of Richardson. Don't get me wrong; he's fine if you like that kind of thing. But he does . . . well . . . go on a bit.'

Though I was currently unqualified to give an opinion on Richardson's prose, I couldn't help but feel Ernest was probably right, judging by the way the heavy book was digging into my thighs.

'I said I'd try it.'

'Good luck,' said Ally, rolling her eyes. 'Honestly, trust him to recommend a book the size of a small boulder. What have you done with him, anyway?'

'I don't know. He just said he needed a quick sec.'

Ernest smirked. 'Probably wanking off in the toilets to some Marquis de Sade.'

'I think maybe he went to buy something,' I muttered, though of course I knew no such thing.

The three of us talked for a bit, with Ernest sharing some additions to his book list while Ally made gentle fun of him. Fifteen minutes after James's mysterious disappearance, curiosity got the better of me and I stood up. 'I'm just going to see if they have any Dorothy L. Sayers novels.' I walked out before I could see their reactions. I didn't know whether the two of them had any opinions on Sayers and wasn't waiting to find out if they did. Looking around me as I came out into the main part of the store, I felt oddly panicked that I couldn't instantly see him anywhere, as if he were a small child who had run off and been out of sight for a little bit too long. I fantasised briefly about the shocked reactions I'd probably get if I suddenly started shrieking 'JAMES!' at the top of my voice, but decided it wasn't worth it, humorous though it might well have been.

'Excuse me, do you need any help?' The young bookseller we'd met as we came in was looking at me suspiciously. Did he think I was a shoplifter?

I was about to tell him I was fine when I saw him. James, outside the shop in the street. He was talking to someone. I couldn't make out a face, but I could tell by the long, flowing, brown hair and shape of the figure that it was a female. James, talking to a girl. And not just talking. She was leaning up against a lamppost and he had his hand on her shoulder.

I walked away from the bookseller without saying a thing, moving towards the door, trying to keep my pace as close to normal as possible. I felt like running. I wanted to interrupt them somehow, to tell him he had to come back inside. To conjure up some emergency that could only be solved by his returning to the little alcove with the sofas and piles of books. I could see her more clearly now and, with depressing inevitability, saw that she wasn't just pretty. She was breathtakingly beautiful. I was standing there, right by the doorway, partly hoping he would see me. But he didn't. He didn't even glance in the direction of the shop. They were laughing together and I caught a few words.

'Oh, come on. You've got to be free at least one night.'

That voice. American. My mother had always claimed she found the American accent 'brash' and said it sounded so 'uncouth'. But hers didn't sound anything of the kind. It was silky smooth, like liquid caramel. He laughed and said something I couldn't catch, then a group of laughing teenagers walked in front of them and started entering the shop. Apparently spotting their open bottles of Coca-Cola within milliseconds, the bookseller arrived out of nowhere and began rebuking them pompously. I thought about waiting, to see if I could hear anything more of their conversation, but the bookseller was now rounding on me, clearly disturbed by my odd behaviour.

'Are you sure I can't help you find what you're looking for?'

I wish you could, I thought, but instead said to him, 'No, I'm fine,' and walked back towards the others, upsetting a stack of teetering paperbacks on a trolley as I went. I wasn't fine.

I cried myself to sleep and felt ashamed when I woke up in the middle of the night, my pillow still damp from my tears hours earlier. I drifted in and out of a sleep filled with vague dreams of James and that girl outside. The American girl. And they were both laughing at me, swinging from lampposts around the streets of Oxford, pointing and jeering and saying things to each other I couldn't quite catch. The dream was just transforming into something darker and more nightmarish involving vampires when a knock came at my door and woke me with a jolt. Seconds later, Ally walked in without waiting for a reply. She often did this and I thanked God every time that she hadn't yet caught me naked.

'Morning, morning, morning!' she said unnecessarily loudly. 'There's a phone call for you.'

I was still slightly dazed with sleep and for a moment didn't have time to process what she'd said. Eventually, it sank in. 'Phone call?'

'Uh huh,' she said, now fiddling with the bookmark ribbon of a critical theory anthology on my desk.

I felt myself growing cold. Nobody ever called me. Something must be wrong.

'Did they say who it was?'

'Mother? Father? Something parental. I didn't take the call. It was that coloured girl from down the hall.'

'She's African–American. From Washington,' I murmured as I pulled myself out of bed and took my dressing gown off the desk chair.

'Your mother?' said Ally, not really listening. She was busy running her hands through the pages of the anthology. 'God, I have no idea how you make sense of this. Have you actually tried reading it?'

I sighed. 'No, not my mother,' I said, then headed to the door, not bothering to answer her question about the book. I left her in my room and walked down the corridor to the phone. The receiver had been left on the top of the unit and I picked it up gingerly, unsure what I was about to find out.

'Hello?' I said, slightly nervously.

'Hello? I'd like to speak to Holly. It's her mother talking.'

'Mum, it's me.'

'Oh,' she gave a small little laugh. 'Sorry, love. You sounded so different.'

She'd mentioned this before and it was becoming irritating. During our brief and awkward short chats on the phone in the past month she'd implied that my accent had become posher, and I wasn't quite sure if this was a dig or something she wanted to encourage.

'I just said "Hello". How could that be so different?'

'Well, I hope you're having a good morning.'

'It's 8.00 a.m.,' I said, glancing at my watch. 'It hasn't really started.'

'Oh, I forgot you students are such late risers.'

That was certainly a dig. She knew I was naturally an early riser and prided myself on it, but I hadn't bothered setting an alarm the night before.

'Is there anything wrong, Mum?'

'Oh no, definitely not. Something quite nice, actually. It's about Christmas.'

'Oh,' I said. 'What about it?'

'Well, you see, our friends the Searles . . . you remember them, don't you? Well, they're going on a cruise over Christmas. The Caribbean. Anyway, they were going with their two sons. Well, there's been a bit of an upset and the boys are no longer going.'

I remembered the Searle family very well. My mother had met them at the local church fete and decided they seemed like good people to befriend. Middle class enough so she felt like it was a good thing to be seen in their company but not so posh as to make her feel intimidated. She'd even tried encouraging me to befriend the two sons, particularly the one closest to my age. We'd gone to the cinema together to see *Total Recall* and then afterwards he'd confessed he wasn't really up for dating and had only gone out with me to be nice. I'd told him I didn't want to date him either and had only agreed to go because I fancied Arnold Schwarzenegger. A bit of a white lie, but it made his eyes widen in a rather satisfying way.

'Sorry to hear that. What kind of upset?'

'Well, one of their boys, the older one, um, well, he's become in the family way with a girl at university. He's at Warwick. Maybe that sort of thing goes on there. Anyway, the Searles have all been in a bit of a state about it and Kieran is refusing to go with them on the cruise, and now his brother, Samuel, your friend, is refusing, too. So they've very kindly invited us along.'

I was taken aback. The thought of my mother on a cruise felt foreign to me.

'That's . . . that's nice of them. I suppose I could bring along my work and stuff . . .'

'Oh . . . oh dear, I'm sorry, love. By "us" I meant your dad and me. I thought you'd probably be busy with all your studies and would want to go out with your Oxford friends at some point. You'll probably have a much better time with some peace and quiet, anyway.'

I tried to digest what she was saying, but it was as if her voice was getting steadily quieter.

'I'm sorry, love. I know we've usually done the traditional turkey dinner for Christmas, but I sort of thought your going to Oxford would . . . well . . . kind of put an end to things like that. You're grown up now and I wouldn't want to hold you back and force you to do all our old-people things. Is that okay?'

I struggled to get the words out, but finally managed to breathe. 'Yes. Okay. I understand. That's fine.'

'We'll be gone by the time you return from Oxford, I'm afraid. We leave on December tenth.'

'I get back on the twelfth,' I said in a monotone.

'I'll leave some nice bits in the freezer for you. And presents under the tree. I've got you some vouchers, too, so you can go out and do a bit of shopping? That will be nice, won't it?'

I didn't say anything. She hurried on. 'I just thought we've never been a big Christmas-type of family, have we? Just us three, chewing away at whatever cheap, leathery turkey your dad's picked up and my burnt potatoes. It's not as if we'll be missing much.'

'Okay.' I didn't want to hear any more. I just wanted her to get off the phone. 'What day do you get back?'

'We'll be back just into the New Year. January sixth.'

'So you'll be gone nearly a month?'

A pause. 'Yes. You see, the Searles are retired now, so they don't really have any time constraints.'

'Surely their sons would have . . .'

'Oh, that's not been a problem. They've managed to extend our tickets without much of an uptick in price. It's all been very reasonable. They . . .'

'That's great, Mum. Really great. I'll have to go. Somebody wants to use the phone. I'm glad Kieran Searle's lack of condoms has made your Christmas complete.'

'Okay, love. Er . . . sorry, what?'

It took her a while to compute what I'd said, but I'd had enough. 'Send me a postcard,' I said, then put the phone down. I went back to my room to find Ally still there, now reading a large Agatha Christie omnibus she must have found at the back of my bookshelf.

'Did you know Hercule Poirot is supposed to be Belgian? I saw that new TV series last year and I swear David Suchet plays him as French.'

'He doesn't. He does a Belgian accent.' I didn't bother trying to sound friendly, but Ally didn't notice.

'Oh well, I've always been rather rubbish with European accents.' She slammed the book shut and leapt up. 'Do you want to go and get some breakfast?'

I shook my head. 'I don't feel well,' I said bluntly. 'I'm going to go back to sleep.'

'Oh no! Dearest!' Ally rushed to my side. 'Do you need a paracetamol? Is it period pains? Or flu? There's definitely something going around. How about I bring you some hot orange juice with a dash of lavender honey in it?'

I stepped away from her and went to lie down on my bed. 'Thank you, but I'll be fine. I'm sorry, Ally, that's very nice of you. I just need to sleep.'

She nodded enthusiastically. 'Quite right, quite right. Have a good rest. Come and join me for *Neighbours* later if you feel better.'

At last, she left me alone with nothing but my thoughts. And they weren't good company.

Chapter 9

Julianne

Knightsbridge, 2019

My mother is on her way out and James is being much more attentive than I am, as usual, helping her with her coat, checking she's got her scarf, demanding to know where Stephen has got to again (he went back upstairs halfway through *The Best Exotic Marigold Hotel*).

'Goodness, I'm not looking forward to going back to my cold, empty old place on a night like this,' she says, fully aware she'll be going back to a warm, comfortable, modern house with her live-in housekeeper.

'I can drive you, if you'd prefer that to the taxi,' James says.

'No, no. I don't want to be a nuisance and Julianne

looks like she's about to collapse. You'd better get her into bed.' She comes over to me and gives me her trademark awkward tap on the back and kiss on the cheek. 'Take care, dear. Try not to let everything get on top of you. Remember some women have a career *and* a home to run. Imagine how much harder it is for them. And say goodnight to Stephen for me. Such a conscientious boy. I'll see you all on Christmas Day.' With this parting shot, she disappears into the night, no doubt confident her final few thinly veiled jibes will have well and truly hit home.

'Well,' James says, 'I don't think you look like you're about to collapse. I think you look as lovely as ever.' He moves towards me and wraps his arms around my shoulders, bringing his body close in to me so that we're touching. I know the signs. He always does this when he wants to have sex.

'She's probably right, I am a bit tired,' I say, slightly stepping away from him, but he doesn't let go.

'Nonsense,' he says, leaning back to look at me. I find I can't meet his eyes, and instead settle for a point on his shoulder. Not getting anywhere with his attempts at affection, he changes tack. 'What was wrong with Stephen? All evening he seemed . . . not like himself.'

I extricate myself from his grip and move towards the stairs. 'What he said, probably. School stuff.'

He nods, looking a bit troubled. 'Listen, I'm sorry the subject of Oxford came up when your mother was here. I realise it isn't always helpful to have her chipping in.'

'No, it isn't,' I say, still not looking him in the eye.

'Let's go to bed. Leave the plates and things for Cassie in the morning.'

I sigh and nod, feeling bad for adding to Cassie's workload, even if such jobs are the very things we pay her to do.

James goes ahead to our bedroom, but I pause on the landing to listen at Stephen's door. I can hear the sound of his television. Knocking softly, I open the door and see him on the bed, hugging his knees close to him, as if he's cold. He's got his pyjamas on, itself rather unusual – he normally only wears them when he's got flu and doesn't want to be lying about in just his underpants when his father and I are bringing him hot drinks, soup and paracetamol.

'Are you okay?' I ask, and he nods. 'I'll talk to Dad about . . . about what you found. There'll be an explanation. They'll be to do with his work, or maybe a computer virus or something. Just . . . try not to dwell on them.'

'Okay.'

I give him a weak smile, say goodnight, close the door to his room and walk over to mine.

James is already in his boxers and brushing his teeth in the en suite. He sees me looking in the mirror and I can tell, from the slightly mischievous look in his eye, that his desires haven't gone away.

I need to talk to him. I can't sleep until I've got all of this off my mind and heard his explanation. He comes towards me now, using the hand towel to wipe toothpaste from his chin. His dark-brown hair is slightly damp from where he's washed his face, a few strands from his fringe hanging limply over the smooth skin of his forehead, making him look much younger than his forty-eight years. I start to say something about needing to talk to him, but he starts kissing me without warning, the scent of mint and his Hugo Boss fragrance mingling, intoxicating, making me almost fall into him. Then it all happens very quickly, as it usually does when we make love. Though I'm not sure making love is the right word for it. As soon as he's got me, ready and compliant, he pushes me away onto the bed so I'm lying on my front. With one hand, he gathers my arms together so they're pinned in front of me, my frame bent over the bed. With the other, he pulls down the bottom half of my clothes, a little roughly, and casts them aside. My face is being pressed into the mattress, the scent of James now replaced by fabric softener and the pine-tree air freshener installed in the corner of the room. I hear the snap of the waistband of his boxers as he hurries to get them down and then, without much warning, always without much warning, there's the sharp suddenness of him entering me from behind. More often than not, I'm aroused, enjoying the sensation, liking what he's doing to me, so that he slips in easily. But today I'm not. And he hasn't asked. He hasn't checked. He hasn't said anything, apart from his usual low grunt as he pushes himself deeper. Surely he can feel I'm not ready? That he might be hurting me? Doesn't he care? He's pushing quicker now, in and out, gathering speed. And then a grey shape at the corner of my consciousness starts to take hold, bit by bit, until something falls into my mind. Two words.

Trial run. The impact of those two words, what they could mean, explodes through my brain. *No attempts to contact police have been made.* I can't do this. I cry out and pull myself up.

'I'm nearly finished,' James pants, still going, stabilising himself by holding on to my shoulder. Or is he trying to hold me still, stop me struggling?

'Stop!' I shout, and again try to get up. He does stop and pulls out of me, too quickly for comfort, and I roll to the side away from him. Lying on my back on the bed, I hear him ask what's wrong and if I'm okay, but my heart is pumping too loudly and my vision is blurred.

'Julianne, talk to me?' He comes into focus now, crouching down beside me, his hands taking hold of mine. 'Are you feeling unwell?'

I let out a splutter – a noise of disbelief. I can't help myself. 'Unwell? Must I be feeling unwell to not want you hammering away at me like that?'

I can feel the shock in his silence. It fills the room. I've never spoken to him like this. I've never interrogated our sex life in such a stark, harsh way. To be honest, I don't think I've ever really wanted to. Waiting for him to respond, I pull myself up so I'm in a sitting position on the bed and wipe my eyes, finding tears clinging to my cheeks.

'I don't know what to say,' James says, standing there naked. 'We were just having sex . . . why did you start shouting?' He has a semi-erection that looks strangely ridiculous now. It's practically deflating before my eyes. He's realising we're not going to start having sex again. Something serious is happening.

'It's the way you were doing it. As if I . . . as if you didn't care about me.'

He walks towards me and lays his hands on my shoulders. 'Julianne, how can you say that? Of course I care about you. I was just . . . you know . . . in the midst of it all. Passion. Arousal. That sort of thing.'

I still can't look him in the eye. 'That sort of thing,' I repeat. It isn't a question. The words just stick in my head and I have to get them out again. Because they seem too vague and leave room for doubt and interpretation. What sort of thing does he really want, does he really like? The thought is making me feel dizzy and I close my eyes.

'Talk to me, please. Tell me what's wrong.'

I might be imagining it, but I think I can hear the faintest hint of irritation in his voice amidst the concern. Even the possibility that he might be frustrated with me makes me angry. I get up and go over to the bathroom, not bothering to close the door. I turn the taps on and splash some lukewarm water onto my face. It soothes something within me, even though my heart is still pounding in my chest.

'Do you prefer rough sex? Violent sex?' I ask the question simply and quietly and for a second I think he hasn't heard me over the sound of the water, but then he answers.

'Violent? What are you talking about?'

'I'm talking about sex.' I reply simply. I'm trying to keep my cool, to sound almost disinterested. It will make this as easy as possible to get through.

'I don't think we really need to discuss this.' His tone

108

is guarded and opaque. 'I think we have a pretty healthy sex life. Compared to many couples our age.'

I stop for a moment, not liking where my brain is going. 'How about with other women?'

I can feel the tension coming off him. Something's shifted. He's still, not moving, but I can tell his fight or flight response has been triggered. I'm stepping over a line here.

'Julianne, how can you possibly ask me that?'

I take in a deep breath. 'I think I can.'

He doesn't reply.

'Is there anything you want to tell me?' I say slowly. Carefully. 'Anything that springs to mind?'

Another beat. Then: 'I don't know what's brought all this on, Julianne. It doesn't sound very healthy.'

I turn off the tap.

'Oh, I'm being unhealthy, am I? Curious choice of phrase, don't you think? Talking about sex, about what turns us on, about what we like to do to each other – is that unhealthy?' I look directly into the mirror above the sink and see him looking back at me from the doorway. He must see the danger in my eyes, as he starts back-tracking.

'No, I didn't mean that. I just mean that . . . well . . . all men like different things . . . and of course women aren't all the same. Everyone has their own preferences and desires and . . . needs. Don't they?'

I find I can hold his gaze now, albeit through a reflection. 'I don't know. Do they?'

A few beats of silence pass between us, then I break

eye contact and wipe my face with a towel. I get up and, without making a sound, go back into the bedroom, pull on a dressing gown that's hanging on the wardrobe door, and walk out of the room onto the landing.

'Where are you going?' James says as I close the door behind me. I ignore him.

It takes me less than a minute to retrieve my iPad mini from the living room and return upstairs. His eyes widen when he sees what I'm carrying.

'Julianne, please, tell me, what is all this about?'

I still don't say anything, but set to work unlocking the iPad, opening up my Facebook messages, taking care to tilt the screen away from him so he can't see it's Stephen's message I've clicked on. I then navigate to Dropbox. It's already signed in to the general family account we use and I follow the file path I've now memorised, all the while expecting him to stop me. He doesn't. He just stands over me as that daunting list of files with the long numbers for names appears on the screen.

I click on the top one, the one I looked at earlier. Up comes the neat, ordered list, the haunting photograph, the mounds of information on how terrible this woman's life is. I look up at him. His face has gone white and his eyes are glistening.

'I want you to tell me what this is. I want you to look at it and try . . . just try . . .' The tears are threatening to come now and I swallow hard. 'Just try to tell me why you would have put something like this in our family Dropbox account?'

He continues to stare at the computer in silence still,

a look of mounting horror on his face. I watch as he casts his eye down the page on the screen, seeing how it affects him. His mouth twitches slightly, but overall his face settles into something strangely blank. Then he reaches down and presses the lock button, shutting off the cold white light that had been illuminating his face. The room suddenly feels very dark.

'Oh, Julianne,' he says. He turns back to me now and his face looks sad. Troubled and sad, as if I've just told him I'm unwell or that someone has done me a terrible, terrible wrong. He steps forward and reaches out, trying to hold me, but I step back.

'No,' I say, quietly but firmly. 'Don't touch me. Just tell me why the fuck something like *that* is on here. This is your one and only chance or I swear to God I'll go to the police.'

He looks even more upset now. 'The police?' He says the words as if he doesn't fully understand what I mean, as if I've just offered him an ice cream. 'Oh God, Julianne, is this why you've been acting strangely all evening?'

My eyes widen. 'Of course it is. What am I supposed to think when I find something as strange as this in a file with your name on it? And there are more of them. This isn't the only one. Who are they? Why do you have all these details on them? Are you having an affair?'

As soon as these last five words are out my mouth, I regret them. And I know they're foolish. Whatever this is, it isn't simple infidelity. If infidelity is ever simple.

'Please, darling, listen to me. Please.'

I stand in silence, ready to back away if he comes any

111

closer. I don't want his hands on me. I don't want him trying to comfort me. 'I'm listening.'

He takes a deep breath. 'Julianne, you know what I do for a living. You know that part of my job is to gather information for our clients. Publicly available information, gathered legally and ethically.'

'This doesn't look legal or ethical.'

He holds up a hand, a habit of his that's always irritated me. 'This isn't from me or my company. It's from a start-up firm we were looking to acquire. It's based in an office block in Mile End and, well, it all looks very promising. It's run by two young women, actually, along with a few men they subcontract to. They're very good, very 'of the moment', one might say. Very keen to see how information can lead to political gain, social reform. This was part of a project of theirs, looking at disadvantaged people in certain parts of London and the South-East. I think they were looking to sell this to a left-wing pressure group.'

His words are tumbling around inside my head. Have I got this so catastrophically wrong?

'We aren't acquiring the firm. We had concerns about their methods – the legality of them. We would never condone people posing as social workers and health professionals in order to get key personal info, like their STI status or drug-use habits. To be completely honest, that kind of thing does go on. Data harvesting through surveillance and undercover work. But those services are usually provided for either rather shady clients paying big bucks or . . .' He stops, as if he's just lost his nerve. Or caught himself before saying something he doesn't want to.

'Or?' I ask.

'Or MI5.'

I look at the floor. 'Right. I see.'

'I think it's likely this company is trying to appeal to clients who don't have the same ethical standards I hold so highly. I can honestly assure you, Varvello would never, ever take part in this kind of thing. If it needs to go on, and I'm sure it does, this is the sort of surveillance the security services should carry out on people they're suspicious about. It shouldn't be done on the general population by a private firm, with the resulting information sold to the highest bidder.'

I can feel him getting energised. He's passionate about his work, about the amazing things that can be done with big data, the influence it can have. It both impresses me and scares me. 'I'm so sorry you had to see it. But please believe me when I tell you it isn't anything to do with me personally.'

I stare at him, watching the pleading eyes, clearly willing me to believe him. He wants to save me, I can see it in his face. He wants to save me from the horror, be my protector, convince me the hell I've been going through is all over now. But I'm not convinced.

'Then why were the files in your family's Dropbox file? Why not in your work account or on your computer? Surely you of all people know how sensitive that kind of thing is? Surely it's illegal your even having it, so easily available?'

He winces. 'It wasn't clever of me, I know. I did it by mistake. I meant to put them in my personal account, but

I was already logged in to this one and didn't notice when I dragged them over to my folder.'

I shake my head. 'I think there's something else. Something you're not telling me. And we can't sort this – we can't properly fix this – until we talk about it.'

He looks at me appalled. 'Julianne . . . there's nothing more to this . . .'

'The truth. All of it. Not some dialled-down version of it.' I say it loudly and firmly and it takes him aback.

'Stephen will hear you,' he hisses. 'Julianne, please can we just forget about all of this?'

'Forget about it? Are you serious? If all of what you're saying is true, surely these would be kept on some kind of secure server or in some other safe place or on a hardrive, only to be looked at by people like you *at work*. Do you routinely just fling files by accident into your family accounts? What else will I find in there if I go digging? Company policy documents? Pension details?'

He's looking a bit desperate now. 'I know. What you're saying makes sense and that's usually the case. But . . .'

'You copied them, James. You took files from this dodgy company and you copied them. You kept copies *for yourself*. And you don't want to know where my mind is going right now.'

'Okay.' His deep, hazel eyes are still fixed on me imploringly, his hands reaching out for me, but I step away from him. 'I'll tell you everything. I didn't want to go into it, but if I really have to, I'll explain. Just . . . sit down.'

I stay completely still for a few seconds, then take a seat on the small, single-seat sofa we have by the bedroom desk we rarely use. He looks put off – apparently he expected me to sit on the bed – but he sits down on top of the covers on his own, the two of us facing each other.

'You know I mentioned the security services?'

I don't reply. Just watch him.

'Well, I have a friend. Someone Ernest and I went to school with. You don't know him. He didn't go to Oxford with us. He works . . . in that area of things.'

He pauses, waiting for me to react, but I still say nothing.

'This is all a bit difficult to speak about. It's sensitive territory. Well, he's the type of person who would have some use for the data this company provides. For his own services. In the interests of keeping the country safe. So I took some of their files to send on to him.'

It takes me a moment to digest this.

'Are you telling me you headhunt data companies for MI5? Let them know when you come across people who would do things for them that ordinary, law-abiding people can't?'

He squirms a little, sitting up straighter. 'I would prefer it if we just didn't talk about this. Really, Julianne. That's all I want to say and, honestly, it's all I think you should know. But you can rest assured I don't approve of such practices and neither I nor my colleagues commission them or have any part in them.'

I'm rather stunned by all of this. I knew this wouldn't be an easy conversation, but of all the places I expected it to go, this wasn't one of them. He's not seeing prostitutes. He's not having multiple affairs with women across London. He's still James. My husband.

Eventually, I nod. The relief spreads across his face. 'Okay,' I say. 'But there's still another problem. Stephen.' He looks as if he's about to hug me, but stops himself at the mention of his son's name.

'Stephen? What does Stephen have to do with this? With any of this?'

The tears come now. I'm not sure if it's relief or still the after-effects of tonight's ordeal, but they pour down all the same. 'Stephen saw the files. He found them. That's how I know about them. He brought them to me.'

His hands go up to his face and for a second I think he's about to scream. 'Fuck,' he says through clenched teeth. He falls onto the bed and kneels forward, running his hands through his hair. 'Christ. I'm so sorry about all this. I'll talk to him. He doesn't . . . he doesn't really think . . . I have anything to do with them?'

I watch him agonise for a second or two before replying. It's as if he's a teenager again; the same eighteen-year-old I fell in love with, but with the quiet confidence stripped away. 'But you do have something to do with them. Don't you? You just explained it to me.'

'Shit,' he says bitterly, rubbing his eyes now. When he sits up they look red and tired. 'I had minimal involvement, Julianne. Please believe that. I know I keep saying it, but I'm so sorry. I really am. I'll talk to him. I'll make sure he understands.'

I'm still watching him carefully. I'm convinced. I think. All the torment of the past few hours is starting to feel like a bad dream. A nightmare. I want it to go away. I go to him and take his head in my arms and hold it to my chest, then lower myself down to his level so I can look him in the face.

'When you tell Stephen, you're not to mention anything about what you just told me. Nothing about the security services. Nothing about spies or MI5. He's a teenage boy. That type of thing should be confined to TV shows and novels. Tell him what you told me first.'

'That I got the wrong Dropbox account?'

I nod.

'I love you.' He says it simply, but I know what he wants in return. Reassurance. Comfort. Absolution.

'I'm sorry I ever thought . . . what I thought,' I say.

He shakes his head. 'It's over. It's okay.' He leans forward and kisses me tenderly. I hold him close for a moment, and then we separate.

'Be careful with how you talk to Stephen. I mean it. I don't want his Christmas ruined over this and to go back to school thinking . . .'

'I promise,' he says.

'And . . .' The words catch in my throat as I say them and come out in almost a whisper. 'There's nothing else? Nothing else at all . . . that you want to tell me?'

His expression turns hard to read and he says, sounding slightly puzzled, 'What else could there be?'

I nod. 'Okay. Let's just . . . let's just go to sleep.'

'Good idea,' he says, and walks towards the bathroom. I watch him, hoping to feel relieved. Hoping to see again the man I love above everything else. But all I notice is the way his hand trembles as he reaches out to close the door. Ever so slightly.

CHAPTER 10

Holly

Oxford, 1990

'I'm not sure it's really my thing,' I said, looking up at her. Ally sat on my bed with a twang of springs, slightly ruffling the corners of the duvet. I tried not to let it bother me.

'Oh, you simply must. Really, Holly. You must.' She did her wide-eyed, I-can't-believe-you're-even-doubting-this expression.

I pursed my lips and looked back at the piece of paper in front of me, the familiar sight of my deliberate, neat handwriting filling its lines. 'I have a lot of work to do. I've already decided not to go to the main Christmas and Winter balls. The official ones.'

Ally gave a noise of contempt. 'Oh, I wouldn't bother with them. Just a mixture of horny eighteen-year-olds hoping to get their first handjob and wannabe politicians who think networking around the Christmas trees will help them become PM.' She rolled her eyes.

'So why should I come to this . . . thing?'

Ally sighed. 'Have you not been listening to me, Holly? It's not a "thing". It's a party. A house party. At the Ashtons'.'

'Where's the Ashtons again?' I asked, thinking it was the name of some nightclub or bar that had passed me by.

More sighing. 'The Ashtons' as in the house owned by Thomas and Linda Ashton. I swear I mentioned this, Holly.'

'No, I don't think you did—'

'Well,' she said, cutting me off, 'Thomas and Linda Ashton are family friends of ours. They're actually Lord and Lady Ashton, but that's beside the point. Basically, their son Rupert went to school with Ernest. He lives in Oxford. Like, actually from here. Not just a student here.'

'But he's a student here, too?'

'Oh gosh, no. Apparently couldn't stand the thought of living so close to home. No, he's gone to St Andrews. But he's back now. They break up for Christmas early. Must be a Scottish thing.'

'Right,' I said, unsure how I was supposed to respond to this.

'So will you come?'

The prospect of spending time feeling even more out of my depth than I did with Ally and her friends filled me with horror. Ever since I'd seen James talking to that girl outside the bookshop, I'd tried my best to distance myself from him and Ernest, something Ally had been rather successful in counteracting. She saw to it that I was invited to every outing and often cajoled and pleaded with me to come along on trips to restaurants ('Don't worry, it won't be awkward, Ernest pays for everyone, absolutely everyone') and to study groups ('I desperately need some help with this essay and I just *know* you'll come up with more useful suggestions than anyone else there!'). So I'd swallowed my inner turmoil and joined in. I'd even discovered that the girl's name was Julianne and that she was from America. I was still having some difficulty in pinning down what relationship – if any – James had with her. When I'd mentioned her to Ernest, asking if James's girlfriend was coming along to one of our meals out, he'd laughed and said, 'Girlfriend? Not James's style. He's more into brooding attraction followed by heavy flirting, culminating in a long night of full, constant and athletic sex. That's how James does it. After that, on to the next girl, with a few months of celibacy in between.' Ally, however, seemed to think there was romance in the air. 'They look at each other in *that way*. I wouldn't be surprised if this was serious.' Ernest had made noises of disbelief and Ally had remarked that he was 'just jealous'. I wasn't sure if Ally's firmness on the subject was a way of telling me to get over my attraction to James or if she just didn't really have a clue. Whichever it was, I often found myself torn in these discussions, both wanting to know more and wishing I didn't know any of it.

'Wouldn't it look as if I were gate-crashing?'

Some violent shaking of Ally's head dismissed this concern.

'Okay, er . . . well, would they mind?'

'Of course not! Rupert said specifically "please bring anyone along", so that is what we'll be doing. You'll love Rupert. He's gorgeous. I would try to set you up with him, but he's gay. Not that that stopped him and me indulging in a bit of heavy petting in the library a couple of years ago. His library, that is. The library in his family home is stunning. I'm sure you'd die for it. He'll inherit it all, one day. He really is quite a catch. I'd go the whole way with him if I was certain he hadn't messed around with my brother at some point.'

I turned around to face her properly, easing the ache in my neck that had come from the awkward sitting position I adopted when writing. 'Ally, why do you keep implying that your brother has sex with men? James, and now this guy Rupert. I know I've mentioned it before, but it . . . it just seems weird.'

Ally raised an eyebrow. 'Weird? Good God, Holly, he went to *Eton*. They all did. What do you *think* they got up to, shut away for years without women during the most fevered part of their hot-blooded masculine lives? Of course they turned to each other; who on earth wouldn't? It would be weird if they kept everything zipped up, don't you think? It doesn't make someone gay just because they enjoy a bit of fun with a close friend. Not that it matters about being gay, anyway; I have pretty strong opinions on that subject. I read an article on prejudice in the newspaper at the dentist's last summer and it made me a firm believer in gay rights. We're now in the 1990s. Not far from the twenty-first century. People need to mind their own business and get on with their lives.'

I nodded quickly, regretting bringing up the subject. 'Okay, okay. Sorry, it's just I feel there's so much I don't really know. How things work. What people do. I just worry about making a faux pas and people laughing at me.'

'Nobody will laugh at you and you won't make a "faux pas",' she said, using an exaggerated French accent for the last two words. 'Rupert and his friends are lovely. And if you did want to get laid – and there's no pressure to – but if you *did* want to . . .'

'If I came along, there wouldn't be anything like that on the cards.' I gave a half-laugh, half-tut. I certainly didn't imagine my first time occurring at some drunken party. Eventually I nodded and said to Ally that, okay, so long as she didn't think I was going to be the odd one out, I would join them at the house party.

I *was* going to be the odd one out. I could tell that as soon as the car Ernest had ordered to collect me, him and Ally paused at the wall surrounding the property to allow the gates to swing open automatically. The house looked like something from a C.S. Lewis novel, the type of place that would have multiple rooms full of secret wardrobes, libraries full of big old leather-bound books and maybe the odd bit of taxidermy. This prediction turned out to be rather close to the truth, and I grinned to myself as we passed a stuffed owl on a table in the cavernous entrance hall. 'This . . .' I said, then stopped myself. I was about to say *This place is amazing* but decided it would be better to keep my wide-eyed innocence to myself.

'Welcome to Rupert's,' said Ally, waving her arms around. 'I love this place. We practically spent our teen years here, didn't we, Ernest?'

'Hmmm,' he said, running his fingers along the top of a small chair as if inspecting it for dust. 'Well, it was all part of your grand seduction, wasn't it, sis?'

Ally tutted and continued her march through the house into the corridor. The abundance of wood panelling and warm, slightly too low lighting threw shadows into the corners and gave the house an ominous feel.

'Where is everyone?' I asked Ernest, looking around. I'd expected the party to be in full swing when we arrived, but the place seemed deserted.

'Oh, we're early. We always get here early,' he said, sounding a little bored. 'My sister likes to feel like she's part of the furniture when people arrive. As if she's too important to walk in at the right time with the ordinary guests. She prefers people to think her presence itself gives the party permission to start.'

I laughed and heard Ally's voice echoing in front of me. 'I heard that.'

Wondering why the much-talked-of Rupert was failing to materialise while his unlocked home was invaded, I followed the two of them down the corridor and deeper into the main part of the house. Eventually, after what felt like several kilometres, we turned to go down a narrow, winding, stone staircase that appeared to lead underground. The further down we got, I could feel the temperature rising and the smell of chlorine hit me.

'Of course he'd be swimming,' I heard Ally say, as if irritated by the predictability of her friend, though I was sure I picked up a touch of something else in her voice. Excitement, perhaps?

The swimming pool itself was, like the house, large and impressive, though better lit, with spotlights shining down onto the water's surface, causing a shimmering effect to dance off the walls. It was a moment before I realised there was someone in the pool, swimming beneath its surface, seemingly gliding along its tiled floor with a swift effortlessness.

A sudden burst of laughter made me look round. Along the side of the pool, hidden from view of the entrance, was a row of sunloungers, and seated on two of them were James and a beautiful girl with dark, red–brown hair. I felt a cold, creeping sensation spread down my shoulders as I realised who she was: Julianne, the girl from outside the bookstore. The girl he had left me and his friends to talk to, flirt with, and, if Ally's words were to be taken seriously, fall in love with. I'd been thankful I hadn't needed to speak to her before today, building her up into some conniving, manipulative monster in my head. I knew I was being ridiculous, but I couldn't help feeling an overwhelming sense of resentment towards her, like she had infiltrated a group even I hadn't properly managed to slot into.

'Oh blast, you got here first,' said Ally, walking over to them.

'We've been here an hour,' said James, lying back on his lounger. 'Rupert's been giving us a bit of a show. The great man-dolphin.' He nodded towards the pool and I heard the sound of disturbed water. A large human mass had just pulled itself out of the pool, like a dripping heap of muscle. The body stood up and, to my horror, I realised it was completely naked. The six-foot, toned and astonishingly attractive figure of Rupert Ashton stood before us, grinning. I tried to keep my eyes on his face and away from his groin, but was uncomfortably aware of the outline of his penis at the edges of my peripheral vision. He had a sharp, harsh jawline, not dissimilar to Ernest's, though with more of a boyish friendliness to him. His hair looked dark, though with the promise of a lighter, naturally highlighted tinge when it wasn't soaking wet.

'Oh my God.' Laughter, an American accent. Julianne was shielding her eyes in mock embarrassment.

'Good grief, put some clothes on!' exclaimed Ally, though she was grinning widely. 'You're going to shock Holly and Julianne.'

'Oh, I'm already shocked!' More American laughter. I'd never really thought about it before, but I decided now that the accent was my least favourite in all the world. It sounded fake, contrived, like someone was imitating a trashy imported sitcom.

'Why do you suppose *I* wouldn't be?' said James from behind me.

'Because you have a penis,' Ally threw back matter-of-factly.

The smiling figure of Rupert was still standing there,

126

the dripping water causing a small puddle to form by his large feet.

'Hi,' he said, putting his hands on his hips and looking squarely at me. 'I presume you're Holly.'

I felt myself blushing. This beautiful naked man saying my name and looking me straight in the eye was causing a strange sensation within me I wasn't sure I wanted to explore right at that moment.

'Put some clothes on,' Ernest said, taking his seat on one of the free sunloungers.

Rupert, still looking at me, shrugged and turned around, offering me a view of his broad shoulders, slim waist and perfectly formed behind. I looked at the ground until he got a bit further away then stole a glimpse at him as he towelled his body and stepped into some bright-yellow Y-fronts. He made his way back over to us, still using the towel to dry his hair.

'People should start arriving in about half an hour,' he said.

'Super.' Ally looked over at me. 'So, what do you think of the strapping young Rupert Ashton?'

I was instantly mortified by her question. The shock must have shown in my face because Ernest cut in. 'Maybe we should all just go up to the lounge,' he said, winking at me. 'Give us a chance to get some drinks and let Rupert get, er, properly attired.'

Rupert laughed and raised his eyebrows at me slightly, as if knowing I'd just been rescued from the awkwardness of Ally's question, then went back to putting on the rest of his clothes.

★

Within an hour, the house was packed with people and there was a vague, monotonous beat coming from an invisible stereo sound system. I was impressed by how quickly the house, which had felt like a gloomy and slightly menacing mansion on our arrival, had suddenly transformed itself into a lively hub of young people dancing, laughing and talking loudly to one another. I stayed mostly in the corner with James and Julianne, trying not to look at her and aware I was becoming a third wheel. She didn't seem sure what to say to me, so we both let James speak, with him musing about how his parents were pressuring him to follow them into politics and how Ernest was keen for him to do the same. 'You've gotta do what makes you happy,' Julianne said, giving James's leg a little squeeze.

I couldn't help but give a little sniff of disbelief. If she really was interested in becoming serious with him, I suspected she'd rather like the idea of being the wife of an MP. Ally had mentioned how he was regularly buying her gifts – expensive gifts – and I imagined there'd be more of that sort of thing if James followed his father into Whitehall. She'd go to posh dinners, have expensive holidays, do a lot of charity volunteering. I was so busy mapping out a fantasy life for them both that I didn't realise Julianne had said something to me. 'What are your plans after graduation, Holly?'

I stared into the distance trying to piece together her words. 'Oh, sorry, miles away,' I said, aware it probably sounded rude. I had no idea how long she'd been speaking for. 'I think I'd like to do something to do with . . . to do with books . . .'

I cringed inwardly to myself at the sound of this and saw Julianne's eyebrows rise slightly, but she covered it well. 'I suppose that makes sense. Considering you're an English major.'

James laughed. 'Major? This isn't Harvard.'

She looked embarrassed. 'Oh, of course, sorry.' An awkward laugh followed.

I sat there, wondering if Julianne's question to me was still on the table for expanding upon in more detail, then decided to take my chance to bail out. 'I'm going to find the loo,' I said, glancing around as if a sign would suddenly point me in the right direction.

'Down the main hallway, turn left. Best knock first. People forget to lock it if they're drunk,' James called after me, smirking slightly, sounding a lot more like Ernest than his usually quiet self.

I nodded at him and walked away. I didn't need to visit the bathroom but wandered in the direction he described regardless. There wasn't anybody inside, thankfully, and I locked the door behind me and sat down on the seat of the toilet, leaning against the cool white wall. I was in a funny mood and couldn't quite work out if I was glad I'd come or if I should have stayed back in my room. I could be putting the finishing touches to an essay plan right now. Or making myself some hot chocolate and settling down with a long Victorian novel or mystery thriller.

After a few moments I walked over to the sink and splashed some water on my face, feeling the silky coolness run down my cheeks. I decided I'd go and find where

Ally had got to. One of the problems with being out in the middle of nowhere was that leaving suddenly became a lot more difficult. I'd been to a number of gatherings and parties since term began as a kind of token gesture – here I am, being sociable – only to slip away after barely an hour and walk back to my room, my books and bed calling me. But here I would have to order a taxi, which would be expensive and conspicuous, or wait until the car Ernest had arranged to drop us off came back, and when that would be I couldn't be sure. Annoyed at myself for not being prepared with a better escape plan, I exited the bathroom and walked back down the hallway to the lounge where I'd left James and Julianne. They were gone. I tutted under my breath and wandered through the rest of the downstairs rooms, searching for someone I knew. Ally was nowhere to be found – I couldn't even hear her laughter. Eventually I found myself at the top of the stairwell that led down to the basement and the underground swimming pool. I could hear the noise of voices – it sounded as if intoxicated people were splashing about in the water. I was about to go down the steps when I collided with something large, moving and firm.

'Oh God, are you okay?'

For a second I thought it was James – the voice was similar – but looking up I found it to be Rupert, dark-blond hair swept back over his forehead and wearing a plain black t-shirt that clung to his muscular frame. I realised I'd clutched hold of it to stop myself falling and his hands had gone out automatically to steady me.

'Yes,' I said, a little breathlessly. 'I'm sorry, I was just . . .'

'Looking for your friends.' He didn't say it as a question, but looked at me knowingly. He seemed to be aware how out of my depth I felt here.

I nodded and he smiled. It was a warm smile, unlike Ernest's smirks or James's cagey, secretive grin.

'Forgive me, Holly, I may be speaking out of turn here, but you seem a little all-at-sea. Is there anything I can get you? You've helped yourself to a drink, haven't you?'

I nodded again, struggling to put together words that might form a sentence.

'Good. Well, if you need anything, just find me. I'll be around. And if I'm not in the house, I advise you to try the pool shed.'

'There's a pool shed?' I asked.

'Yes. By the other pool. The outside one. It's covered for the winter. Round the back of the house. Knock three times if it sounds like I'm inside and have company, if you get my drift. But honestly, I mean it. I can have one of my drivers take you home if you need a get-out-of-jail-free card.' He winked at me, then moved out of the way so I could pass him and continue down the steps. 'Oh, and Holly – you're welcome to go down there . . .' He nodded to the stairwell that led to the indoor swimming pool. 'But be warned . . . people are getting friendly.'

I nodded again, feeling a little confused, then realised what he meant. 'Oh,' I said.

'Oh indeed. Take care.' He disappeared out of sight. I stared down at the turquoise-blue light that was filling the stairwell and listened to the noises of merriment. I should have asked where the others were, I thought to myself, but then realised he surely would have shared this information, had he known it, when he guessed what I was up to. I decided to press on and take the last remaining steps in my stride, and walked with purpose into the echoing pool room. People were splashing about in the water, many holding plastic cups of something or other, shrieking and laughing. A group of boys had found a ball somewhere and were playing a vague form of catch with each other, laughing whenever it hit a group of chatting girls at the side. Most of the boys, from what I could make out, seemed to have stripped down to their underpants, and a few of them were naked, but the girls seemed to be wearing stylish little bikinis, presumably brought with them in their clutches or handbags in preparation for this very activity. Over on the sunloungers, meanwhile, Rupert's warnings were proving to be spot-on. They seemed to have been commandeered by couples in varying states of undress; some of them were kissing enthusiastically.

I turned away and started to walk around the edge of the pool in the opposite direction from the copulating couples. Around the other side there was another door, leading up a small flight of steps and out into the garden. The cold night air hit me in a rush as I left the chemical stuffiness of the pool and walked out onto the pavement. This side of the garden was dark, but there seemed to be Christmas lights hung up in the trees nearby, so I spent a good twenty minutes walking amidst them, staring up at their tasteful golden glow. I tried not to let them, but I couldn't stop thoughts of my mother and Christmas coming into my mind – how she had so casually said they were abandoning me and seemed to think I wouldn't care. Or hoped I wouldn't care. Though the air was cold, it felt as if the Christmas lights were warm on my skin, making me feel better. Eventually, after walking around to the far side of the property, making sure to follow the lights and not stray too far into the darker areas, the thin woodland, I discovered the outdoor swimming pool. It was even larger than the inside one, though there were no sunloungers in sight and the water's surface was covered, with leaves speckling the white material. A little way beyond the pool I could see a little collection of wooden huts, which I presumed were used for changing.

Remembering what Rupert had said, I found myself drawn towards the huts. I could talk to him and perhaps ask if he could call me a taxi discreetly. Arriving at the first of the huts, I peered through the doors tentatively. Though Rupert hadn't been clear as to why he might be hanging out in one of these cold-looking buildings rather than the main house, I guessed it was either for smoking pot or more of the shenanigans I'd seen at the side of the pool inside. The first one, however, seemed to be empty. I walked to the second of the three, situated a few metres along to the left of it, though the door was round the other side. This time I could certainly hear something, though couldn't quite make out whether it was male or female. Then I heard it. Low and tight and breathless.

'Fuck. Oh God . . .'

It was a man's voice. And unless I was mistaken, he sounded like he was moaning in pleasure.

'Ahh. Slower, slower. That's it.'

On the last of the two words I felt myself go cold. I knew that voice. I took two steps forward so I was nearly in front of the French windows. What I saw confirmed my suspicions. James was inside, seated in a chair, with his head leaning back. One arm was raised behind his head and the other was resting on the shape bobbing up and down around his crotch. He had his trousers and underwear around his ankles and the girl had her dress undone at the back. I knew even before I saw her red-brown hair that it was her. Julianne.

I felt the anger rising in me like bile; words I'd never thought, never felt, never even thought of employing pushing themselves to the front of my mind as if fighting to be spoken out loud. I wanted to go in there and pull her off him. I wanted to drag her out of the shed onto the concrete. I wanted to shame her. Call her out for her actions. But a niggling voice inside my head was saying something different. She's just doing what everyone else here is doing. You're the one who's outside in the cold wandering around on your own. You're the one who's unwanted, unloved, uninvolved and on the outskirts of even her own pathetic excuse for a friendship circle. For a second, I thought I really was going to burst in and surprise them in the act; then I glanced up and almost screamed. James had lifted his head so he was facing upright and was staring at me, straight in the eyes. I wanted to move, run away and leave this horrible place, but I couldn't. He was smiling. Looking me in the eye and smiling, and Julianne, with her back to me, was totally oblivious to my

134

presence. He opened his mouth in a silent moan, letting the smile spread at the corners. His breathing was getting shallower and when he climaxed he kept his eyes on me the whole time. The grin dancing around his lips never left his face. Then he winked at me.

In a rush, the real world seemed to return around me and I stepped backwards, away from the glass door, tripping over as I tried to turn around at the same time. I landed with a thud on the pavement floor, wishing I'd managed to fall into the nearby grass. My left elbow scraped the rough surface with speed and I felt the skin tear.

'What was that?' I heard Julianne's smooth voice from inside the shed.

'Probably a fox,' James replied, and I heard her laugh, as if the response was somehow funny.

I pulled myself up, wincing slightly as my elbow straightened out, then stumbled away from the shed towards the last of the three, situated a little distance from the other two, closer to where the line of trees joined the swimming-pool area. Not bothering to check to see if it was occupied, I clattered through the French windows and dropped to my knees, the tears arriving instantly.

'Holy Christ!' someone exclaimed.

I looked up and suddenly a light came on out of nowhere, causing my vision to swim. I wiped my eyes and, blinking, made out the shape of a man, hand on the switch of one of the tall standing lamps.

'Well, I didn't realise you'd be dropping in quite so literally as this,' he said. Posh, similar to James's voice. Calm and confident.

'Rupert?' I said, feeling a little confused.

'The one and only,' he said and smiled.

'Sorry to break up the party here, but we're kind of in the middle of something.' This second voice made me start and I stood up, realising it had come from another male who was leaning over the arm of a chair. It took me a second to realise what was going on, but when I saw that both he and Rupert were naked, with the latter positioned behind him, their bodies touching, it hit me.

'Oh God,' I said, embarrassed and angry with myself for just walking in. 'I'm sorry.'

I looked away quickly and went to leave. I'd never seen two men even kiss, let alone do what they were doing, though I was vaguely aware of the mechanics of it.

'It's okay,' Rupert said. 'Wait.'

'Carry on, it's fine,' I said, walking out of the shed and back into the night.

I heard Rupert murmur an apology to the other boy and come after me. He pulled me round by the shoulder so I could face him. 'You look upset,' he said.

I couldn't help it. The tears continued rolling down my face and I sniffed loudly.

'Hey, hey,' he said, and pulled me into an embrace. I felt my cheek meet his bare chest and I heard the beat of his heart. I'd never been this close to a naked man in my life and was surprised at how much I liked it. How much I wanted him to hold me tighter and not let me go.

'Why the crying?' he asked quietly, rocking me gently.

I didn't know what to say so just kept silent, allowing the slow movement to calm me a little.

'Holly. I'm sorry to be a bore, but it's damn freezing out here and I haven't got a stitch on me.' He was starting to shiver and lifted me away from his chest. 'Apart from this,' he said with a hollow laugh, looking down towards his penis. He reached down and I heard a slap of elastic as he chucked away the condom. 'I'm going to have to put some clothes on before I get pneumonia.'

I nodded and managed to find my voice. 'Of course. Sorry.'

'Stop apologising,' he said. 'Do you want to come back in?' He was edging back towards the shed door. 'Don't worry, Timothy won't bite. I'll make it worth his while later.'

I allowed myself to be led back into the shed, which was marginally warmer than the night air. Inside, Rupert seated me on a chair – identical to the white wicker one James had been perched on minutes earlier while Julianne pleasured him. The other boy, Timothy, made a noise of disbelief as I settled myself down, but Rupert spoke quickly.

'I'm sorry, Holly is just a bit upset. I'm going to take her home.' He pulled on his bright-yellow Y-fronts, jeans and black t-shirt, along with a thick cream cardigan. Timothy didn't say anything, just sighed and bent down to pull on his own briefs, then started to pick the rest of his clothes up off the floor.

'I think I'll be fine,' I said, sniffing again, wishing I had a tissue. 'I'll just go back to the house.'

'Nonsense,' Rupert said, heading for the door. 'Come

on. Let's get you back home. We'll have a chat on the way.'

Before we left, I looked back towards the other boy, who was now fully clothed, seated on one of the chairs and in the process of lighting a cigarette.

'Don't burn the place down,' Rupert called after him.

The car was comfortable and warm. A BMW, I noticed when I got in, not that I cared much. Rupert asked if I'd like some music on, but I shook my head and said I'd prefer not, if he didn't mind. He said he didn't. After driving in silence for a while, I turned to him and asked, 'Why are you being so kind to me?'

He laughed at that. 'Why shouldn't I?'

'I mean,' I said, trying to choose the right words, 'not many guys would abandon having sex halfway through to drive a random girl they barely know back home through the night.'

'It's not that far to your dorms. And anyway, I like driving.'

I didn't reply and he seemed to decide the evasion wasn't going to work. 'I don't really like what Ernest's lot do. Him, James, Ally – they're careless. Careless with other people. People who aren't like them. I've seen it before. Don't take this the wrong way, but you aren't the first. They used to do this when I was at school. They'd find someone – a pet, a plaything – someone a bit different to themselves, someone from a different background or just not part of their little club. They like impressing people, bewildering people, pushing them out of their depth.'

138

I let these words sink in. *A pet, a plaything.* Is that all I was to them? 'Ally's not like that,' I said.

'Hmm.' Rupert kept his eyes on the road, but he looked sad. 'I like to think she isn't. But she left you alone at a big party full of people you've never even met, didn't she?'

I was confused and leant back in my seat to look at him. 'What do you mean?'

'I mean I saw her getting into a car with Ernest about an hour ago. Heard her telling people they were going to pick up Peter, but I know that's not true. Peter's at home in London with his parents.'

'But . . . maybe they just . . .'

'Just forgot? Too drunk to remember? Or just didn't care?'

I shook my head. 'Ally isn't like that,' I said again.

'Okay,' he said. It sounded final, but I could tell he wanted to say more.

I let silence fall again until we were nearing the road leading up to the accommodation, then I said something that had been on my mind all evening. 'Everyone was having sex. As if it didn't matter. Those people in the swimming pool, stripping off, apparently not bothered at all. And James and Julianne . . . I saw them. She was using her mouth on him. And . . . and . . .'

'And me?' he said, with a quiet laugh. 'Yes, that isn't exactly rare at house parties.'

'Really? Am I just naïve, or does it all seem rather . . .'

'Rather what?'

I shook my head. 'It doesn't matter. I'm clearly just sheltered. Out of my depth, as you say.'

He drew in a breath. 'I didn't mean anything bad by it.'

'It's fine,' I said, though it wasn't. 'I'm just glad to be back here. And I do appreciate you bringing me. You didn't have to.'

'You're welcome.' He turned the car into the driveway and along the small path towards the entrance. 'Sweet dreams. I hope our paths cross again.' He smiled at me.

'Me too,' I said, though as I said the words I somehow knew they probably wouldn't. 'Goodnight.'

He didn't drive away until I was inside with the door closed. Safe.

CHAPTER 11

Julianne

Knightsbridge, 2019

My mother used to struggle to sleep when I was young. I used to wake up and hear her tidying the already immaculate kitchen, bleaching the surfaces so they'd probably pass even clinical standards. Dad used to hate it. 'Not being able to sleep is the sign of a guilty conscience,' he always used to say, frequently within Mom's hearing, which I'm sure exacerbated the issue. Her insomnia was only cracked when a family friend I called Aunt Joan, even though she was no blood relation, finally said to her, 'I've got the cure. It couldn't be more simple. Just don't give a damn. Don't worry for a single second you can't sleep. It doesn't matter. Don't overthink it, don't dwell on it, don't *try* to sleep.

Think about something else, read a book for a bit, and if you can't sleep just shrug it off. The worst comes to the worst, you'll be a bit tired the next day. That's life. No big deal.'

Lying here, trying to sleep now, I think of Aunt Joan and wonder what she'd advise if she knew what was keeping me awake right now. Whether she'd tell me to shrug it off. Not to care. To not give a damn and just go to sleep.

Any attempts to quiet my screaming mind are falling flat. Nothing can drown out the noise. A thousand images push themselves to the front of my thoughts, jostling for space. Some are just words, taken from those documents I'd read. *Sex worker. Illegal substances. HIV and hepatitis. Trial run.* Others are things James said to me during our discussion before bed. *Sensitive. Surveillance. MI5.* Then my mind starts to spin towards other memories, ones of us. Our wedding. Our honeymoon. Our happiness. And other times. Times when he's had to work late. Hours in front of the computer upstairs while Stephen and I are watching TV. The times he's stopped a phone call in haste when I've entered the room. And, with a horrible sense of painful inevitability, a time when I was at my lowest at Oxford. Me, accepting the apologies of a tearful James. And then looking at a half-clothed girl, lying in a bed.

Part of me was tempted to bring some of this up when we first got into bed. But then the minutes ticked by and James's breathing became heavy after about half an hour. Longer than normal – he's normally dead to the world as soon as his head hits the pillow – but he's still able to push aside the events of the past few hours enough to allow his mind to close down and let sleep envelop him in its comfortable clutches. I, meanwhile, am left fending off the darkness alone. And it's so, so dark in my head, I can hardly bear it. At 4.00 a.m., after hours of lying awake, I get up and go over to the walk-in wardrobe, opening the door as quietly as I can. I don't risk turning on the light inside and I don't need to. Feeling around along my row of coats, I quickly get to my Jaeger Cocoon with the large, smooth-knit collar and feel inside the top breast pocket. There, I feel a small rectangle of cardboard and pull it out. Keeping it clasped in my hand, I leave the wardrobe, take my phone off charge by the bedside, and make my way out of the room and downstairs, listening all the way for any stirring from James or Stephen.

The Christmas lights are still on throughout the house – probably the first time we've forgotten to turn them off in years. Even though this is the second year we've had 100 per cent LEDs, which don't overheat, James still gets concerned about us waking up to a burning house around us, or, even worse, not waking up at all. The twinkle of the big tree in the corner of the lounge draws me to it, like a moth to a flame, and I stare at it for a while before reaching for my phone and looking down at the card in my hand. I dial the number.

'Hello, you've reached Myanna Thornton-Smythe. I'm not able to take your call right now, so please leave a message and I'll get back to you as soon as I can.'

For a second or two I panic; then, when I start, the words seem to clump together as I say them. 'Hello, my name is . . . Julianne Knight . . . I wanted to . . . Last year you approached me about . . . about my husband. You said one day I would realise and when that day happened . . . I should call . . . and . . . .I told myself the day wouldn't ever come . . . but I kept the card, all this time. And I think I need to . . .' My tears roll down my face as I try to keep the sob from my voice. I cut the call. Regret swells within me. What have I done? I stare at the phone, as if hoping there is a way I can eradicate the last couple of minutes, turn back the clock, but the screen just goes blank. And then it lights up with an incoming call.

'Shit,' I say out loud. My finger hovers over the cancel button. Then I click answer.

'Hello,' I say, my voice quiet and faint.

'Julianne. It's Myanna. I just heard your message.'

Her voice is strong and confident, as if this were the middle of the day and I'd been put through to an office, rather than woken her up in the middle of the night.

'I . . . I'm sorry . . .'

After a few beats of silence, Myanna says, 'It's okay. Take your time. I'm very glad you've called me.' She pauses here, perhaps hoping I will start speaking, then says, 'Perhaps you could start by telling me what prompted you to get in touch. I'm really pleased you kept my number.'

'I don't know . . . I don't know what I'm saying, really. It's nothing. This is nothing. I'm sorry.'

'Julianne, don't apologise. And this isn't nothing. You've phoned me in the middle of the night. That's a good thing — a very, very good thing. You're not alone. If you just talk to me, I think I can help.'

'Forget . . . please, forget what I said. On the voice message I left you.' My heart is beating so loudly I swear the phone will pick it up and my knees start to give way. I lower myself awkwardly so I'm sitting on the floor like a child. 'Please just delete the message. I'm sorry . . . I was wrong . . . I'm sorry to bother you.' I take the phone away from my ear, tears splashing onto the screen as I hit the red button. Quickly, I navigate to the call log and add Myanna's number to the blocked list, then let the phone fall on the carpet. I sit there, crying by the Christmas tree, as time slips past me. Things filling my head. Images clawing at the sides of my consciousness. I fall in and out of sleep, curled up on the carpet, the heated flooring mitigating the discomfort. Then, eventually, when I hear the clock on the mantelpiece quietly chime 6.00 a.m., I pull myself up with an effort and get my balance. I should go back to bed. Or start doing something, something normal. James will worry if he finds me sitting on the lounge floor, spaced out and crying before dawn, like a disturbed child.

I decide to heat up a pain au chocolat and take it back into the lounge to eat on the sofa. Turning on the TV, I navigate to Sky's Christmas movies section, select *Home Alone*, and enjoy the first ten minutes of the McCallister family trying to get themselves organised for a family trip to Paris over the holiday period. As the film goes on, I gather up some of the shopping bags of gifts I've had stashed away and spend an hour or so doing some wrapping. Though sitting on the sofa, hunched over the coffee table, is unkind to my back, the simple activity is therapeutic and I feel the tension leaving my body as I snip and cut and stick down the paper over socks, books and, for my mother, a new KitchenAid stand food mixer. I am just folding down the last bit of paper over the box when I hear a noise on the stairs. Moments later, James walks in.

'You're up early,' he says, coming over to rub my shoulder. 'You're watching *Home Alone?*' He sounds slightly amused.

'It was just on,' I say, not entirely truthfully. I finish wrapping the big box surrounding the mixer and set it on the coffee table.

'Are you okay?'

The question hangs there, waiting for me to answer. Although the air around me is comfortably warm, I feel slightly chilly.

'Julianne? Is everything okay?'

I turn round and look at him, taking in the whole man: his messy bed hair, his muscled torso underneath his navy-blue t-shirt, the long outline of his penis, clearly visible against the tight cotton of his white boxer briefs. And his face. That kind, handsome face I've known all these years, and the pleading look filling his eyes.

'Yes,' I say, giving a small nod. 'Everything is okay.'

Chapter 12

Holly

Wickford, Essex, 1990

It didn't take me long to unpack. As my journey back for Christmas was to be by train rather than car, I'd only brought some essentials. There were enough clothes at home for me to wear – especially if I was going to be sitting round the house for a month – and the local library was only ten minutes' walk away if I needed any further light reading. The only books I'd brought back were the novels I knew I was going to write about for homework over the holidays, along with a few academic texts I'd borrowed from one of the university libraries. I was cross with myself for not going back to buy Samuel Richardson's *Clarissa* – a novel of over a thousand pages would have set me up very well. I had been tempted by a new volume of Penguin English short stories at the small station bookshop, but didn't have the correct change and had to run for the train before I could find a cashpoint.

Once I'd got all my clothes in the drawers in my room and the books on my desk, I set about vacuuming. The rest of the house was scrupulously clean and tidy – ever since Mum had gone part-time on reception at the dental practice she had filled her time with exceptional levels of house care. What had once been a cluttered, ever-so-slightly dusty house had suddenly become as beautifully kept as a showroom property, albeit one on a limited budget in a not very affluent part of Essex. Clear surfaces stretched before me as I wandered through the rooms. The tables, nightstands and bedroom floors were all free from dust and clutter and I got a strange sense of pleasure thinking where I'd spread out my lecture notes and essay plans while I worked on my assignments throughout December.

The Christmas tree in the lounge looked fuller and more expensive than usual and underneath there was an overflowing sack of presents and a stocking hanging by the chimney loaded with gifts. Most of the presents in the Santa sack appeared to be book-shaped. I suspected Mum had gone on a bit of a spree in the WHSmith in the high street. Maybe she did feel a little guilty about abandoning her only child over the Christmas holidays. Dad's most overt input, meanwhile, was a bag of Bassett's Liquorice Allsorts – a bumper pack – on the mantelpiece next to the hanging stocking. They were our favourite, and when I was young he'd come home from work with a bag of them every Friday, which we'd share while watching a film on the telly, while Mum did the ironing. I felt sad, thinking about this now, so left the lounge and went into the kitchen. The fridge was packed with a range of long-life microwavable ready meals. Apparently my parents presumed this was what a student lived on while away from home and would naturally expect upon their return. Though the pictures on the front looked appetising, the glistening grey-brown mass behind the clear cellophane that greeted me when I closely inspected the 'Ultra-Quick Sausage and Mash' brought to mind some graphic scenes of decomposing bodies in a made-for-television forensic crime drama I'd watched earlier in the year. I decided I wasn't hungry just yet.

The days of December went by at an excruciatingly slow pace. I finished my essay assignments within six days, working long into the night on many occasions, kept going by coffee and Lucozade. I knew as I was doing them that I should space them out, that I'd miss the work once it was gone, but I'd always worked this way. Once I was in the zone, I found it hard to break away and do something else.

I had thought about contacting a couple of school friends to see if they wanted to do something, but, though it pained me to admit it, I really didn't want anybody to find out about my situation. Seeing the look of, first, confusion, then shock, then pity and concern in their eyes when they found out I'd been left by my parents over the holidays made me feel nauseous. I just knew I couldn't bear it.

149

On Christmas Eve, however, I was forced to confront this horrible reality. As I arrived back home from the corner shop I was alarmed to find a hooded figure standing on my doorstep, knocking loudly.

'Can I help you?' I said, slightly nervously, and the Adidas-coated black mass turned round. Peering from underneath the hood was a face I recognised.

'George!' I exclaimed, almost dropping my carrier bag.

'Hol,' he said, and smiled.

I looked George Treadway up and down, though there wasn't much to see other than the oversized coat, jeans and trainers he was wearing.

'You going to invite me in?'

I nodded and smiled, moving awkwardly past him to unlock the front door. Inside the house, he pulled off his coat and hung it on the hook. Only then did I notice the transformation. George Treadway had been the invisible boy at school for the whole of his time there. Usually seated in the middle somewhere, away from the eager learners at the front and the dickheads messing around at the back, he had managed to always blend in so students and teachers alike never really noticed his existence. This was probably the reason he and I became firm friends. Now, however, I saw he had changed. Though never a bad-looking boy, I noticed a slight coating of stubble on his face, emphasising a now-sharper jawline. His once-skinny frame was firmer, thicker, and his arms and chest showed considerable definition, even underneath his *Ghostbusters* t-shirt.

He seemed to notice me staring and grinned. 'I joined

the Territorial Army,' he said. It was clear he expected me to be impressed, so I returned his smile, then asked, 'The what?'

'The T.A. Territorial Army! They protect Britain from invasion. Come on, you must have heard of us. You with your Oxford degree and all.'

'I don't have a degree yet,' I said distractedly. 'So do you go off to fight? Are we about to be invaded?'

He rolled his eyes. 'No, it's mostly just keeping fit and training exercises. It's really good, though. Get to hang out with the lads – made so many great mates. It's the best thing I've ever done.'

I smiled again, not sure what else to say. We were still standing in the hallway and it felt weird talking to him like this. He reached up and ran a hand through his now almost non-existent, close-trimmed brown hair. 'So, do I get a cuppa?'

'Yes, of course, sorry,' I said, walking down towards the kitchen and starting to fill up the kettle.

'I was going to ring you, but thought I'd just come over. I . . . I hope you don't mind.'

He was clearly starting to feel a bit awkward now, too.

'No,' I said, trying to make my tone breezy and light. 'It's a nice surprise.'

'I've brought some Christmas cards. They're in my coat pocket. I'll get them in a sec. I got one for your parents, too.'

'That's sweet of you,' I said, watching the kettle boil instead of looking at him. 'I . . . I was going to call you, too. It's just been a bit . . .'

'Bit busy? Well, it's Christmas, isn't it? I get you. Don't worry, Hol.'

An awkward silence followed. 'Where are your parents, anyhow?'

I drew in a breath, buying myself some time as I added the water to the mugs. 'They're on a cruise. The Caribbean.' I hazarded a glance at him now, to see his reaction to this. His eyebrows rose and he looked confused.

'What? Why? They never . . .'

'Never go anywhere, I know.'

He nodded. 'So why have they . . . ?'

'I don't fucking know, to be honest.' My own words shocked me, and I suddenly realised I was crying. With a surge of heat in my face, I felt anger course through me. All it took was a quick movement and I sent the two mugs of brewing tea crashing to the floor, the brown liquid and fragments of stoneware going everywhere.

'Jesus Christ,' yelled George. He rushed over to me from the doorway, taking hold of my shoulders as I cried and cried and buried myself in him. He smelt of men's shower gel mixed with the vague hint of cigarette smoke. I heard his heart beating and was reminded of being held close to Rupert's naked chest, over a month ago now, as he shivered in the cold and I sobbed as I was doing now. George, however, wasn't shivering, and the softness of his t-shirt felt better somehow than Rupert's bare skin. I realised this was the first time George had hugged me – indeed, the first time he'd ever really touched me at all. Neither of us had been very tactile people at school. Some friends would hug each other every day as they greeted one another at the school gates, but he and I, and the rest of the invisibles we hung out with, always kept our distance slightly.

'Maybe you should go and sit in the lounge. Sit by the Christmas tree for a bit while I clear up in here.' His voice was deep in my ear.

I nodded and shuffled off in the direction of the lounge. I sat, as instructed, by the tree, a little entranced by the dancing coloured lights in front of me. Pink, green, blue, green, gold. I lay back on the sofa and listened to the oddly comforting sounds of George mopping up the spilled tea and carefully picking up the bits of broken mug and dropping them into a container.

When he came back into the lounge he glanced at me, seated on the sofa, with a slight air of trepidation, as if I might start torching the tree or ripping up the carpets.

'I'm okay, honestly. I'm sorry for the outburst.'

He nodded, but didn't look convinced.

'Holly, what's going on? You're alone at Christmas, you haven't been in touch for literally months – I'm not criticising – and you seem to be, well, a tad on edge.'

He perched on the arm of the sofa I was sitting on and I saw a hand coming towards me. Realising he was proffering tea, I reached out and took it, our hands brushing slightly as I tried not to touch the hot part of the mug. 'I made a fresh batch,' he said, stating the obvious. We sipped in silence for a few minutes, then finally I attempted a response.

'I don't really know. To be honest, all of it is just . . . just so shit.'

More raised eyebrows. It was the swearing – I know it surprised him. Though no stranger to a 'fuck' or even a 'cunt' himself, he'd always playfully criticised me for not even dropping a minor expletive. Now, back from grand old Oxford, I'd let two slip out in the space of twenty minutes.

'Have you and your parents had a row or something?'

I shook my head. 'No. In fact, that would be easier. All I got was a phone call from Mum saying the two of them were joining family friends – the Searles – on a cruise over Christmas.'

'I didn't know you were family friends with the Searles.'

'We're not!' I said, louder than I meant to. 'We hardly bloody know them. Well, Mum and Dad do now, apparently. Mum's wormed her way in over the past year. Anyway, how do you know them?'

George grimaced. 'My mum cleans for them. I remember them, as she broke a vase once. She was really upset about it even though they seemed all right about it at the time. But then she overheard the missus telling her husband that the "idiot of a cleaner" had smashed it. Not nice, hearing someone call you names behind your back like that. So she's had a bit of a downer on them since. The property is lush, though. Six bedrooms. Apparently one of their sons has got this girl pregnant . . .'

'Yes, I know. That's why he and his brother dropped out of the cruise and my parents have gone along instead.'

'Ahh,' said George awkwardly. 'Yeah, that is a bit shit.' He nodded to the presents under the tree. 'Looks like they've left you some things to unwrap, though.'

154

I made a noise of disbelief. 'It's just guilt, wrapped up with a bow.'

'I'm sure they do care for you. In their own way.'

I tried to return to the calm I'd felt a few moments ago, but the anger was winning again. 'No, actually, they don't. It's not "care", it's something else. Do you know what it is? It's resentment. It's insidious, nasty resentment. Most parents would be proud their daughter had got into one of the best universities in the world and was on track to get a first in her first year. But no, not them. They see it as a mark of their own failings. The only joy they get from me going to Oxford is being able to boast about it to the Searles while having cocktails in the Caribbean sun. That's the life they've always wanted – or rather what Mum's secretly wanted, and now she's told Dad he'd better sodding well go along with it.'

George was clearly torn about whether to comfort me or let me rant on as I steadily became more upset. He leant forward but spilt some of his tea on his knee so aborted, looking around nervously for the coffee table on the other side of the room.

'Well, at least you have Oxford,' he said quietly. 'That's got to count for something. Maybe you don't need your parents any more, Hol. If that's really what they're like, fuck 'em. You go and be your own version of brilliant and if they don't like it, well, it's their loss.'

I knew he was trying to be sweet and encouraging, but it just made things worse. 'Oxford? I don't *have* Oxford at all. If anything I feel just as alienated there as I do here.'

He looked puzzled. 'Surely you have friends?'

'You would have thought, wouldn't you? But actually, I've kind of come to the conclusion they're the biggest bunch of frauds and louts I've ever met. Posh–louts, really. Ones who have only ever known an easy life and think it gives them the right to act however they please. They swan about their parties, taking drugs and getting pissed. They have sex in public. Like, on display. And no one seems to care.'

He gave a small chuckle. 'Sounds like a good laugh to me.'

'It isn't a laugh,' I snapped. 'Do you know who these people are? These are future judges and MPs and prime ministers. These are the people who will be dictating to others how they should live their lives. They will be at the very top. Or they'll become semi–fascist columnists for some right-wing newspaper, lying about immigrants or spreading hate about homosexuals while they themselves shag anything with a pulse.'

I paused for breath. George looked rather stunned. 'Don't you think you might be reading just a little too much into it all? From what I hear, most people go to uni to do all those things you've just mentioned.'

This stopped me and made me think. He was right, to some extent. I tried to speak slowly and calmly. 'I know, it's just I thought . . . I thought it would be different.'

He nodded. I looked over at him. 'So is it like that in the T.A.? Drink, drugs and casual sex?'

He blushed slightly. 'It has been known. Not so much on the drugs front – we take care of our bodies.'

'So that's a yes to the sex?' I wasn't sure why I was

pursuing this line of inquiry, but I couldn't help being interested. Though we'd never talked explicitly about the subject at school, I'd sort of known he was still a virgin like me when he left. I'd certainly never seen him with a girl, nor was he one to go out partying with the types who enjoyed drunken fumblings behind garden sheds.

He looked embarrassed. 'Well, now you mention it, that side of things has got, er, slightly more active since school.'

'Girls in the army?' I asked.

'Friends of friends, more like. The other blokes I train with seem to have them on tap. Girls, I mean. I never really thought I'd be one for all that but, well . . . turns out it's rather fun.'

'*All that?*'

'Yeah,' he said, looking a bit sheepish. 'As in going back to one of the lads' flats with lots of beers and some girls. Messing around. Having a laugh.'

'What does having a laugh entail?' I asked.

'Well, y'know . . .'

I shook my head. 'No, I don't. Do enlighten me.'

He looked uneasy, but shrugged and said, 'Threesomes, blowjobs, spin the bottle, that kind of thing. Listen, Hol, I'm not sure we should be talking about this right now. You don't seem . . .'

'But I want to talk about it,' I said. It was true, I did want to. It seemed surprising, if not downright shocking, to me that people – Ally, Ernest, James, Julianne, Rupert, even innocent and quiet George – could treat a subject

157

like sex, a subject I had built up into some kind of behemoth of importance in my head, with such dismissive irreverence. As if it was nothing.

'Okay,' he said, and it sounded like he was choosing his words carefully. 'What part of it do you want to talk about?'

'So, when you're sharing a girl in a threesome with one of your army mates, do you know her name? Does she know yours while she's being penetrated by you?'

'Jesus, Holly!' He looked shocked.

'You're the one who brought it up, mentioning your threesomes.'

'No, Hol, to be honest, you're the one who seems a bit fixated on the subject. So what if people want to have a good time? This is 1990, not 1890. There shouldn't be any shame in it. And maybe . . . maybe . . .'

I turned fully to face him. 'Maybe what?'

'Well, maybe if you were getting some you wouldn't feel so left out?'

I stood up, the fury back and raring to go. 'Oh, so I feel left out, do I? I'm secretly gagging for it, am I? Because all girls must be, is that what you're saying? We all secretly want it, craving to be dominated by horny young louts?'

'Horny young louts?' He couldn't help but laugh. If I hadn't got myself so worked up, I probably would have done the same, but riding along on the surge of emotion racing through me, lighting me up inside, I walked over and kissed him. I didn't really know what I was doing, but all of a sudden our lips were locking and I was pressing his mouth open with mine, forcing him to reciprocate,

158

which he did, allowing me entry, my tongue connecting with his, then his arms taking hold of me, pulling me into the embrace. After about a minute he drew away, breathing heavily. 'Fucking hell,' he said, looking at me as if he was half-scared, half-impressed. 'Now, that was a surprise.'

'It shouldn't be, should it? It's just sex, after all. Doesn't mean anything.' I threw the words back at him, wanting them to hurt, wanting them to upset him, but he just looked at me.

'That wasn't sex,' he said quietly, slightly rubbing his lip. Had I caught him with my teeth?

'Fine,' I said, shoving him to the side so he fell off the arm and onto the sofa. I got on top of him. 'Show me then.' I started kissing him again, more forcefully than I had before, letting my body rub against him, feeling him growing hard underneath me.

'Holly, is this really want you want?' he said quietly into my ear.

I brought myself up so I was pinning him to the sofa with both hands, holding him down. 'Yes,' I said. 'I want us to do it. Everything you do to those girls, I want you to do it to me.' I brought one hand down to his groin and started rubbing, feeling his jeans now stretched tight by his protruding erection.

'Go on then,' he said, glancing down to where my hand was resting. There was an air of defiance in his voice and challenge in his eyes. He didn't think I would do it. Quiet Holly. Kind Holly. More at home with her books than at a party. She'd never sucked a cock or shagged a boy at school. Well, here I was, going to do exactly that. I moved down towards his waist, slipping off the sofa and kneeling on the floor. I unbuckled his jeans and pulled them down to his knees. He was wearing Spider-Man underpants and I almost laughed at the incongruity of his stiff penis distorting the webbed face of the iconic superhero. I pulled these down, too, and before I could allow myself to be intimidated by what was underneath, I took hold of it and lowered my head.

The groan of pleasure he let out surprised me; that I could make someone sound so enthralled, so deeply happy – it was a foreign feeling to me. I went at it for a while, improvising and pretending I knew what I was doing, having never received any instruction on how best to perform the act and only glimpsing it occasionally in films. And being done to James. The image of him seated in that pool cabin flashed into my mind, the head bobbing in his lap, that look on his face. I tried to put it out of my head and focus on what I was doing. When my jaw started to get tired, I pulled myself back up, triumphant and slightly amazed I hadn't run for the hills when I'd first pulled down his pants. He had his eyes closed and looked slightly sleepy.

'Don't stop,' he said. He tried to guide my head down again, but I resisted.

'I want to do all of it. I want you to have sex with me.'

He made a doubtful noise. 'I think this is fine . . . I think this is enough for now. Please, don't stop.'

'I'm not carrying on,' I said firmly. 'You want more, you do the work.'

He laughed at this and pulled me up onto him, helping

me take my top off and pressing his face into my breasts. I tried to reach around to unclip my bra, but he had me down on my back on the sofa before I could get it undone. He unbuttoned my jeans and pulled them off with my knickers in one swift movement. He then descended upon me, kissing my neck. Part of me couldn't believe this was happening. This was George: the boy I'd played Scrabble with in the school library at lunch and went round to tea with when we were twelve. George who used to forget his P.E. kit and try not to cry when they gave him a lunchtime detention. And now here he was, positioning his penis so he could enter me, slowly and carefully, then all the way, making me let out a short, sharp noise of discomfort.

'Sorry,' he whispered. 'Does it hurt?'

'Slightly,' I said. 'But it's okay, I think.'

He started moving in and out, his weight heavy on top of me, his muscular arms, so different to the bony, weak things I'd become used to seeing, now gripping me tight. I reached my hands down his back and then, in what seemed to me like a daring move, took hold of his bare buttocks as he thrust into me, feeling the muscles under his skin tense and tighten as he pushed. It didn't go on very long after that. His breathing became shallow and he pushed his face hard against mine, the stubble on his jaw coarse against my skin. I realised I liked it. 'I'm going to cum,' he grunted, and he started thrusting deeper and quicker. I wasn't sure if he was asking permission or just giving me a heads-up, so I let him carry on until I felt him go very tense and he let out a low, deep groan. I felt a warmth inside me, then cold as he pulled out and rolled onto his side. There wasn't much space against the cushions on the chair, so I got up, staggering slightly as I felt around for my knickers and t-shirt. Once I was dressed I turned to look at him, sprawled on the sofa, his Spider-Man pants in a tangle around his knees, and his jeans draped untidily over the side of the chair, a pool of loose coins and debit cards scattered on the floor underneath them. He was still breathing heavily, lying on his front, his face resting on a cushion, eyes on me, watching, seeing how I'd react. Eventually he asked if I was okay and I nodded. He sat up then and I noticed his penis was still partially erect as he pulled up his briefs and set about turning his jeans the right side out. He kept glancing at me, standing awkwardly in the centre of the lounge. Eventually he spoke.

'Was that okay?'

I nodded.

'Are *you* okay?' he said quietly.

I nodded again. He seemed awkward now, struggling to get his jeans on, covering up his bare legs, much closer to the George I used to know – just a glimmer of him peeking out from beneath this strange, sexually confident young man sitting before me. He stood up and said, 'Do you want me to go?'

I instinctively nodded again, then apologised. 'I'm sorry, I just think I should be alone right now.'

He seemed a little put out. 'You sure? I think *The Italian Job* is on TV today. We could watch it together. Have some mince pies.'

I glanced at the TV, as if it might have heard him and

162

spring into life at any moment. 'I don't think so. I don't have any mince pies.'

'That doesn't matter.'

'No, really.'

He seemed to get the message. Once he'd got all his clothes and shoes on and was standing by the door, ready to leave, I did feel a twinge of regret. Maybe it would have been nice to have some company on Christmas Eve night. I was just about to say something, tell him I'd changed my mind, when he said, 'It's probably best if I get off. Promised my mum I'd help her with some Christmas prep. Got the family round tomorrow.' This stopped me saying anything at all. I didn't know if he meant it as a dig. It wouldn't have been George's style, but then again I never would have thought casual sex on the lounge sofa would have been his style either. Everything was so confused.

'Merry Christmas, Hol,' he said, giving me a small smile. Then he was out the door and walking away, zipping up his black Adidas jacket against the cold.

I walked back into the lounge and looked around. Everything was exactly the same as it had been, aside from the sofa. The cushions needed straightening. As I walked over, I noticed there was a key difference – something that certainly hadn't been there before. On one of the seats there was a small patch that was slightly wet to the touch. I looked closer, inspecting it. Translucent white residue clung to the surface, flecked with tiny marks of red. Semen and blood. Slowly, putting pressure on the spot, I wiped it harder into the fabric of the sofa, watching it grow into a larger dark, damp patch. I stood back to take a look when I was finished. I hoped it would leave a stain. A rough image swam into my head; of my mother settling down on the sofa to watch *Countdown* when she returned in the New Year, wondering how that strange mark had ever come to be there. I smiled to myself, then turned on the TV to watch *The Italian Job* alone.

Chapter 13

Julianne

Knightsbridge, 2019

Things aren't fine. They're far from fine. And on top of that, I've still got presents to wrap, food to buy, people to see. No more crying on the floor in the lounge in the small hours. No more phone calls to people I don't even know. Just from a practical perspective, I don't have the time. But no matter how busy I am, that strange, niggling feeling is in the back of my mind – this draining, clawing creature perched on my shoulder that's only become larger since speaking to Myanna. I keep thinking of that painting by Henry Fuseli, showing a woman lying on a bed with some sort of demonic manifestation sitting on top of her. The image floats into my mind so often I end up googling it on my phone, irritated I can't remember the name of the piece. When I see its title, that cold chill returns to my spine. It's called *The Nightmare*.

I'm just coming back from a quick nip out to Whole Foods when I see Stephen sitting on the stairs, head in his hands.

'Honey, are you okay?' I ask. I've tried to talk to him twice now since the other night – the night of the discovery – but he's either hurried away or James has been within hearing distance. Aside from a quick iMessage I sent him telling him everything is explained and he's not to worry, we haven't communicated properly in two days.

He just shrugs at me and says, 'I don't know.' He's mumbling, unable to look at me. One of the things I've always loved about my son is his effortless confidence, his ability to meet people's eye, to talk with ease and charm. He's a miniature version of James in that way. And now he's been reduced to this. Lost, monosyllabic, sitting on the stairs as if he doesn't know what to do.

Our housekeeper, Cassie, comes through into the hallway. She's got rubber gloves on and her hair is tied back. She greets me with a warm smile. 'Let me take those bags from you, Julianne,' she says, picking up the ones I've already put down, catching two apples as they start to slip out.

'Thank you,' I say, giving her a distracted smile in return, not wanting to take my attention away from Stephen. I wait until she's gone back through into the kitchen then go over to him and sit beside him on the stairs.

'Dad's at work,' he says.

'I know,' I reply. I put my hand on top of his and give it a friendly squeeze. He doesn't pull away, but his hand remains limp and oddly lifeless.

'I just thought you'd like to be sure. In case you wanted to do anything.'

'Do anything?' I say, confused.

'Anything without him being here.'

I stare at him closely, but he's still staring directly ahead, not looking at me. 'Stephen, what do you mean? I told you there's nothing to be worried about. Everything's fine. We don't need to do anything,' I say. He says nothing. 'Come on, it's Christmas. Look, I know . . .' I lower my voice, though Cassie's got Radio 4 on in the kitchen and I can hear her opening cupboards and unpacking the shopping. 'I know what you found was strange. I found it disconcerting, too. But I spoke to him about it, and honestly, it's all fine. It was just some work project he was doing and he put the files in his Dropbox by mistake.'

'I see. So that's sorted then.' He doesn't say it like a question. It's a pointed statement, said bluntly and coldly. He's suspicious. Suspicious of his own father. He thinks a man he's loved his whole life might be hiding some awful secret. It devastates me. But there's a small part of me that's scared of something different, something I'm afraid of even admitting to myself: it comforts me that I'm not the only one with doubt. That I'm not alone with my torment. That Stephen, too, suspects the full truth hasn't yet been told.

'Yes. He just put the files in the wrong folder. Honey, please . . .' I say, leaning in to hug him. 'I know this has been a bit of an odd thing for us to deal with. The file on that woman was distressing to read. It was from another company your dad's firm was going to do business with, but they decided not to. Because of that file. They decided it was unethical. Everything with your dad is fine. Truly. It's all figured out.' I'm making myself sound more sure than I am, but I know it's what I need to do. This isn't Stephen's battle. This shouldn't be something he has to worry about. 'We can just ... carry on with Christmas. We've got the Kelmans coming for dinner tomorrow, Grandma and Grandad on Christmas Eve ...'

He sniffs and shakes his head. 'Can't let anything get in the way of that.'

I'm not used to sarcasm from him and it stings. 'I didn't mean ...'

'Files,' he says, cutting across me.

I don't understand him at first, then he says it again, 'You said file. It's files. Plural.' And then I remember. That long list of files. Loads of them. And I've only seen two. Stephen's looked through more than me.

'They're not important,' I say to him, and eventually he looks at me. His eyes make me want to cry. The look on his face takes me back to that moment a couple of days ago when he came into the kitchen and told me he'd found something. It feels like a lifetime ago now. Eventually, he moves to lift himself up off the stairs.

'If you say so,' he says, then walks away, up towards his room. I hear the thud of his bedroom door closing, and I'm left sitting on the stairs on my own, the theme tune of *The Archers* drifting in from the kitchen and a tight knot in my stomach, twisting away at my insides, that I fear will never go away.

I'm sorting out the remaining presents I have to wrap when my phone sounds a ping from my pocket. It's Ally Kelman, asking if she can bring anything tomorrow. She always does this, regularly asks and offers to help, then turns up either late and empty-handed, or early and sits around watching me getting the place organised. I read through her message again, trying to focus.

Popping into Selfridges later so can pick something up? Unless you'd like to join? Naughty afternoon champagne bar trip? x

I'm in the middle of messaging back an apology, saying I've got too much to do, but then I stop. Do I really want to stay here in this suffocating house? And I've been meaning to pop into the shops to find something for James's mom. I bought her a scarf earlier in the year that I thought she'd love, only to see a photo of her on holiday in Norway wearing an identical garment. I've been planning to find something else for weeks but it keeps slipping my mind. And maybe I could talk to Ally. Not tell her anything explicit. Just a distraction, a moan about James, her usual no-nonsense approach to life. It could be what I need. She's been a good friend over the years, and God knows I've been a kind ear and shoulder to cry on during her recent divorce.

I text back. *Sure. Although can we go to John Lewis? I have something to return. I can be there in an hour?*

She messages back immediately. *Okay! See you at the café.*

I go up the stairs and knock on Stephen's door. 'I'm

just popping out to John Lewis,' I say to the wood. For a moment I think he's going to blank me for the first time since he was a child, but he doesn't. He eventually murmurs back, 'Okay.' I hesitate, wondering whether to go inside, but I can't face a repeat of our conversation earlier. Not yet. After a quick exchange with Cassie before I leave about wine supplies, I wrap up warmly and head out and across the cold street. I decide to take the underground rather than the car, but regret it after waiting on the Knightsbridge Piccadilly line platform for ten minutes for a delayed train. After I finally get to Green Park I decide to ditch the Tube and continue my journey above ground. The buzz of Central London is immediate and infectious. The Christmas lights of The Ritz glint in the gloomy December afternoon light and there are people with bulging shopping bags everywhere. It feels like it might snow and I wrap my coat around me, setting off up Old Bond Street. Under normal circumstances I'd love this. The festive season is my favourite time of year and I'm never usually bothered by the crowds and endless Christmas music playing in the shops. But now it's as if I'm watching myself in a movie rather than real life, feeling secondhand fake emotions rather than the rush of the real thing. Everything's muted, dialled down, diluted.

I reach Oxford Street after a fifteen-minute walk and cross the road to John Lewis. I have ten minutes before meeting Ally, so start to browse the cosmetics on the ground floor, but after a few seconds there's a tap on my shoulder.

'Hello! I thought I was going to be late but managed to dodge the tourists.'

Ally looks the same as she always looks: dishevelled in an expensive, beautiful sort of way. Her flowing blonde hair is down today, pouring over her bright-red coat, messy and perfect at the same time, her face flushed from the cold.

'Hiya,' I say, returning her smile. 'How's it all going?'

'Oh gosh, such a hassle. I still have a ton of shopping to do. Why do I always leave it till the bloody last minute? I must be some sort of masochist or something.' She lets out her loud, disarming laugh. 'Anyway, come on, let's get a drink.'

'A non-alcoholic drink,' I say. 'I'm definitely in more of a hot chocolate mood than a champagne mood. If that's okay?'

'Lead the way!' she says brightly, not caring that her loud, theatrical voice is making staff and customers stare.

We journey to the café on one of the upper levels, Ally remarking on the cascade of Christmas lights hanging in the air near the escalators, 'You should have these in your house, Julianne!'

In the café, I get my hot chocolate and Ally opts for a cappuccino; then we find a corner and begin to talk.

'The bitch is at it again,' Ally says, without even taking a sip of her coffee. 'All over Facebook and Instagram. They're in Miami.' She says the last word with wide eyes as if she's never heard of anything so ridiculous. When I don't respond immediately, she adds, 'As in Florida.'

'I know where Miami is.'

171

She laughs again. 'Oh, of course you do. Probably went there all the time when you were back in the States, did you?'

'Well, no, Chicago's not exactly—'

'Anyway, look at this.' She brandishes her massive Samsung smartphone, the screen filled with the warm glow of an evening on the beach, a couple in the centre embracing. 'That's HIM. And her. Thunder-tits, as I like to call her.'

I study the picture. In another context, it might have been quite sweet, and because of the soft lighting the age difference between Ally's ex-husband and his new twenty-eight-year-old girlfriend isn't as plain to see. I'm not really sure what to say, although that rarely matters with Ally.

'I was tempted just to comment underneath "Twats", but thought that might seem childish.'

'A bit,' I say, blowing on my hot chocolate. 'What is it she does again?'

'She's a mindfulness coach. I know. I'm not even fucking joking. As far as I can make out, she doesn't have any formal qualifications. So she's poking around in people's heads, telling them to think of waterfalls and whatever nonsense, and she doesn't even know what she's doing. That would worry me, if I went to see her to deal with my stress. Like going to a dentist who just hacks up teeth for a hobby.'

She pauses a moment to have some of her cappuccino, then raises her hand and points upward, as if she's just remembered something important. 'Oh my God, I completely forgot to say. That guy I went on a date with.

Cameron. It's a thing. We're a thing. He's coming tomorrow. To your dinner. If that's okay with you, of course.'

This rush of information takes me by surprise. 'Er . . . wow, that's great.' To be completely honest, the addition of another person at such short notice isn't exactly ideal, but I'm used to this kind of thing with Ally. She's presumptuous, and always gets away with it. I just nod and smile, as I do now. 'No problem. Bring him along.'

'Super,' she says. 'I can't wait for you to meet him. He's young. I thought two can play at that game. The sex is really rather surprising. I'd forgotten how creative people in their twenties can be. And how blasé. The other night he lost his erection during sex and just shuffled off to get some Oreos. No embarrassment, no awkwardness. Older men act like it's a sign they're knocking on the doors of the retirement home. I think young people just take it in their stride. Watch a bit of porn to get themselves in the mood again. We didn't watch porn together that night, though – we shared the Oreos while watching *Planet Earth II*. Have you seen that episode with the snakes and the lizards?'

'No, I haven't,' I reply. 'You say you watch porn? Like, together?'

Ally shrugs. 'Yeah, sometimes. Not that often. He likes it and I don't mind. Especially if I'm going down on him while he's watching it happen to a guy on-screen. I always try to make sure the girl in the video looks wildly different to me so he won't start comparing us.' Another loud laugh. 'I'm not sure I'd be able to compete with those youthful Californian blondes.'

Normally I'd take this kind of conversation in my stride,

173

laugh at some of the more outrageous details and try to steer the conversation into less colourful territory. But today's different.

'Aren't you ever worried . . . when you're dating new people . . . that you'll, I don't know, discover something you don't like. Something you find unpalatable?'

Ally's eyes light up mischievously.

'Only mildly so. Having sex in public. Getting caught. No more than most people. We don't do it in public, I hasten to add. None of those is my scene.'

'No, I'm not necessarily talking about sex.'

She raises an eyebrow at me. 'What do you mean? Political things? Like, discovering they're far-right racists on the quiet?'

I'm not sure how to phrase this, whether I'm being stupid, going too far. 'I suppose. Or, like . . . having a secret life. A side you don't know anything about. And then when you discover it . . . other things start to make sense. And it preys on your mind.' I realise I've been looking at my hot chocolate the whole time while talking, but when I look up, Ally's eyes are averted, too, staring at a space across the table.

'Well, I suppose that can happen,' Ally says, her voice not as smooth as normal. I shouldn't have taken the conversation into such serious territory, I think. 'My twat of an ex-husband obviously had a not-so-secret love of enormous breasts. I suppose that's my only experience of that kind of thing.'

Ally's still not looking fully at me. In fact, I'm sure she's deliberately avoiding my gaze.

'I'm sorry, I don't really know what I'm talking about. It was just something I was watching on TV. Made me think.' I try to say it brightly, aware my voice is probably sounding false. Something about the mood between us has changed slightly. I would have expected her to pounce on my words, asking if I've found something out about James. But she doesn't. Instead, she changes the subject.

'Let's talk about something fun,' she says, putting a hand on mine, her smile spreading across her lips. 'Like my plans for a cruise with Cameron in the spring.'

We talk for another forty minutes, Ally showing me on her phone all the places she and her new man are going to visit. Eventually, I tell her I must get going and we gather our things and make our way down towards the entrance. At the doors, I stop still. 'Oh damn,' I say, 'I was supposed to find something for James's mom.' I look back at the busy shop floor. The thought of going back in makes me feel so tired, I think I'm going to collapse in a ball on the floor. Ally doesn't seem keen on lingering.

'You know, darling, I'm going to have to dash. I've got a thing with a few former colleagues in bloody Hornchurch of all places – sodding miles away. One of them decided to move out to the suburbs so we've apparently all got to risk our lives in the depths of East London. Practically Essex, you know.' She says 'Essex' in the same wide-eyed way she'd said Miami. 'Plus, I still don't know what I'm going to wear. Got to go home and try a few bits on. I'll see you tomorrow, though. Can't wait. Your Christmas do is always the highlight of my calendar.' She leans in to give me a hug and an air-kiss and I say goodbye. She's gone, lost among the bustle of shoppers.

I linger for a moment then take a deep breath and walk back into John Lewis. Just before I walk into the main part of the ground floor and back towards the escalators, I hear someone running up behind me and suddenly I'm being pulled around. The force of it startles me greatly and I draw in a sharp breath. But when I see the person who's touched me, there isn't any hope of drawing in another. I can't breathe at all. A woman stands before me, her face white, her hair pulled back tightly as if she were about to go to the gym. Indeed, her whole attire suggests sports activities – she has an Adidas tracksuit and running shoes on, and a hoody that looks like it's seen better days. Anyone would think she was a teenager or university student, if the lines in her face didn't show so clearly she'd passed thirty-five.

'Julianne.' She says my name in almost a whisper and as soon as she's said it I know exactly who she is.

'Oh my God,' I say, and take a step back. I'm instantly knocked aside by a man carrying a lot of bags, but I hardly feel it. I just stare at the woman in front of me. 'Holly.'

'Hello.' Her tone is flat and her eyes keep darting about. 'I was waiting for Ally to go. She hasn't changed, has she? She looks just the same.'

I'm still trying to breathe, my legs unsteady, dimly aware shoppers are trying to push their way around us. 'It must be . . . twenty years . . . or more. I can't . . . I can't stop and chat,' I say, trying to act like there isn't anything weird at all about this meeting. 'But I hope . . .'

'She said you called her. Myanna. She said she tried to talk to you a year ago but you didn't respond and then she got bogged down in something else, something to do with ISIS trafficking women; important, of course, but it was frustrating as I really felt something was happening and then nothing came of it.' She's gabbling now, getting her words out in a rush. 'But you called her two days ago. She's going to help me. Help us. She's got the time and the resources now.' Her eyes are wide and I can't help it — I'm frightened. Frightened by all the things she's saying. 'She's been trying to get in touch with you but she thinks you've blocked her number or something. Have you?'

I feel the temperature around me changing, my skin going cold, my legs threatening to give way. 'I don't know what you mean,' I say.

'I'm the reason she got in touch. I told her. I said you might help us. You might be willing to talk.'

I stare at her in horror. 'Talk about *what*? What's there to talk about? I don't know what any of this is about . . .'

'Don't you? Please, Julianne. We can go somewhere right now and . . .'

'I can't,' I say, forcing myself to straighten up and breathe slowly. 'I'm busy. Tell your friend not to get in touch with me again.' I walk away from her, back out of the doors of the shop and onto the street.

'Julianne!' She screams my name. People around me stop and stare, causing other people to knock into them, but I carry on going. I don't stop. I push on until I reach Oxford Circus Underground station, then force myself to steady my pace and walk calmly behind the flow of shop-pers and commuters heading home. It's only when I'm safely on the Victoria line, sitting in a miraculously vacant seat, that I let my guard down and start to cry.

Chapter 14

Holly

Oxford, 1991

Part of me had wanted to never talk to them again when I got back to Oxford. That was the New Year's resolution I had made to myself when I got on the train in London. I was going to focus on my studies, maybe make some new friends, rekindle my friendship with Rachael and Becky. They'd been a little cool with me since I'd become more and more unavailable. I even considered joining a society or two. Something different. I'd never been much good at sports, but maybe there'd be something about learning a new language or art. I managed to get myself into a pretty positive frame of mind and then set forth devouring Emily Brontë's *The Tenant of Wildfell Hall*. I'd made my way through nearly two-thirds of the book when I arrived at the station, and planned to keep my place with one hand and lug my travel bag off the train with the other. However, as I stepped on to the platform, a gust of unusually strong, icy wind sent the book flying out of my hand and onto the damp, gritty floor.

'God's sake,' I said under my breath, then saw someone stooping to pick it up. I knew the blonde hair immediately.

'Christ, this looks dry! Couldn't you have found something a bit more lively to read to ease you into January?' Ally shook the book a little to get rid of a few specks of dirt and held it out to me.

'Were you on the train?' I said, taking the book from her, not bothering to say thank you.

'I was indeed! Didn't see you, though.'

'Were you in first class?' I asked, starting to walk towards the ticket barrier.

'Guilty as charged.' She let out one of her barking laughs and stuffed her hands into her expensive-looking and rather eccentric blue and pink coat.

'Well, that explains why then.'

I thought this might remind Ally that there was supposed to be at least a suggestion of awkwardness between us. After all, I had fled Oxford without a word of goodbye to any of them, but either she didn't realise or was determined not to show it.

'I just popped to London for a bit of shopping. Been back here for four days now, but I was craving some retail therapy. Mother has been driving Ernest and me insane over the whole Christmas holiday and he's got all tense and weird about his studying, so I took myself off to Harrods for a nose around the sales.'

I looked her up and down but she didn't seem to have any bags of shopping with her. 'Didn't find anything you liked?'

'Oh, heaps of stuff. Simply heaps. But it's all being sent on. Some of it here, the rest back home. I have this mortal fear I'll be the madwoman running for a train who sends showers of clothes skidding across the station platform and there'll be security guards and ticket inspectors scrabbling to pick up my bras and whatnot. Do you ever have that?'

'As in, has it ever occurred to me, or do I ever worry it will happen?' I wasn't really in the mood for Ally's silly little problems of privilege and fully suspected this particular fear was actually a lot of nonsense, and she had the clothes sent on because she was lazy rather than being worried about dropping them.

'It hasn't really happened to you, has it? Oh Christ, I'm terribly sorry if it has.'

'It hasn't.'

'Well, I just always think it's better to be safe than sorry.'

Outside the station Ally again sidestepped any awkwardness when I went to walk back to the dorms by immediately striding up to a taxi, brushing away my objections with a swish of her hand and a cry of 'Nonsense! Get in!' I found myself being driven through the familiar streets towards our halls. Inside, I walked past Ally's room, determined to get going with my unpacking, but to my irritation found her behind me as I unlocked the door, following me in, talking animatedly about the huge row her father had had with a famous, award-winning novelist at their house on Christmas Eve ('I can't tell you his name, I'm afraid, but the surname starts with a B') over something as trivial as the year of the wine they were drinking. She continued talking while I was unpacking and, though I was only half-listening, I stopped dead when she said, 'James was sorry not to see you before you left, you know.' I paused in what I was doing and turned back to face her.

'Was he?'

She grinned. 'He was indeed.' And she winked at me. I felt myself blushing and turned back to the clothes I'd been folding. 'Oh, come on, Holly, it's plain as day to anyone that you fancy him and I think he fancies you in his own way.'

I didn't say anything for a minute, then replied very quietly: 'I think he's got his hands full.'

Ally made a 'hmm' sound, as if weighing something up in her mind. 'I must confess I'm not as taken with Julianne as I would like to be.'

'He isn't your brother,' I said. 'Surely he doesn't need your approval.' It probably sounded a bit harsh, but Ally carried on talking.

'I know, yes, I really should just mind my own business. But he needs someone . . . I don't know . . . with a bit of backbone. I'm not convinced she has any. No spark. She's pretty enough, of course, but I don't think she has any fizz. Do you know what I mean?'

'She certainly had some fizz at Rupert's party before Christmas.'

The words were out of my mouth before I had time to really consider how sensible they were.

'Oh really?' Ally said, sounding curious.

I nodded. 'I saw them together. She was giving him oral sex.'

Ally looked at me blankly for a second, then guffawed with laughter. 'Good God, Holly, you make it sound so clinical. Well, I'm sure they weren't the only ones getting a bit fruity at the party. And while we're on the subject . . .' Her face turned slightly pained, as if she were preparing to address a subject that was unpleasant to her. 'I need to offer you an apology. I had a ghastly headache that night and demanded then and there that Ernest get the car to take us home. I felt absolutely awful that we had just abandoned you like that. Rupert gave me a bit of a telling off about it when we saw him over the holidays.'

I wasn't sure where to look, so chose the floor. 'It's okay,' I said, even though it wasn't and I didn't believe her headache excuse for a moment. 'I survived.'

'Can we make it up to you? We're going to a bar tonight. The Scarlet Cape, it's called. I know, it sounds like a brothel, don't get me started on the name, but it's honestly rather fun. They do really nice cocktails. Ernest and James are coming, and Peter, finally. And, even better for you, Julianne is *not* coming. She's got an exam soon and needs to *go study*.' She said these last two words in an imitation of her accent, and then pulled a face, as if the idea of revising for an exam was some strange American phenomenon that had yet to cross the Atlantic.

'Honestly, Ally, I think I'm fine. I'm really not in the

mood, and I mean it this time. It's nice of you to ask, but I really would rather finish this.'

She wouldn't accept the declined invite at first, but after badgering me for a bit she nodded and said, 'Fair's fair. We'll be heading back to Ernest's room after, probably around midnight, post-drinks drinks. If you can't sleep or get bored of sorting out your knickers drawer, do join.'

I told her I would bear it in mind.

I went to bed early that night, determined to wake at the crack of dawn and go to the library, but instead spent the two and a half hours tossing and turning, unable to find the right thoughts to guide me into the usually comforting world of sleep. Images of Ally, sitting on my bed and talking about James and Julianne, kept swimming into my mind, no matter how hard I tried to think of something else. James's eyes. That confident, almost challenging, gaze he had held me in as he allowed Julianne to do *that* to him. That thing I had wanted to do to him the moment I met him, and more besides. I thought of my time with George on the sofa at home and how plain it had all felt. How strange yet mundane, unusual yet uninspired. It wasn't what I'd expected. It wasn't enough.

I got up and pulled on my clothes. It was just past midnight. Though I'd have preferred to have spent some time getting ready properly, I quickly pulled on some black jeans and a light-blue cotton jumper over the white t-shirt I'd worn in bed. On top of this, I picked out my thickest winter coat from the wardrobe and set off down the corridor, out of the building and into the night. The courtyard was coated in a thin layer of snow and I crunched my way across it, walking the short distance down the road to where the boys' halls were. A young man held the door open for me on his way in, removing the obstacle of gaining access after hours without a key, and I remembered where Ernest's room was easily enough. I stopped in front of it, knocked and, thinking I'd heard a voice call out from inside, opened it and walked in. Darkness greeted me. I took a step back outside into the dully-lit hallway, disconcerted. Were they all sitting in the dark? Then I heard voices to my left and realised it must have been another group of students I'd heard. Ernest's room was empty. Though not as bitingly cold as the January winds outside, the corridor was far from warm, so I decided to wait inside. I'd been invited, after all, I thought as I turned the light on and settled myself on the bed.

Ernest's mattress was softer than mine and dipped quite a bit as I put my weight on it. I glanced around, taking in the books I had examined on my previous visit and the general untidy feeling of clutter and disorder. On the floor by my feet were the familiar scattered items of clothing and, within them, a fold of maroon fabric. I reached down and retrieved it. James's tracksuit bottoms, the ones he had been wearing when I'd seen him emerge from Ernest's bed all those months ago, were in my hands. Weighty, extremely soft, no doubt a premium brand. I brought them closer to me and saw a glint of white poking out, then something fell on my lap. A pair of men's underpants. I jumped up, as if they were a tarantula, and let them fall to the floor.

My heart was beating and I glanced at the door, convinced someone would step in at any moment and declare I was a pervert and shame me in front of hundreds of my fellow students. But no such thing happened. I nudged them gingerly out of my way and sat back down. Still clutching the tracksuit bottoms, I gave in to my overwhelming desire: I brought them to my face. His scent – that strange, elusive, manly scent – a mixture of his aftershave and something else, something more primal, filled me as I drew in a breath. I let my mind hang there for a moment, picturing him, his face, his smile, his eyes, that look as he leant back and watched me watching him being satisfied in the most pleasurable way possible. I was excited, I could feel it between my thighs, and I desperately wanted to put my hand under my jeans, but I couldn't bring myself to do it here. I thought about later. What I'd do to myself when I got back to my bed. I'd almost decided to return to my dorm and pretend I had never arrived here when the noise of a door down the corridor closing made me start.

'Let's get you into bed, young man,' said a posh male voice. Ernest's voice.

'That sounds promising,' another said, and I knew it was James.

'With the American and the Pauper forsaking your needs, I think I'm the best you're going to find.' Ernest laughed to himself, but James cut across him.

'Don't call her that. Really, don't.'

Their voices were getting close and, in a second, I hit the light switch, and then felt my way to the wardrobe, relieved to find there was more than enough space amidst the jumble of shirts for me to stand. I didn't know what I was doing, why I hadn't just stayed seated. But now I was in there, I was scared to come out in case that was the first thing they saw when they walked in: me, emerging from Ernest's wardrobe like the freak they no doubt thought I was.

I watched from the slit as the two boys entered the room and turned on the light. Ally wasn't with them, nor was Peter. They were both stumbling a little. Alcohol, it seemed. But not enough of it to make them hit the bed straight away. Ernest crouched down at his desk, picking up some papers from the floor and putting them in his bag. 'Darthall's bloody Proust essay tomorrow. Fucking hate Proust. Had to force myself to finish it.'

James merely murmured in response. He pulled off his jumper and shirt in one apparently effortless movement, his subtly toned body exposed. 'Can we turn off the light?' he said.

'Just a sec.' Ernest finished sorting out his papers and then hit the switch on the wall. The room went dark again, though they were both clearly visible from the light pollution streaming in from the window. A strange, weak, orange glow washed over James's torso. He unbuttoned his jeans and pulled them off. My heart felt like it was doing gymnastics in my chest and I felt sure they'd hear its relentless pounding if they didn't hear my breathing first. James stood there in his briefs, then pulled them off, too. The shock of seeing him completely naked over-whelmed me for a couple of seconds. I felt like a deviant, a voyeur – a horrible, sinking feeling of guilt mingling with the prickly rush of a teenage girl brushing up against the boy she likes at the school disco. Here I was again. Always on the outside and unable to look away. I shouldn't have been there. I didn't want to be, and yet I did, desperately, want to carry on staring. Shadow fell on his crotch as he turned, covering any frontal nudity as he got into the bed. Ernest started to remove his clothes seconds later. He, too, removed his briefs, and I got a brief glimpse of his penis as he turned around. Before he got into bed, however, he picked up a pair of what seemed to be boxer shorts from his drawer and put them on. They were together in bed. Both boys. Ernest and James. The latter completely naked, the other in just his pants. They lay quite still for a while. After what seemed like an eternity, the two shapes seemed to mingle and I realised Ernest had pulled himself close to James. He put his arms around his friend so he was hugging him from behind.

'You in the mood?' said a voice, which I took to be Ernest's. James gave out another barely audible murmur. Ernest's visible arm was drawn back under the sheets and I could see it travelling under the covers around James's body. It began to move rhythmically. My legs had become part of the wood of the wardrobe and I couldn't move. I watched them get further entwined, with Ernest's chin pressed up hard against James's shoulder. He moved his leg over him and the covers were pulled back. Ernest stopped what he was doing and pulled his hand back closer to himself to pull down his underwear, his skin glowing a strangely bright white in the light from the window. I only vaguely realised what he was doing when James let out a loud moan – the most definite and true noise he'd made since he entered the room; a strong, almost animalistic, noise that at once suggested pain and a deep, deep pleasure. Ernest was now gripping his shoulders and James's body seemed to have gone long and tense, his feet, still partially hidden by the folds of the duvet towards the end of the bed, pointed sharply outwards. As he relaxed, and allowed himself to be taken without any evidence of tension or pain, their bodies seemed to go through a kind of merging. It was as if they weren't people any more, just shifting, swirling shapes. The moonlight, the streetlamps, their otherworldly, glowing figures: it was all strangely cinematic and, in spite of my shock at what I was witnessing, there was something beautiful about it all that kept me hypnotised. It shook me, shocked me and, in an odd way, moved me. James's moans were starting to build and Ernest's heavy breaths and grunts to grow shorter, more staccato. Eventually he appeared to tip over, his full weight pressing against James, his arms gathering him up, holding him tightly. James didn't resist, but let out a low sound, a half-cry, half-gasp, that sent a rush down my arms, and then another noise – a slow, satisfied sigh.

They stayed there, still, for almost a minute, motionless apart from their steadily slowing breathing. Then James turned, extricating himself from Ernest's arms, and rolled over to face him. He reached out and held his face in his hands, gently running his fingers along his jawline.

'Is this where you get all sentimental?' Ernest whispered.

'I don't know what you mean,' James said, with a quiet laugh.

'You always do after you've finished.' Ernest embraced him and James followed his lead, allowing their faces to meet. He kissed Ernest gently on the lips, taking his time, his hand reaching around the boy's neck, pulling him into him. Ernest didn't resist and kissed him back. The tender nature of it made me want to cry although I wasn't sure why; then I realised I was, the tears dropping lightly onto my hand. They carried on, holding each other, their mouths connected, and I knew why I was crying. Nobody had ever kissed me like that. Deep, hard, honest, unflinching, with an intimate understanding that comes from a long-term familiarity between the participants.

When the boys finally drew apart, slowly, still looking at each other, Ernest said quietly, 'It's not enough any more, is it?'

'It's still good, though,' James replied, staring at him intently. 'Better than nothing. But we'll have some more fun soon. Something new.'

'If you don't lose your nerve again,' Ernest said, letting his hand glide over James's face.

'I won't. I promise,' he said.

Ernest seemed to be studying James, though his face was in too much darkness to see his expression fully; then he drew him in closer so James's head was resting in between his shoulder and neck, just like men had done to women in countless films. They fell asleep like that, woven tightly together, their naked bodies half-covered by the sheets, their legs like tangled roots, poking out at the ends. I don't know how much time passed. An hour, maybe two. But eventually I couldn't stand still any longer. I gently pushed open the door of the cupboard, thanking God it didn't creak, and tiptoed to the door, taking it off the latch as quietly as I could. I kept glancing back at them, but their eyes were tight shut and their breathing steady. Once I was in the corridor, I pulled the door to, afraid I'd wake them by closing it. I hoped they would just think they'd forgotten to close it properly in the morning. I walked back to my room, across the courtyard, up the steps, down the hallway, through the door, into bed. Still fully dressed, but I didn't care. The tears came soon enough and I didn't try to stop them, partly confused as to why they were there, partly not wanting to admit the truth. I just let them fall onto the pillow. Slowly, as I cried, the words of the two boys floated in and out of my consciousness: 'We'll have more fun soon . . . something new.' What more could they do, I thought dully. What was it they were looking for? These questions rose and fell, gently pricking at my mind, until eventually the numbing anaesthetic of sleep took me away.

Chapter 15

Julianne
Knightsbridge, 2019

Cassie's vacuuming the hall carpet when I arrive back home. As I step through the door and start unwinding my scarf, looking down so she won't see how red my eyes are, she shuts off the Hoover and starts talking about a plate she's broken.

'I'm so sorry, it just slipped off the counter. As if a poltergeist had pushed it.'

I attempt a weak smile. 'It's fine,' I say. 'Honestly.'

'Oh, and you had a visitor. A woman. A couple of hours ago now, just after you'd left.'

I freeze on my way to the stairs. 'What? Who?'

Cassie shrugs. 'I don't know, I'm afraid. She wouldn't

leave a name. She just asked if Julianne lived here and I said "Can I help you?" and she just kept saying "I need to talk to Julianne". She looked a bit manic towards the end, saying she'd hoped to catch you. I said you'd nipped out to John Lewis and didn't know how long you'd be. She went off after that.'

She'd followed me. The realisation makes me shiver slightly, although in the back of my mind I'd already known it to be true; we hadn't just bumped into each other on Oxford Street by coincidence.

No doubt noticing the look of worry on my face, Cassie starts to garble. 'I'm sorry if I shouldn't have said where . . .'

'It's all fine, Cassie. Thank you.' I walk up the stairs without meeting her eye and carry on until I've reached the bedroom.

After a moment sitting on the edge of the bed, staring into space, I go back out onto the landing and tread quietly towards Stephen's room. I can hear talking coming from inside. I try to make out the words but they're too muffled, so I knock gently. 'Darling? You in there?'

'I'm just on Skype to Will,' he replies.

'Right, okay,' I say through the door. 'Are you . . . Is everything . . . Do you need anything?'

'I'm fine, Mum.'

I nod, even though he can't see me. I give it a few seconds and hear him carry on talking, so I return to the bedroom. James is still at work, then he's got a Christmas gathering with former colleagues. Alone with my thoughts, I know I can't just sit here, feeling powerless. I'm in the dark and, as my mother always used to say, when you're in the dark, make sure it's you ruling the darkness, not it ruling you. As a twelve-year-old girl, I used to find these bleak nuggets of wisdom from my mom disturbing. Now, for the first time, I'm truly glad of something she taught me. At least she didn't sugarcoat things. That's always been James's problem, throughout our marriage. If it was something he wanted to make a point about, he'd say it, like with our clashes over Stephen going to Oxford. But so many times he'd put a happy gloss on a subject, as if he were afraid of inspecting it more closely. His swerve away from politics and into his job in data services, my decision to leave my job in publishing, our inability to have any more children and the choice not to pursue treatment, the discussions about relocating to the US and possibly bringing our then-tiny son up as an American child . . . he'd charmed his way through all these points in our lives, smiling and comforting but never really offering any answers, quick to extinguish any upset or discontent before it could properly develop. Without me realising, he'd become evasive. Elusive. Private. As if he were frightened of me looking too closely at the fabric of our existence. Now I am looking at it. And I'm not sure I like what I see.

I don't think I've ever used the lock on the bedroom door – not even when James and I are making love, confident in the knowledge Stephen wouldn't just barge in at night. But I use it now. It slides into place, barricading out the world downstairs, giving me space to think and time to do what I need to do. First, I need my iPad, currently on charge on the bedside table, on top of an Agatha Christie novel I've been leisurely making my way through.

Settling back amidst the pillows, I take out the charger and unlock the iPad, the bright screen making me blink in the dim room. I navigate once again to Dropbox, and then to James's folder. It's empty. There is no trace of the files Stephen and I looked through. No long list of numbers. Just a clear, white column of nothing.

This shouldn't really bother me, I tell myself. If it's true the files were meant for someone in the security services, James would be foolish to leave them in there now. He'd already made a preposterous mistake leaving them so unprotected to start with, let alone once his wife and son had stumbled across them.

I instead go back to the home screen and launch the Chrome app. I locate the private browsing mode and find my way back to the search engine. In the box I type the name of James's company, Varvello Analytics, and wait. The animated front page blossoms into view, showing loads of numbers and letters flickering across the screen, flashing and changing until they finally settle into the company logo. I then have the option of choosing which area of the site I want to look at – commercial or political. What is it I'm looking for, I think to myself. There isn't likely to be anything useful to me on his company webpage. What am I trying to find?

Reassurance. The word falls into my mind as soon as I've asked myself the question. And then something arrives just as quickly: Clover Shore Construction.

Why would a data analytics company – even one of the kind James had mentioned, one that didn't really abide by the ethical standards of UK law – have 'construction' in their name? Perhaps this is some kind of tech language I'm just not aware of. I try googling the company name but nothing obvious comes up on the first page of results. There are other companies with similar names, most of them building firms, from skyscraper construction to conservatory design. I'm almost about to give up, but then, many pages into the search results, I do hit upon something. A local newspaper in Dagenham had used the words in an online piece nine years ago. And the title of the article makes me feel instantly sick: *Young woman, twenty-one, raped by four unknown men on Dagenham building site.*

I click on the piece, even though I'm terrified what I'm going to read. My eyes dart across it quickly. The woman, Anna Svoboda, a Czech immigrant, claimed she couldn't remember how she had arrived at the building site, but alleged she had been sexually assaulted multiple times by a group of men. She hadn't been able to see their faces, since they had kept a bag over her head for the duration of the assault. My eyes then fall on the words I have been looking for: *The site, located near Dagenham marshes, is registered to the company Clover Shore Construction, which is no longer believed to be in operation. It was used as a storage facility for building equipment, but has remained abandoned in recent years.*

It can't be a coincidence. In a desperate rush, I copy the name of the young woman and paste it into Google. There are many Anna Svobodas listed on Facebook and

LinkedIn and Twitter, but there's no way of telling which is the right one. Most don't list their ages, and there is no photograph of the woman with the news article. I try searching the name of the police inspector who has given a statement about 'bringing the perpetrators to justice' at the end of the piece. This time, the results are even weirder: there's nothing. Not a single thing. No results at all. It's as if he doesn't exist.

A knock on the bedroom door sends a jolt through my bones so forceful it's as if someone's shaken me. 'Julianne?'

It's Cassie. I hide the device under the pillows and run to the door. 'I'm here, I'm here.' My flustered appearance doesn't go unnoticed.

'Oh, are you okay? I'm sorry, I didn't mean to disturb you.'

The fact Cassie has felt the need to apologise to me twice in one day – a first for her – probably says a lot about the way I'm behaving. 'No, not at all. I was . . . I was resting.'

Cassie nods, looking both puzzled and unconvinced, but presses on. 'Well, a package has arrived. It looks like it's from Apple. It's quite weighty, but light enough to carry. I've left it on the kitchen table, but I can bring it upstairs?'

'From Apple?' I'm not sure what she's talking about.

'Yes. I presumed it was a Christmas present or something. You haven't ordered anything?'

'No,' I say, shaking my head. 'Maybe Stephen has, or . . .' A lump appears in my throat. *Or my husband*, I think. 'It's fine,' I say. 'Just . . . leave it there. I'll talk to James about it later. Maybe I'm getting a new iMac for Christmas.' I let out a short laugh, but Cassie looks concerned again.

'Goodness, I hope I haven't spoiled a surprise.'

It takes another bout of reassuring words to convince Cassie everything's fine and she can return to whatever she was doing downstairs. Once she's gone, I sit on my bed and think. A new laptop has just arrived. Surely, if this were anything suspicious, he would have bought it in secret. It must, therefore, be a purchase he was going to make anyway?

Unsure what else to do, I close the private browsing tab and, in a rather pointless act, but just to be on the safe side, delete all browsing and search history. After that, I turn the device off and replace it on top of the book next to the bed. I'm trying not to panic, to rein my mind in, stop it jumping to terrible conclusions, each more outlandish, more strange, more terrifying than the last.

I eat alone in the kitchen – a gluten-free Carbonara with chicken Cassie's prepared – but I hardly taste it. Stephen gets a Deliveroo in; he just hops down the stairs, collects the package (Nando's, from the smell of it) and disappears back to his room. I'm slightly hurt he didn't ask me if I wanted to get a takeaway.

After eating, I get up and take hold of the box I've been staring at for twenty minutes. It is indeed from Apple; the branding is obvious and, through a slight slit in the side, I can see the words MacBook Pro written in their iconic font. Should I confront James again? Or just wait and see what he says about it when he comes back?

Eventually I leave the box where it is on the table, go into the lounge and try to focus on an old episode of *Inspector Morse* on ITV3. I give up after the fourth commercial break and head back upstairs. I should be getting things ready for tomorrow, with everyone coming for our Christmas gathering, but the place already looks showroom-clean thanks to Cassie, and I can't bear the thought of writing Christmas cards and sorting out presents right now. Why do we even give presents to our friends still, I think, as I undress and get into bed. We're adults in our forties. We all have everything we want. We don't need any more things. Everything is perfect. Isn't it?

I fall asleep quickly, probably a symptom of my insomnia the night before. James wakes me when he comes in, even though I can tell he's trying to be quiet. He's not drunk, as far as I can make out. He always drops either his toothbrush or watch if he's drunk. Today, he cleans his teeth quietly and calmly, then takes his watch off and lays it gently on the table on his side of the bed. I turn round to face him, opening my eyes slowly.

'Hey,' he says, giving me a sweet smile. I just look at him.

'Are things okay?' From the light in the bathroom I can see his eyes glinting in the darkness, a look of worry still lingering there. He knows I'm having doubts. He knows there's still something to be afraid of.

I just keep staring at him. I'm not in a position to reassure him. And I don't want to talk about this now.

'Get some sleep,' I say, turning away from him. 'We've got all your friends coming tomorrow.'

I know the 'your' will sting him. He's always wanted me to think of the Kelmans as my friends, too, and it's true Ally and I have been close for almost twenty years now, but I'm not in the mood to be kind. And the thought of spending hours with them, attempting to be polite and having a jolly Christmas, makes panic spread through my body. He doesn't say anything now, just slips into bed next to me, the brush of his legs grazing mine, his flesh still cool from the December air outside.

'You had a delivery today,' I say, still facing away from him. I listen hard to hear if I can detect any reaction, but he's silent. Then he just says, 'Thanks.'

'I think it's a computer.' I don't say it as a question, but it is one really. And I think he knows what I'm asking. In the quiet darkness, I hear the brush of him moving against the duvet. His hand settles on my shoulder and rubs it. Firmly.

'You're wonderful. You know that, don't you?'

I have no idea how to answer this, not without turning round and facing him properly. Perhaps I should. But I say nothing. The two of us lie there, silent and separate in the darkness, until sleep arrives and saves me from my thoughts.

Chapter 16

Holly

Oxford, 1991

It took me over a week to reveal to anyone what I had seen in Ernest's room. In the days that followed, I went from being overwhelmingly shocked to strangely numb. In these moments of numbness, I tried to prod myself – a cerebral pinprick to a memory that seemed like a dream. Sometimes it resulted in the glimpse of a jarring, explicit detail – the noise James had made as his friend entered him from behind, or the way Ernest clung to his shoulders as he pressed himself close. Other times, my mind closed up, refusing to give up such details, as if the memory itself was harmful to my wellbeing. It felt like a self-preservation mechanism. Only years later, after hours of talking to a therapist about my feelings surrounding sexual activity, would I be able to articulate and unpack the causes behind my naivety concerning the whole subject. Or perhaps innocence would be a better word. Innocence, spiked with a judgemental edge I had obviously inherited from my parents. The weight of all this baggage was a burden I didn't know I was enduring, and the relief I would feel when I did finally shift it off my back would be astonishing.

Overall, the shock I felt at the time, witnessing James and Ernest's night-time antics, helped me commit to my New Year's resolution, or at least a diluted version of it. Though I was still polite and civil to them all, I never sought out their company. The nights watching *Neighbours* with Ally now seemed like a distant memory from a half-forgotten time. She never invited me now, nor did I offer to come. This stung at first, then I remembered it was me who had chosen to distance myself from her and her weird brother. If you keep saying no, eventually they stop asking. Then I noticed something that, temporarily, drove all concerns about the sex life of Ally's brother out of my head.

My period hadn't come.

When I realised I was late I experienced one hour of instant, white-hot panic. Then it subsided. People didn't get pregnant their first time. Surely they needed to have lots of goes before? And I wasn't eating very much – my diet had become rather poor since Christmas, with me picking at meals at dinnertime rather than properly eating them. I just wasn't hungry. Maybe that was the cause of my out-of-sync menstrual cycle.

Denial is a funny thing. There's a way it wraps itself around your shoulders in such a welcoming way; you hold it close to you and don't let go. It becomes part of you. I was being stupid. And I think I knew it, deep down. But it saw me through for a time.

The truth about what I had seen during my night-time adventure did come out eventually, however, when Ally walked through my door one unseasonably warm February afternoon, holding an enormous stack of books. 'I thought you might enjoy these!' she said as she precariously hobbled over to my desk and set the titles down with a loud thump.

'Er, thank you,' I said, slightly bewildered as the books landed in front of me. 'Where are they from?'

'Oh, Daddy is chums with someone at Penguin. You know, the publishers.'

'I know who Penguin are. I'm doing an English degree.'

'Well, they always send over a load of books to the house every now and then of their recently published stuff to my Dad and he for some bizarre reason said I'd probably benefit from upping my reading of contemporary literature, so low and behold this turned up this morning and I must say I'd rather build my own coffin than work my way through that lot. Then I thought, I know who'd like these! So here they are.'

'That's . . . that's very nice of you.'

'Splendid. So, now you can tell me what's been eating you up over the past few weeks.'

Her words hit me like a bullet. I didn't think Ally was observant enough to notice such things. I blinked at her, not saying anything, hoping I'd misheard, but it was no use.

'Come on. Can't wait around all day. Let's go for a walk. It helps one talk. My mother always says so. Probably why she always walks alone so nobody can hear her.'

I wasn't sure I understood the reference, but agreed to her request. She led the way with purpose out of the halls and towards a green quad area situated by one of the closest university libraries. A small group of girls sat at the far end on a bench, text books open on their laps, but apart from that it was deserted. We started walking a slow circuit around the still leaf-bare trees and Ally opened with: 'So, where shall we begin? Is this about James?'

I didn't have a clue whether to lie or tell the honest truth, so nodded in what I hoped was a casual, non-committal sort of way.

'About you having the hots for him?'

I drew in a breath, 'I don't have 'the hots' for him.'

She laughed. 'Oh Holly, you don't have to deny it. I think every girl fancies James at some point.'

'Just the girls?'

The question hung in between us for a few seconds, then Ally said, 'Sorry?' as if she'd misheard.

'Just the girls? As in, are you sure it's just the girls who fancy him?'

Ally looked at me, clearly not understanding. 'Well, I'm sure some middle-aged mothers probably have the odd fantasy now and then.'

'I'm talking about your brother, Ally.'

Ally stopped and stared at me. 'What are you talking

about, Holly? Ernest doesn't fancy James. Yes, I joke about it, but they're not into each other in that way. As in . . . I don't know . . . not in a romantic sense or anything. Nothing like that.'

I stopped walking too and looked over at her. 'We've spoken about this before. You implied they were intimate. I just never really knew how intimate.'

Ally still looked baffled. 'Holly, I really don't know where you're going with this?'

'I saw them.'

Her eyes widened. 'What? Saw them where?'

'Together. In bed together. That night, when you said I could join you lot back in Ernest's room, after you went to that bar – The Pink Koala or something . . .'

'The Crimson Cape,' she corrected, rolling her eyes.

'Whatever. Well, I did go there. To Ernest's room, that is. I waited for a while in his bedroom. The door was unlocked and I was cold. And then they came back without you – just him and James.'

'I know, I was getting tired. Decided I needed my bed. Did you guys have a row or something? Oh goodness, I abandoned you again. I'm so sorry . . .'

'We didn't have a row. I hid in the wardrobe.'

She paused for a second, then laughed. A loud, very Ally laugh. 'Oh god, Holly. You do kill me, sometimes. Why on earth did you . . .'

'Because I didn't know what else to do. I regretted it though. Because when they came in . . . they . . .' The awkwardness of what I had started to say had begun to catch up with me and I suddenly became very mindful of the fact that I was, after all, talking about her brother. 'They got into bed together and . . . did things. Together.' I emphasised the final word until I saw the dawning realisation in Ally's face.

'Oh Holly,' she said, then laughed again.

'Can you stop saying my name like that. I'm not a child.'

Like most of my blunt responses to Ally, this didn't seem to hit home. She just continued to laugh and then pulled me over to one of the empty benches. 'Come on, sit down.'

I did as I was told and looked at her, frowning, waiting for an explanation.

'Holly, is this really what's been bothering you?'

I nodded.

'I swear we spoke about this. It's nothing to worry about. James and Ernest are just two horny Etonians that haven't kicked the habit yet.'

I wasn't convinced. 'When we spoke, I didn't think you meant . . . well . . . the things they were doing.'

Ally just shrugged. 'What did they do?'

I grimaced. 'It feels weird telling you. Ernest's your brother.'

She waved a hand, 'Oh, nonsense. I'm not squeamish. I've seen things, goodness knows the stories I could tell you. So what did they get up to? Oral? Full-on shagging?'

I nodded again. 'The last one.'

Ally sighed. 'I don't like the be the one to trample on your innocence, Holly, but it really isn't as unusual as you'd think. I suppose, for someone who hasn't seen that much of that sort of thing it might be a little, well, odd to witness. But I promise you, it's just a bit of silliness between two old friends.'

'It didn't look like silliness. It was . . . intense.'

'Sex is always intense,' she said, casually. 'Or at least is should be if you're doing it right.'

I didn't know what to say to this, so let Ally continue.

'The upshot of all this is that boys are rampant horny devils who would fuck anything with a pulse, given half the chance. I once saw James give my brother a hand job in the library one summer holiday when I was fourteen and they were fifteen or sixteen. I was amazed, but then I asked them about it afterwards and they said they did it all the time at school. Don't be so shocked. And please don't tell me you believe the whole nonsense about it being bad for one's soul or they'll go to hell or something. That's just bigotry.'

'I'm not a bigot. And I'm not religious. Not really. My parents are. But I'm not my parents. Not at all.'

'Glad to hear it. Things are changing, Holly. You need to open your eyes.'

'I know they are. And my eyes are open. I'm just . . .'

'Not sure you like what you see?' Ally finished the sentence for me and sighed. 'I'm not stupid, Holly. I realise you probably didn't have much exposure to all this when you were growing up. But guess what, some boys like other boys, some girls like other girls . . .'

'I know they do. I'm sorry, I didn't mean to sound—'

'And some,' she continued, interrupting me, 'just do it for the sheer fun of it. Honestly, Holly, all the stories and rumours you've heard about boy-on-boy action at single sex private schools? They are all true. They just love it.'

'I haven't heard any stories,' I murmured, picking at a bit of dirt stuck to the bench.

'Well, now you've got one to tell. More than one, in fact.'

I looked up at her. 'What do you mean?'

'Well,' she said, slightly quieter, and I had the sense she was avoiding catching my eye, 'you're making a bit of a habit of this, aren't you?'

I pulled an affronted expression, but had a slightly mortifying feeling I knew what she was implying. 'A habit of what?'

She smiled and for the first time it looked more like a smirk than her happy, carefree grin. 'First James and Julianne at Rupert's party, now James and Ernest in their bedroom from your view from the wardrobe. You've become quite the expert little voyeur.'

I stood up immediately. 'That's sick. You know it's not like that.'

Ally tutted and stood up too. 'I didn't mean anything by it. I'm sorry, I shouldn't have worded it like that.'

'No, you shouldn't have,' I snapped, feeling myself going red.

'Look,' she said, clasping hold of one of my hands, 'Let's go via the little corner shop and get some chocolate, then feast in my room in front of some tacky Australian soap? How does that sound? No talk of sex or boys or anything like that. Sound like a deal?'

I stared hard at the floor for a few seconds, then looked at her again, feeling less angry now. 'OK,' I said.

She grinned. 'Perfect. Walk this way.'

I didn't look at her as I walked, nor did I really bother to talk to her either. I think she thought we were OK. And part of me really wishes we were. How I would like someone I could properly talk to about everything that was in my head. My frustration at my parents. That I constantly felt like an outsider here at Oxford and a stranger back at home. That I was becoming increasingly worried about the absence of my period and what this might mean for my future and any choices I might have to make because of it. But it didn't seem like Ally and I were ever destined to have that kind of friendship. She wasn't a bit like me. I watched her as we walked, standing tall and confident, pleased that she'd managed to make the poor confused commoner alright about the thought of her brother fucking the night away with his lifelong male friend. I was starting to hate everything about them. All of them. It wasn't the fact James and Ernest were two males. I was prepared to put my initial shock at the gay sex down to my sheltered existence up until now (and, in no small part, growing up with my parents). If James and Ernest were genuinely gay I could have understood. But that would have been too normal for them. Too mainstream. It was their arrogant belief that nothing ordi-nary applied to them. All of them. Ally, too. They seemed to think they were members of some exclusive club who had been handed a get-out-of-jail-free card at birth. They didn't have to 'be' anything; they didn't have to subscribe to the set lifestyle the rest of us were saddled with. If the time came, I vowed I would tell them what I thought of them. For now, however, I decided to keep a dignified silence and allow Ally to treat me like a child she'd successfully talked down from a tantrum.

Chapter 17

Julianne

Knightsbridge, 2019

'Julianne? Where are you? Ally's here.'

James calls up the stairs, but I'm already down in the kitchen helping Cassie. I come through, wiping my hand on a tea towel, and smile at Ally.

'So sorry, got caught up with something. Ally, let me take your coat.'

'I've got it,' James says, stepping in to take it and hanging it up. I hang the tea towel on a vacant peg next to it. James looks at me as if I've just stripped naked, then back at the towel, clearly mortified I would do something so odd. I ignore him. I'm not sure I care any more.

Ally, who either hasn't noticed the odd gesture or

chooses not to comment, embraces me in a hug. 'Oh Julianne, how are you?'

'Kind of the same as yesterday,' I say in an attempt at a bright voice. Well, it's true, I suppose.

She laughs as if I've cracked a joke, then steps aside, revealing a young man like a magic trick. He's just standing there, staring blankly at me. I'm taken aback, then realise who he is.

'Julianne, James, this is Cameron, my new man.' It's like she's just got a new car and is eager to show it off. Cameron, on the other hand, seems less than eager. He is good-looking and it's clear right away why Ally finds him attractive, but he must know what we're all thinking: God, he's so young. Must be mid-twenties at the very most. He's wearing a nice patterned shirt – the kind I occasionally used to buy for Stephen, until James turned up his nose at them, describing them as 'very high street' – and chinos, and is shivering slightly, apparently arrived in from the cold without a coat. I shake his hand and welcome him and he gives a thin smile, all the time looking around him. It isn't just his age that sticks out. He isn't used to wealth. James will have noticed that immediately. I can sense James wanting to catch my eye, but I avoid his gaze.

As Cameron and Ally go into the lounge, the doorbell rings. 'I'll get it,' I say, and look towards the disappearing figures of Ally and Cameron, making it clear to James he should be following them.

'Julianne, many greetings of the season.'

Ernest steps inside the house before I've said anything,

followed by his wife, Louise. In all the time I've known him, Ernest has been one of those men who seem desperate to assert their own attractiveness whenever possible, something that, to my slight irritation, he's rather good at. Louise, on the other hand, is loveliness personified, but I'm aware James finds her irritating. She comes across as a bit too eager to please and, although her refined accent makes it sound as if she's been bathed in money, it's hard to believe sometimes that she's one of us, or rather one of James's group of friends. Under her slightly ditzy temperament shelters a brilliant mind, apparently, or so Ally always says. She even beat us both with her degree, graduating four years after we did with a double first in history. Maybe that's how she maintains her confidence in front of us all.

Ernest, now an MP like his dad, and godfather to my son, is talking very animatedly. 'Such a sodding nuisance, this weather. The road at the end of your street is like an ice rink. Not sure what the Royal Borough of Kensington and Chelsea think they're doing, but they aren't doing enough. Why haven't they gritted the road? This is London, for God's sake. Nearly lost control of the car.'

His wife laughs. 'A bad workman blames his tools.' She chuckles and turns to me. 'Lovely to see you, Julianne, it's been too long. God, you look lovely, as ever.'

I smile and thank her, even though I'm sure I probably look as haggard as my mother suggested two days ago. Louise looks a little tired herself, but Ernest seems to be bright-eyed and crackling with energy. He has his typical white-shirt-and-tie affair going on, as if he's just walked out of a constituency meeting. Even back when we were students, he would wear crisp white shirts while lying around in his dorms reading or nipping out for drinks.

'How are you, Julianne?' He reaches forward to kiss me on the cheek. He's always been a bit of a charmer. Blond and traditionally handsome, Ernest has a striking presence that never quite hides what I always think is a slightly cruel-looking edge to his face. His hair has been combed over today and the angular shape of his shoulders suggests that, amidst his time in parliament, he still finds time to work out a lot. He and James used to play squash together, but over the past couple of years their meet-ups have become more about food and alcohol than fitness.

'I'm good, thank you, Ernest,' I say. 'It's been too long.'

'Certainly has,' he says, his deep, posh voice resonating through the hallway.

'Come on into the lounge, I'm just finishing up with the food.' I go to walk back towards the kitchen.

'Oh, you're not cooking yourself, surely?' he says. 'Whatever happened to your housekeeper? Catherine or Cara or whatever her name is?'

Why is it nobody can get her name right? Just like my mother, I suspect Ernest doesn't really think of house staff as real people, but rather another breed altogether.

'Her name is Cassie. And I didn't want to leave it all to her. There's rather a lot of us.'

I lead the Kelmans further into the house and James arrives smiling at the entrance to the living room. 'What are we drinking these days?' he asks, sounding happy and

216

merry. His friends are here, back around him. Just where he likes them.

The living room is warm and Christmassy, with the fire crackling in the grate and the big tree glinting with yellow lights. Usually I would be soaking up the atmosphere, but today it feels like I'm on mute, unable to appreciate the season I look forward to all year round. James is pouring out wine and brandy and Ally and Cameron are eagerly accepting. I stand in the doorway, momentarily unsure where to go or who to talk to. That feeling of mounting dread that's been clinging to me for the past two days isn't going away, and it's now mixed with a sense of helplessness I can't shake off. It's as if I'm a visitor in my own home. Everything's been turned upside down.

'Julianne, James was just telling us about Stephen's plans for Oxford. You must be so proud.' It takes me a second to realise Louise is talking to me and I stare at her stupidly for a moment before managing a smile. 'Yes, it's certainly, um, on his radar.'

James turns to look at me, as I'd known he would.

'*On his radar?* I think it's a great deal more important to him than that. It's his overall goal.'

'Hmmm,' I murmur. James stares at me, but I look away quickly.

'Where is the dear fellow?' Ally says, looking around.

'Exactly what I was thinking,' James says, still looking at me. 'He seems to be spending an awful lot of time shut in his room these days.' James says it with a laugh, but I can detect a slight note of uneasiness in his voice.

'I wonder why,' I say under my breath, but everyone's attention is suddenly focused on me. 'I mean . . . school-work. He's still consumed with coursework and exam revision. And . . . he's got a cold.'

'Has he?' James says, looking puzzled.

'Yes,' I say firmly. I can feel this getting weird and the others must be able to tell. Thankfully Ally starts talking about her trip to Hornchurch yesterday and how three of her five friends at the dinner all had terrible seasonal flu, and how she was furious they'd exposed her to it.

All of a sudden I feel a deep, burning sense of urgency within me. I can't take it any more. I can't stand it. I leave the room without another word, turn down the hallway and walk up the stairs. Stephen's bedroom is at the end of the landing on the first floor. I walk towards it and pause outside, listening. There's no sound at all. This is unusual in itself. I knock on the door. There's a rustling sound, as if someone's turning over in bed. Has he gone to sleep? I don't bother to knock again, and instead open the door. He's lying on his bed, his arms around one of his pillows.

'I wanted to check you were okay,' I say, going over to him and putting a hand on his shoulder.

'I'm fine. Really. Go downstairs. I'll be there in a minute.'

I'm not quite sure what to say. He nods, looking lost and on the verge of tears.

'I'll be down soon. I will. Just give me a sec.'

I offer him a small smile and go back towards the door. 'Come down when you're ready, but there's no rush. They'll be pleased to see you. They've all been asking after you.'

He just nods again. Unable to think of anything else

to say, I offer one last encouraging smile and go to close the door. Then he speaks.

'You've forgiven him, have you?'

I stop where I am, half in his room, half on the landing. I backtrack and close the door and lean against it. 'Your dad loves you.'

'That doesn't answer my question.'

I raise a hand to my face. 'Please, Stephen. Can we not talk about this now?'

'When can we talk about it?'

'We already have.' I'm struggling not to cry, focusing my eyes on a small space on the floor.

'He spoke to me. Earlier this morning. Did you know he was going to?'

I try to keep calm, but I can't help the quick intake of breath. Stephen notices.

'He said he was going to,' I say. 'Look, whatever you think . . .'

'He didn't deny it. I listened carefully to what he said. He just said I need to focus on the "bigger picture" and that things sometimes don't make sense when you're young and the most important thing is me getting into Oxford. I asked him why those files were in his personal Dropbox if they were to do with his work and he was just evasive. No attempt to make an excuse. He just kept mentioning Oxford and how I had a duty to the family to do well and I mustn't get hung up on distractions.'

I clench my hands behind me to stop them trembling. 'Well . . . I know your father and I may not see eye to eye on Oxford . . .'

219

'This isn't about fucking Oxford.'

I flinch. I can't help it. I don't remember ever hearing Stephen swear, certainly not in anger. Maybe when telling a joke or quoting something, but this is different. It sounds harsh and ugly coming from him. Before I can comment he gets up off his bed and walks over to his chest of drawers and opens the one on the top left. I see him lift up a pile of boxer shorts and retrieve something from underneath. He holds it out.

'What is this?' I say. But I can see what it is. It's a USB drive. I hold out my hand and feel the ground shift beneath me as it drops into my palm.

Without talking, Stephen walks back to his bed and sits there looking up at me.

'I don't want to look at what's on here,' I say firmly.

'He's deleted everything, hasn't he? Deleted or moved the files. I've tried to get back on and I can't.'

I go to speak, to tell him off for trying to access the files again and read through those documents without telling me, but he carries on.

'It doesn't matter. I saved them to this when you went back downstairs. Thought I'd put them on a USB. Just in case. Have a look at the files on there. The later ones. There are more people on there. *Different* people. You'll see. And be sure to look at the calendar.'

Calendar? This makes me hesitate before replying, but I can't go into all this with him now. I need to close down this discussion.

'Stephen, there is no point—'

'Funnily enough, that's what he said. Part of his lecture.

"There's no point making a fuss about nothing." Well, I don't think this is nothing.'

'I think he meant that it wasn't anything . . .'

'Fine.' He says it simply and turns away from me. 'Keep up the party line if you want to. Keep the pen drive. Throw it away. I don't care any more.'

He lies back down on his bed, head buried in the pillows. I take a step towards him, then find I have nothing left to say. After almost a minute, I go back out onto the landing and gently close the door behind me.

'Ah, Julianne, perfect timing!' Ally exclaims as I walk through the door to the living room. 'I was just talking to my idiotic brother about grammar schools. You remember? You made your point so perfectly last time we spoke about them and I wanted to tell him about it but couldn't remember quite what you said. Ernest is dead set on them, aren't you?'

Ernest looks slightly embarrassed. I wonder how much Ally has drunk in the short time I've been upstairs.

'Well, the PM is rather keen on . . . I think the general feeling is that we need a clear and definite direction . . .'

'Oh, that's right, use the PM as an excuse. Tell him, Julianne.' She looks at me, waiting for me to leap to her defence.

'I . . . er . . . I . . .' My head is swimming and I'm finding it hard to pin the words down and form them into a coherent sentence. 'I just feel that it will do more harm than good.' Even as I say the words I know they sound lame. Ally clearly thinks so. I can see her expression fall in disappointment. Usually, I would rise to the challenge. I secretly like winding Ernest up a little. His smug superiority occasionally rubs me up the wrong way, though I normally try to remain friendly for the sake of his friendship with James.

'I thought the whole concept of them would be right up your street, Julianne. You're all about social mobility aren't you? You were able to pay for your child to go to Westminster, Julianne. Grammar schools, on the other hand, are free. Are you to deny all those people you apparently care about the chance of free education just because of some hang-up you've got about these schools? I would have thought you were fairer than that, Julianne.'

He's still smiling, to keep a veneer of playfulness to the conversation, but nobody is fooled. He's deliberately tried to rile me. And it works.

'Should the thousands of children whose parents can't afford to hothouse them through an unfair exam be sent to allegedly second-rate schools? Should they be branded as stupid simply because they can't tick the right boxes, like performing animals, before they even know their true selves? It's not about helping the disadvantaged, as you well know. It's about making sure all the middle class kids don't have to rub shoulders with the rest of society. I would have thought *you* were fairer than that, Ernest.'

Silence greets this. I realise too late that I have turned a conversation into a rant, and made myself look rude at best, and deeply hypocritical at worst.

'Anyone for some wine?' James says after a few beats have passed.

'Lovely,' says Louise, holding out her glass. She is grinning enthusiastically. Always overcompensating, I think to myself, then immediately feel awful for being so horrible. She can't help it that her husband is a self-satisfied jerk.

'I've been so looking forward to this, Julianne,' Louise continues. 'The real highlight of my season.'

The statement only emphasises the awkward tone I've helped set.

'How's Stephen?' she asks, clearly grappling for a lifeline now.

'Oh, he's still in his room . . . I'm not sure if he'll be down. Hopefully he'll come and say hello if he's feeling up to it.' It's the best I can come up with on the spot. I sense James glance at me.

'He seemed well enough earlier. I'll go up and speak to him,' James says and goes to put down his glass.

'No.' I say it louder than I mean to. Everyone stares at me again.

I feign a laugh that fails to sound anything close to convincing and say, 'I'm sorry. I'm so sorry, everyone. Stephen's . . . Stephen's having a bit of a tough time. He's . . .' I put down my glass of wine to buy myself a couple of seconds of extra time. I straighten up, then speak slowly. 'He's broken up with his boyfriend. He's rather upset. I said he could be excused from dinner.'

More silence greets this. Ally is the first one to finally speak: 'Oh God, really?' Her eyes are wide. 'But . . . they seemed so . . .'

'So happy, I know.' I nod and raise my eyebrows, as if

I, too, am shocked by the news. 'But that's young love for you. Never does run smooth, does it?'

Ernest grins. 'Well, it did for you two.' He motions at James. 'Oxford's cutest couple and all that.'

I'm keen to avoid the inevitable Oxford retrospective so early in the evening, but welcome the change of subject. 'I know. God, all that feels so long ago, doesn't it?'

'It does!' Ally exclaims loudly. 'But at the same time, it could be yesterday.'

Everyone nods, even Cameron, seated next to Ally on one of the sofas, even though I have no idea which university he went to. I feel a pang of embarrassment for him, thinking how intimidating we must all be to him; almost lifelong friends, talking about politics and days gone by, not to mention my weird and untruthful announcement about my son's love life. I decide to offer him a lifeline by diving straight in with a question.

'Cameron – which school did you go to?'

'She means university,' said James, rolling his eyes, but smiling.

'How do you know I didn't mean school, as in before university?'

'That's the problem with Americans; you never really know what they mean,' says Ernest, winking at me. I blank him.

'Go with university,' I say, smiling with Cameron. 'It's less of an elitist question.'

'Is it?' he says, chuckling awkwardly, looking around him as if slightly afraid. 'I went to Canterbury Christ Church University.'

I'm completely at a loss as to what to say to this. Ernest, however, can't resist plunging in.

'Really? I thought that only gained university status about fifteen years ago.'

Cameron nods enthusiastically, apparently relieved someone here has some knowledge of the place. I'm not as easily taken in, and look over at Ernest with a sense of mounting resentment. How have I put up with him all these years?

'Yes, almost,' says Cameron. 'I think it was around 2004 or 2005. I went there a few years after it changed.'

'Christ, that must make you . . .'

'I'm twenty-nine,' Cameron says, with another nervous chuckle.

'You *know* how old he is because I bloody told you,' Ally says, scowling at her brother.

'And what did you study?' I ask.

'Teacher training.'

'Oh goodness,' James says. 'How awful we must have sounded going on about grammar schools when you actually work in the education system.'

'Oh no, I'm not a teacher. I never went into it after uni. I work for an online magazine.'

'Really?' Louise beams at him. 'That must be exciting. Is it something like *BuzzFeed*?' She says the word as if it's a new foreign phrase she's just learnt and can't help but feel proud of having mastered.

'It's . . . a bit different. It's called *Kennel Grader*.' He sounds a little sheepish now. Louise, on the other hand, seems even more interested.

'Oh, is it about dogs?'

More embarrassed laughter from Cameron. 'It's . . . well
. . . it's actually about hot women. Each week, the site
looks at women in the media, like on *The X Factor* or
Love Island or just celebs in general, and grades them in
hotness.'

If I thought the silence that met my attack on the
education system earlier was awkward, it pales into insignificance compared to the one that greets Cameron's
revelation. Eventually, I recover the use of my vocal cords.

'You mean . . . it's called *Kennel Grader* because . . . ?'

Cameron grins. 'Well, it's like *The X Factor* is a kennel;
we just grade the members.'

More silence. Then Ally says, 'I'm really looking forward
to dinner, Julianne. Smells glorious. Is Cassie managing
okay? Shall we go and help her?'

I stay where I am, leaning on the mantelpiece, and the
room turns from Cameron to stare at me.

'Are you fucking serious?' I say, making no effort to
disguise my disgust.

'Darling, shall we go and sit down in the dining room?'
James is hovering at my side now, apparently nervous I'm
about to make a scene.

'That's great, Cameron. I'm sure your parents are proud
of what you've done with your teacher-training degree.
Keep hold of this one, Ally. He seems like a right catch.'
I turn and walk out of the lounge.

'Where are you going?' James calls after me.

'To check on the food,' I snap back.

I take refuge in the downstairs bathroom for a few

minutes, splashing cold water onto my face, not caring that it's probably ruining the little make-up I'm wearing. When I open the door, I jump and step back; my husband's tall build is filling the doorframe, waiting for me.

'Jesus, Julianne. What's wrong with you? Why do you keep disappearing? And what the hell was that flare-up all about? I was mortified. Ernest and Ally were mortified.'

'They'll live,' I say, planning to go straight on into the living room, but he moves to block me. 'We need to go back to our guests,' I say. 'Can't have them sitting there *mortified*, can we?' I push past him, leaving him in the corridor.

I decide to tackle the awkwardness head-on. 'Sorry, guys.' I start talking immediately as soon as I walk in, causing the four of them to break off from their suspiciously quiet conversations. 'It's been a long and stressful few days — Christmas and all that. I shouldn't have let it spoil the night.'

A brief silence greets this, then Ally leaps up. 'Of course, Julianne, don't worry about it. Honestly, I give Cameron grief about his fucking atrocious job every day. He's used to it, aren't you, Cameron?'

Cameron, who's gone a bit red, just nods and looks at his glass of wine.

'He's only at that vile place while he tries to get a job at *GQ*. He knows someone who knows someone and they're sure they'll be able to squeeze him in somewhere.'

I nod and put on a smile. 'Well, that's great. I hope it goes well, Cameron, if you get the job.'

He gives a little nod.

More awkward silence.

'Ally, how far did you get with that Netflix series? You recommended it to me the other week. The one about the prison?'

Ally seems momentarily taken aback by the question, but then blinks and smiles. 'God, I love it. I can't stop. I'm on series three in just two weeks.'

'Two weeks? Goodness.' I'm aware I'm sounding over-the-top and falsely cheerful, but my real self feels miles away. Out of the corner of my eye I see movement. It's James.

'Just spoken to Cassie. Food shouldn't be too long now.'

It irritates me he's spoken to Cassie. I think he flirts with her. Never to the point where I would worry about it, but enough for me to get a bit prickly. Very prickly today, it seems. I feel hot and uncomfortable and decide to venture away from my strange stance by the mantelpiece. Keen to keep some distance from Cameron, I take a seat near Louise. Neutral territory. I listen for a while as Ally, James and Ernest muse unenthusiastically about whether there'll be snow by Christmas Day. Louise, while still smiling cheerfully, doesn't seem desperate to take part. I seize the opportunity to engage her in conversation.

'How is Jasper doing?'

Louise turns round and beams at me, apparently thrilled to be asked about her son. I feel guilty for not bringing him up sooner.

'He's great. Really good. Loving his travels.'

'Stephen misses him. He always looked up to Jasper as an older brother. Still does, I think.'

Louise smiles. 'I know. I hope Jasper keeps in touch. They still email, don't they? Or whatever it is kids do these days.'

I nod, though I'm only guessing. 'Oh, I'm sure. I think they Facebook each other.'

'Julianne . . .' Louise says, then glances at the others, who have now moved on to discussing local council politics with more fervour than the weather. She turns back to me, pausing as if she's choosing her words carefully. 'Is there anything wrong?'

'Yes,' I say. The word escapes me before I know what else to say. 'I mean, no. I mean . . .' I put a hand to my face, scared my eyes are starting to shine.

'Julianne, what is it? Is it about Cameron and his magazine? Because if it is, I thought you were rather magnificent.'

'Oh . . . well . . . thank you. I don't think I've ever been described as magnificent before.' I, too, glance at the others, but they're still talking.

'I hate that sort of thing as well,' she says quietly.

I nod and try to smile. I'm cross with myself that I'm struggling not to cry. Though I have been known to well up when confronted with a nice gift or a sad film, I'm usually good in a crisis. I can carry out what tasks need to be done, and then deal with any emotional fallout later. But this is different. I can neither deal with my situation, nor face the emotional consequences. I'm trapped in some kind of hellish purgatory, pretending to my friends that all is happy and fine and making up excuses for snapping at them.

'I'm sorry, Louise, I just need to . . . send a text.'

I need to focus on something that isn't another person. Calm myself down so I can attempt to remain normal for the rest of the evening.

'Oh, of course, no problem,' Louise says, sounding a tad confused.

I pull out my phone from my pocket and instantly lower the brightness level so as not to draw too much attention to myself. I tap on the WhatsApp icon and open up Stephen's message thread. Typing quickly, I send a brief message explaining I've made up a story about him and Will breaking up and that, if he comes down, he needs to play along. I'm not expecting him to reply straight away, but the message comes up as read and the text by his name says he is typing.

Why didn't you just say I was unwell?

I read his message with dismay. He's right. Why the hell didn't I just keep to the story about him having a bad cold? Why did I have to drag his relationship status into this? I type back a reply.

You're right, I'm sorry. Didn't think. It's OK if you stay upstairs. Just to warn you, Dad will probably come up to check on you at some point.

I am tempted to add that it would be best not to mention anything to do with the files he's found, but decide there isn't any need. If he were going to talk to him, he would have gone to him straight away. But he came to me. And now we're in this together and I'm struggling to find a way to cope with it.

A new message arrives.

I'm coming down.

Christ, I think, glancing around, expecting him to appear instantly or apparate like a character from *Harry Potter*; but then I hear the sound of movement coming from upstairs.

I stand up and announce to the room at large: 'Stephen's coming down.' Conversation stops and faces turn to me. I'm acting weirdly again. James's eyes meet mine and I can see he's both embarrassed and getting more and more irritated.

Again, Ally is quick to fill the silence. 'Super! Glad he's feeling okay to join us.'

As if on cue, the sound of footsteps is heard from the corridor and then Stephen walks in, a little tentatively. Everyone looks at him in silence for a moment, then Ally jumps up and embraces him. 'So sorry to hear you've broken up with Will. What a miserable thing to happen at Christmas. The same thing happened to Ernest in 1987. That Polish girl, Franciszka, left you high and dry at that carol service in Winchester, didn't she? Christmas Eve and he was left standing there all alone. Humiliating, wasn't it, Ernest? In fact I think you said you were going to kill yourself, and then you vanished and everyone worried you had; but in the end we found you in one of the back rooms of the cathedral drinking church wine.'

Ernest looks pained, but smiles at everyone. 'I was sixteen or seventeen. And her name was Francesca. My dearest sister has made her more Polish than she actually was.'

Everyone laughs and I feel an overwhelming gratitude towards Ally. She's always been able to do this; breathe life into a room like a scented candle. She drives me crazy, but right now I want to hug her.

'Well, it must have been her surname I was thinking of,' Ally says, not to be put off. 'And of course, you're talking to a woman who's just divorced the world's biggest twat. Everyone could see it except me.'

I see James glance awkwardly away. We'd never liked Arthur and had been rather pleased when, out of the blue, Ally announced they were separating. Though he was never exactly nasty, Arthur had been the type of man who felt he needed to make his presence known. One of his biggest insecurities seemed to revolve around his wife refusing to take his name when they were married. 'Why do I want to be owned by a man? Branded by him, my identity erased?' Ally had said very openly when he'd made one dig too many about it at a previous dinner party. Whenever we went out to a restaurant with the two of them, we would have to sit there as he complained loudly to anyone who'd listen about the state of the country, the job market, the class system and the regrettable decline of the aristocracy. He was generally unfriendly and borderline cruel to anyone he considered outside his immediate social class – everyone from waiters and caterers, to my housekeeper and, on some occasions, me. Ally used to tell him off loudly whenever he became particularly horrid, leading to a number of very public blow-ups. The news of the divorce had made James and me sigh with relief.

'Sit down, Stephen, dinner won't be long,' I say, not looking him in the eye. If I do, I might not be able to

232

keep up this pretence for much longer. No matter what I say and do, I'm determined to make sure there are no more outbursts and no more opportunities for people to ask me what's wrong.

'Mum?'

The word makes me jolt around quickly – way too quickly, and I jog Louise's arm, sending drops of wine spilling onto the white carpet.

'Oh God!' she exclaims, putting her hand under the glass to catch the remaining drips sliding down its stem. 'I'm so sorry.'

'It's not your fault,' I say. 'It's fine, honestly, don't worry about it. This carpet's seen worse, I can tell you.' It's a lie and everyone knows it, staring down at the completely spotless cream pile which was only fitted a year previously.

'I'll get some kitchen roll,' says James, glancing at Louise, still holding the dripping glass. As he exits the room, Ernest's voice cuts through, loud and authoritative: 'Doesn't white wine work as some kind of remover if you spill red? Or is that a myth?'

'A myth, I think,' says Cameron quietly.

Ally makes a sound of disbelief. 'You just say that because you can't bear the thought of wine being poured away.'

In all the wine commotion I've forgotten what caused it in the first place. I glance over at Stephen, who is staring into the distance, his eyes glazed over.

'What did you want me for, Stephen?' I ask, and he comes to, as if from a dream, looking at me blankly.

'You attracted my attention?' I say, trying to keep my voice level.

'It was nothing. We were talking about holidays. I was telling Ernest about the difficulty we had in Istanbul.'

'Oh, that. Yeah, that was . . . that was scary.'

'At least it was only a bomb scare, or so I hear? Nothing actually . . . well . . .'

'Went bang? No. Pretty scary, though, being caught up in something like that,' I say, trying to cast my mind back a few months and remembering the blind panic I'd felt when I was separated from Stephen and James during an evacuation of the airport. 'We really shouldn't have gone at all.'

Ernest nods. 'James bully you all into it, did he?'

I shake my head. 'No. I wanted to go.' I've always been vaguely aware of Ernest's attempts to portray his best friend as a domineering husband and force to be reckoned with. The truth is, it was me that pushed to go to Turkey. I was the one who'd talked down the terrorism fears, said we'd be fine as long as we weren't cheap about it. My love of travel had got us into difficulty in the past, but this was without doubt the most traumatic escapade we'd experienced. 'It was my mistake. I'll be more cautious next time.'

Next time. With dismay, I realise that next time is already planned out. We're going on a Scandinavian cruise in April. Just the two of us. The thought of being trapped with just him on a cold sea mortifies me right now. Thinking about any future with James beyond this evening makes my stomach contract. It's as if a black sheet has been draped over the days, months, years stretching ahead. They haven't been deleted. They're just marked as unknown territory. A no-man's land of years spent in the company of a man who, when I think about it, I perhaps don't know at all.

Something brushes past my leg and I look down, straight into James's eyes. He's arrived at my side without me knowing and is bending down to pat a square of kitchen roll on the carpet. I expect him to be annoyed with me, but his voice is kind. 'All right, dearest?' It's a gentle reminder of all the years that have gone before. All the warm, comfortable, blissful years. I've had it so easy. I only realise this now, when contemplating an uncertain future. How I've drifted through married life. How I gave up my job in publishing when Stephen was born and was very happy to fill my days with shopping, reading, doing up whatever house we were in at the time, going out to lunch, volunteering for charities, all the while not realising how I had, potentially, just handed over the keys of my life to this man. What would I do if it all fell apart? What would be, when it all came down to it, the point of my existence? A mother, of course, and a good one at that. But would that be it? Would it be enough?

A touch on my leg. He's still looking at me. 'Fine,' I say, quickly, not meeting his eyes. 'That won't do anything, though.' I nod at the kitchen roll. 'I'll get Cassie to have a look at it tomorrow morning.'

'That will be a fun Christmas Eve for her.' He sighs, getting up and walking back over to his seat.

As if the mention of her name has conjured her, Cassie appears at the door of the living room and raises her eyebrows and smiles, her way of saying it's time for everyone to be seated.

'Dinner's ready, everyone,' I say, getting up. I glance at the clock on the mantelpiece. 7.40. In previous years, the Kelmans have normally left around 11.30. Ally, on the other hand, is a bit harder to get rid of and usually announces she's staying to help clear up. Hopefully she'll be keen to get her new, sexist boyfriend back home this year. At the most, it looks as if I have between three and four hours to get through. And in the back of my head I can almost sense an uncomfortable weight, pulling me down, and my hand travels unconsciously to my pocket where the thin little USB drive sits, waiting.

Chapter 18

Holly

Oxford, 1991

My dad occasionally said to me when I was young that you can't go through life without spilling a bit of milk. This stuck in my mind. Not because of its intended effect, to reassure me that people make mistakes and things don't go to plan. But rather because it introduced me to the threat of milk spilling. At that point in my life, when he first started saying it to me – I was probably around six or seven – I had never spilt any milk. That sounds ridiculous, but it's true. It was probably because the adults had always poured milk out for me. And through the years that followed, I was scared that one day it would spill.

I don't remember when it was that the white, translucent

liquid actually splashed onto the ground, but I remember with soul-tearing pain when it happened metaphorically, in real life. When the time came for me to go from outsider to victim and the stumbling block that would come to define not just my time at university but my entire life, the analogy about the spilt milk became important to me once again. First, it showed me I had been right to fear. Right to be wary of impending disaster, in whatever form it might take. Right to know it would finally happen. Right about the fact that the milk and the glass could never be put back together again. Second, it encapsulated my overriding sense of emotion surrounding what happened on the 19 February 1991. Guilt. I felt guilty. I blamed myself, just as one does when one is carrying the glass from the countertop to the table and it slips from your grasp somewhere during that short journey.

I had become quite comfortable in my silence when Ally and I were back in her room and starting to demolish the chocolate we'd bought. She spoke, as always, giving a running commentary throughout the naff American film we were watching about why she didn't believe detectives would act this way in real life and how, if she had directed the movie, she would have made sure the women in it didn't have faces like broken car bonnets. I nodded on occasion, but mostly kept quiet.

'You don't mind if the boys join us, do you?' Although it was technically a question, she said it as if my not minding were a foregone conclusion. I gaped at her, the memory of our discussion earlier in the afternoon rushing back with a nauseating jerk. She wouldn't bring it up, would she? Ally, however, didn't even avert her eyes from the television screen, just continued to watch as the central character, a cop, tried to break down the door of his ex-wife's apartment, claiming he was going to 'sort her out' if she didn't stop seeing 'that asshole' from her work.

'I didn't know they were . . . when did you ask them?'

'Oh, before I invited you back,' she said casually. 'And Julianne might join, too.'

Again, the casual tone. No eye contact. It was as if all our conversations about the boys, about Julianne, about what I had seen, had disappeared into thin air; erased from her memory. Perhaps she thought it would embarrass me further to mention them. But surely this was worse – inviting me back here and then having them turn up?

'Okay,' I said. 'I'd better get going anyway. I have an essay to do.'

'Please, Holly, stay.' She said this with an exaggerated look of horror, as if I'd told her I was off to commit a murder.

'No, really, I need to . . .'

The noise of the door bursting open cut me off. Ernest had kicked it violently, causing it to knock into the wall. 'Ho, ho, ho. Santa's here and bearing gifts,' he said in a low, booming voice, sounding more like his eccentric sister than his normal cool self.

'It's no longer fucking Christmas,' she said in response, then leapt up to take from him the multiple bottles of wine he was carrying. James and Julianne were behind him, the former trying to get past him as he blocked the entrance. Once inside, they both settled themselves next to me on the bed, with Ernest on the chair.

'Hi, how's it going?' Julianne beamed at me, and I tried not to think about the last time I'd seen those lips at work.

'Going . . . er . . . going good,' I replied lamely, giving her a small smile.

'Glad you're joining us. It feels like months since we've seen you!'

I noticed she was using *we* as if she and the rest of them were now a whole unit. I would have liked to remind her I'd known her boyfriend before her – even if only for a matter of weeks – but felt that would take things into the realms of playground bitchiness. And it was a little too early in the evening for that.

'Peter's coming,' said James. He seemed to say this to the room as a whole and I realised he hadn't made eye contact with me once since he'd arrived, or indeed at any point since the time in the cabin at Rupert's party.

'Christ, I better bloody hope so. He's so flaky.' Ally gave a hollow laugh as she went around decanting some of the wine into plastic cups – the type you'd see at a children's birthday party. 'Would you care for some, Holly?'

My mind started spinning back, worries floating to the surface. My period still hadn't come. I could tell by the way I felt when I woke up each day that something wasn't right. But I didn't want to think about it. I couldn't think about it. 'Fine . . . I mean, sorry . . . yes, please.'

'Ah!' Ally said loudly as she handed me one of the cups. 'I can hear someone coming. Peter's here!'

Peter had indeed arrived and everyone set about greeting

him like a returning war veteran. I was fairly confident I was even flakier than Peter when it came to not turning up for engagements, and I only got a small smile from him as he shuffled in, looking mildly embarrassed.

'Come on, Holly, sit on the floor with me.' Ally's orders occasionally got up my nose a bit, but in this instance I was rather pleased to have an excuse to move away from The Loving Couple of James and Julianne and sit on the pillows on the floor with her. As the hour passed, I found myself growing more relaxed, helped along by the wine, and even surprised myself by laughing at some of Julianne's jokes about British/American differences and how we all sounded like aristocrats to her. 'Hate to tell you this, dearest, but the Kelmans sort of are,' James said, raising his eyebrows. Ally shook her head, as if mildly repulsed. 'Only distantly, and even then it's tenuous.'

At approaching eleven o'clock, a couple of hours after the others had joined us, Ally got up and reached for one of the now-empty wine bottles. 'Let's play spin the bottle.'

This was met with a groan from Ernest and a noise of disbelief from James. 'Honestly?' he said, rolling his eyes.

'Oh, come on, where's your sense of fun?' Julianne said, kneeling on the floor. 'Do you know, I'm for ever glad this dorm-room tradition has crossed the Atlantic thanks to trashy teen movies.'

'Is it an American tradition?' I asked.

'It's fun and cheap and involves sex, so, yeah, I like to think it is!'

'Involves sex?' Ernest said slyly. 'Sounds like we've been playing it wrong all this time.'

'You know what I mean. Seven minutes of heaven and all that.'

I'd heard of these party games, of course, but had never taken part. In fact, I'd never really been invited to the parties where they'd been played.

Ally, ever the ringleader, was to keep order throughout the game. On the first few spins, the top of the bottle landed somewhere between two people, as we weren't able to sit in a proper circle in her less-than-spacious room, and she had the deciding vote about whose turn it was. Most of the initial 'dares' were actually more 'truths', where Ally would pose a question, usually about the chosen one's sexual, alcoholic or drug-taking experiences. If I'd been sober, it would have all seemed preposterously childish, but on this rare occasion the alcohol seemed to be lifting my mood rather than making me morbid. When the bottle finally landed on me, I wondered where Ally would go with the questioning, considering she knew full well about my lack of experience in any of the areas she was busy exploring with the other participants. Before she could speak, however, Ernest cut across her.

'Last time you had sex. Describe the last time you did it.'

Peter, sitting quietly next to me, let out a high-pitched giggle, then hiccupped, causing everyone else to laugh. He brushed a lock of ginger hair out of his eyes and started refilling his cup with more wine.

'Okay,' I said, meeting his gaze head-on. 'It was on Christmas Eve, on the sofa by the tree. Missionary style. He came pretty quickly.'

Ernest looked shocked for a moment, then a grin spread across his face. 'Nice,' he said, looking a little impressed. 'And who is "he", may I ask?'

'Just a friend from back home,' I said, suspecting the story might lose whatever shine it had if I described George in more specific detail.

I batted away Ally's probing questions as to who this friend might be and just told her she wouldn't know him since he wasn't at our university, which sounded better than the simple truth that he wasn't at any institute of higher education full stop.

When the bottle swung round to James, it became clear that Ernest, tired of his sister's commanding role, was keen to take the game up a notch. 'James can have a dare,' he said, 'a proper one.'

It was Julianne's turn now to let out a nervous laugh. 'Oh, this might be interesting.'

'Have a wank. Right now.' Ernest winked at his friend as he said it, but James shook his head automatically.

'Not a chance.'

'Oh, you're so crude,' Ally said to her brother.

'You chose the game,' Ernest said.

'I'm tired,' Ally announced, slurring her words slightly, yawning and leaning away from me so her head was resting on the chest of drawers behind her.

'You can't sleep through the main event: James's dick.' When he said the last word, Ernest shot me a look and raised his eyebrows once. I found myself laughing. 'No, don't make him.' I looked over at James, who seemed both amused and embarrassed.

'While you guys all debate my boyfriend's penis,' Julianne said, also having trouble getting her words out, 'I'm going to pee.'

'Just down the corridor to the left,' Ernest said. 'My sister likes to live like one of the real people, so doesn't have an en suite.'

'You don't have a fucking en suite,' Ally murmured, her eyes closed, shifting slightly into a more comfortable position.

'So, come on then,' Ernest said, his attention again on James. 'Don't disappoint us.'

They shared a look for a beat longer than seemed natural, and if I had been thinking clearly, I would have thought more of it, but then James was standing up and unbuckling his belt and I felt my stomach do a flip.

'Challenge accepted,' he said, pulling down his dark-blue jeans, his white underwear standing out against the natural tan of his skin.

'Good sport,' Ernest said. I had the feeling he was looking at me as he said this, but my gaze was locked on James as he put his hand underneath his pants and started to play with himself.

'You can lose the underwear, no ladies are present,' Ernest said after about a minute of James tugging away at himself. I glanced over at Ally, now quietly snoring into the wall.

'You're forgetting me and Ally,' I said in what I hoped was an indignant voice.

'I don't think I am,' Ernest murmured. He winked again. 'Not sure where Julianne's got to.'

I half-felt I should go and find her in case she was sick or something, but I was rather transfixed by what James was doing to himself, albeit hidden under the cotton of his briefs. Something in me also wanted to stand up to Ernest; prove to him I wasn't going to fail at the first hurdle or back out when things got intense. I could hold my own, I thought, as I looked back at James and boldly demanded he remove his underwear.

'If the lady insists,' he said, and now, finally, he did look me in the eye as he exposed himself, pulling his pants down to his knees and moving his hand over his penis – larger and thicker than George's, I noticed – back and forward with his right hand. He wasn't fully erect and within seconds Ernest was commenting, 'Not quite the full shilling down there at the moment?'

Peter let out another of his strange, childish giggles and James smirked. 'I think I need a bit of help.'

I thought he was joking and laughed, too, but Ernest didn't – he just faced me, smiling.

'Did you hear him, Holly? James said he needs a bit of help.'

I felt myself blushing, the heat flooding into my cheeks. Could he really be suggesting what I thought he was? I stared blankly at him, worried to make a presumption.

'What are you waiting for?' James smiled at me and now I saw the same look in his eyes he'd had that night by the pool at Rupert's house. A challenge. A dare. An invitation to set the record straight and refute any idea that I was this sheltered, prudish, insignificant person, lost in their posh, exciting world of decadent deeds. I probably

shouldn't have done it. Years later, it would be those tanta-
lising seconds that stayed with me the most; the moments
in which I could have just folded my arms and refused
to be part of whatever game they were playing, even
though it wouldn't have changed anything. It wouldn't
have stopped them. But for me, in that moment, I didn't
want to back down. I didn't want to be the shy girl they
were going to scare away. I wanted to be bold.

Slowly, I got up, feeling the room spin slightly as I
stood on my feet and then walked the few steps over to
James. Sitting next to him on the bed, I reached over and
took his penis in my hand. I let it rest there for a moment,
feeling it swell as my fingers closed around it, enjoying
its generous length and girth; then I started to move it
up and down. James didn't make much of a sound, but
let his breath out in a slow, steady stream, his head falling
back as he supported himself on both hands. I could feel
Ernest staring at us and Peter was making an odd sound,
somewhere between coughing and laughing, as if he
couldn't quite believe what he was seeing.

'Nice,' Ernest said. 'Now, what do you say we let my
sister sleep in peace and take this back to your room?'

I paused what I was doing and looked over to him.
Then nodded. 'That sounds good to me.'

As we walked to the room next door, me and the three
boys, I felt as if I was floating on air, moving without
moving, just one thing present in my mind: I'm going to
do what I've wanted for so long; I'm going to have sex
with James.

I looked around me blearily as we entered, taking in

246

my deep-blue bedcovers, the books lining the shelves and the top of my desk. Then I turned around to the two boys and said, 'So, we carry on playing?' I knew there was more on the cards now, but I wasn't sure how to initiate it. An excitement coursed through my veins, red-hot and eager. The desire I felt for James, which had been building ever since that moment in the cabin, had reached a peak I'd never imagined possible. I was alive, electric and full of a confidence I hadn't known I had within me. 'We carry on playing,' said James, looking at Ernest. Something about that look they shared snagged slightly in my mind, like a very quiet, almost imperceptible warning bell, ringing in the distance. But I wasn't in the frame of mind to care. I was sitting on the floor, and someone put the empty wine bottle in my hands – I think it was Peter – and then I was spinning it round so the whole thing became a circular blur. James and Peter sat on the floor in front of me, Ernest on the side of the bed. We waited for it to stop spinning. It stopped at Ernest.

'My turn,' he said, looking at me. 'What will you have me do?' His eyes sparkled, as if daring me to push boundaries. 'Take off your trousers.' I laughed, for some reason finding this hysterically funny, even if the dare was high-school-level tame. I was feeling very lightheaded now and had to steady myself, even though I was already sitting, so as not to drop forward onto James's lap.

'As the lady commands.' Smirking, he stood up and undid his belt, pulling off his chinos, letting them drop to the floor. He was wearing rather tight-fitting Polo Ralph Lauren briefs. I could see the outline of his penis faintly underneath the material and this made me laugh even more. I didn't care that I probably sounded like an excitable fifteen-year-old girl. In fact, I'd got to a point of revelling in my own silliness. This was fun. I was having fun. Letting go and having fun, as Ally had suggested. James was staring at me now with a strange look in his eye. Ernest came down to sit on the floor with us and picked up the bottle. 'I was kind of hoping for a handjob too,' he muttered, and I shook my head, smirking back at him. He spun the bottle in a gentler, calmer way than I had earlier and watched its slow progress. I knew before it even settled that it would probably land on me. A one in four chance, maybe, but it seemed to have been decided in the stars before he'd even set the bottle down. 'Time for you to get back to work,' said Ernest quietly. He looked at me and then glanced at James, as if making up his mind about something. Then finally he said: 'Give James a blowjob.'

I shrieked with shock, hand clasped to my chest as I shook with laughter. Peter laughed, too, though it sounded awkward and false.

'I'm serious,' he continued. 'You do want to, don't you?'

I stopped myself laughing, though it was an effort. 'What do you mean?'

The knowing grin was back. 'Well, it's been rather obvious to everyone. Unless of course that was all for show.'

'Why would it be for show? I gave him a handjob, didn't I? I think that counts for something.'

I heard Peter let out a breath, as if he'd been holding it from either tension or anticipation. James looked at me and my heart leapt. 'So, Holly, what do you say?'

'Say to what?' My vision was spinning slightly.

'To Ernest's dare.' His voice was calm, cool, matter-of-fact.

He wanted me to. James wanted me to do it. I could see it in his eyes; he was daring me. Seeing if I would go so far or if I would shirk away. It was a test.

'Go on then. Get it out.' Instead of laughing this time, I said it with a firm confidence, meeting James's stare with a smile. After what seemed like a million years, his hands travelled to his flies. He hadn't bothered to do the belt and buttons back up; he'd just pulled up his jeans so he could walk to my room. As they once again travelled down his legs I could see he was at least partially erect already. He laid his hands back down on the floor, waiting for me to do the rest. I shuffled across so I was next to him and reached over. He was still wearing his briefs, the protrusion of his erection pressing against the front of the material. I put my hands under the waistband and he raised himself off the floor so I could pull them down. When his cock came in sight my head started swimming more than before. This was a dream. It must be a dream. I settled the crumpled bunch of his jeans and boxers around his knees, my heart pounding as I looked at his naturally tanned bare thighs. They looked muscular and smooth, with a fine layer of hair.

'Much as I'm sure we all love admiring James's John Thomas . . .' Ernest's drawl cut across my thoughts '. . . I

think it might be time to press on with the main event.'
I didn't acknowledge him, but lifted my hand, supporting
myself on the floor with the other. I took hold of his
long, hard shaft, feeling it react once again to my touch,
and felt James's whole body tense. I steadily started to
move my hand up and down, pulling his foreskin back
and forth over his tip. Then I lowered my head, keeping
my eyes focused up at him, watching his head go back,
that smile I now felt I knew once again dancing dreamily
around his lips. I heard Peter shifting around and letting
out small, staccato laughs.

I don't know how long it took but it wasn't long. It
became obvious that a certain kind of tension was building
around James's hips and he gripped hold of my head – not
roughly, but with strength – guiding me up and down in
a faster motion. He filled my mouth and made the same
noise I'd heard him make when Ernest had taken him in
his bed a few weeks previously. I held him there for a few
seconds after, then pulled myself up, wiping my mouth
with the side of my hand. I couldn't stop smiling and found
this strange. Shouldn't I be embarrassed, or full of regret?
Shouldn't I feel that odd, empty feeling of dissatisfaction
I'd felt when George had cum in me on the sofa at
Christmas? I didn't feel any of these things. I felt elated
and turned back round to Ernest and Peter. The sight of
them initially took me by surprise. Both boys had their
trousers and underwear pulled down and were masturbating,
Ernest slowly stroking his penis and Peter going quicker,
squinting slightly, as if orgasm was in sight but just out of
reach. In any other context I'd probably have been shocked,

appalled even, but in this instance all I felt was mild amuse-
ment at how strange they both looked.

'Great show, Holly,' Ernest said, and his voice sounded
strange. Practised, almost, as if he was reading the lines of
a script. I sat back down on the floor, leaning up against
my bed, looking up to where Ernest sat.

'Thanks,' I said. 'I think I need to sleep now. You guys
can sleep here if you want.'

Ernest laughed – an odd-sounding, cold laugh. 'Oh, I
don't think we're quite ready to stop playing yet.'

That was when I felt the first real stab of worry. Not
that I felt particularly in danger, but rather I was encoun-
tering something that didn't fit with my developing new
sense of self. I was the brave one, the wild one. The one
who sent the boys on their way after I'd had my fun. I
didn't want them to think they were the ones making the
rules. Not in my room, not after I'd just impressed them
all to the point of obvious physical arousal.

'Ernest, I need to sleep,' I said, slightly grumpily. I stood
up and waved an arm. 'Go back to Ally's room if you
want to wank the night away.' I gave him a nudge, but he
took hold of my hand as it made contact with him. His
strength and force took me by surprise and I tried to pull
back, but his hand had me in a tight grip.

'Holly, Holly,' he said, then made a quiet tutting sound.
'We can't have this, can we? Not when one of us has
been satisfied but the others are left wanting. Think of
little Peter here. It's his first time. You wouldn't want to
take that away from him, would you?'

I stared in alarm at Peter, who had stopped masturbating

and was now standing. His small frame, which I'd once considered weak compared to Ernest's and James's – a slight against his masculinity – now seemed strangely sinister; like an insect that sneaks up on you. His penis, surprisingly long, though very thin, stood erect between the ends of his shirt and his jeans were sagging around his waist, threatening to fall down without his belt holding them up. He looked at me with an urgent glint in his eye. Then Ernest said three words that sent a bolt of panic through me.

'The door, James.'

I instantly looked over at it and saw it had been open all this time. Anyone could have seen us. James did as instructed and turned the lock. I was too disconcerted by what was happening to do anything.

'Holly, we have a few requests,' Ernest said slowly, getting up off the bed and coming over to me. 'First, that you scream. Or try to. We will then silence you. It's important for us that you're not just a ragdoll, silent and lifeless. That leads me on to our second point. For this to work, you need to struggle. And I mean really struggle. Do you understand?'

I was paralysed to the spot. I tried to open my mouth but, before I could say anything, Ernest grabbed me tightly and threw me sideways onto the bed. Movement returned to my limbs with the shock and I struggled to get up, but Ernest and then James, too, pushed me back down. I wasn't sure what was happening; my vision started to blur and I thought I was going to be sick. I retched, but nothing came up, and then a pair of hands was at my waist and the nausea was replaced with fear; fear so strong it was almost white-hot, almost a physical thing, almost something I could touch, something I was being pressed against.

'I'm going first Holly, okay?' Ernest was quiet and almost kind-sounding. His face swam into view and came close so he was talking into my ear. 'You're doing very well so far.' His words repulsed me, as if he were a doctor and I was a child getting an injection. I felt James's hand on my shoulder could smell his aftershave. I turned my head to look at him and managed to get out a cry, but he put one of his hands over my mouth and I moaned against it, tears springing from my eyes.

I lost all sense of time during the course of it. I think I kept blacking out, as every time I opened my eyes there was a different face in front of me. I didn't know how many times each one did it to me, but I think some of them went more than once. And eventually I could feel them slowing down, their energy flagging. Mine did, too. I stopped fighting. The fear, which had helped me continue to fight back, steadily became like an anaesthetic. The idea of fight or flight became an unrealistic fantasy. James was the last one to finish. I knew it was him by his scent and the sound of his breathing, even though my eyes were closed. Then something strange happened. I heard a voice at the door. Someone was trying the handle and James was leaving me, going over to the door. I opened my eyes at that point and tried to make sense of my surroundings. There was my room, exactly the same as before. Ernest and Peter were asleep on the floor, back to back. And James was standing by the doorway. It sounded like a woman was crying. I couldn't work out who it was, but I could see James hadn't put on his pants or trousers. He was just wearing a t-shirt, and I remember thinking how peculiar he looked, standing there with his lower half completely bare, his buttocks exposed, talking to someone. Then he went outside and I could hear him walking down the corridor.

I think sleep came at that point. Or another blackout – it's hard to say. But when I woke and looked around, the sleeping boys on the floor were gone and a girl sat beside me. I had trouble focusing on her face – it kept blurring the more I tried to make it out.

'The night seems to have got a bit out of control,' she said. Her accent was American.

Chapter 19

Julianne

Knightsbridge, 2019

'Have you started the second season yet, Julianne?'

I barely hear the voice to my side. I can barely hear or think about anything. Except one thing. The slight pressure on my thigh of something digging in. Something small. The case of a USB drive.

'Julianne? Are you still with us?'

I plunge back into reality with a jolt. Not for the first time this evening, everyone is staring at me looking slightly worried.

'Er . . . Sorry . . .' I look around, trying to work out who's spoken. 'Miles away. Very rude of me.' I laugh awkwardly.

'What were you thinking about?' Ernest asked. 'You looked, well, haunted.'

Everyone gives a polite laugh and stares at their chicken fillets and sweet potato.

'Oh, just, you know . . . Christmas.' I laugh again, waving a hand as if to say *it's nothing, please stop looking at me.* They don't seem convinced. 'Still so much to organise. It's like, as soon as I've done one task another just arrives out of nowhere.'

'Oh goodness, I know what that's like,' says Louise. 'It's like trying to beat the Hydra. And I still do all the stockings for the boys, even though they're probably too old now.'

'You still get a Christmas stocking, don't you, Stephen?' James says, smiling at his son, probably trying to coax him into the conversation. Like me, he's been staring into space for most of the meal, looking like he's just been diagnosed with something terminal. He just nods.

'What type of thing do you put in a stocking for a seventeen-year-old boy?' asks Ally. 'Condoms and vodka?'

More awkward laughter, though Stephen doesn't react. He just looks at his plate and starts moving a lump of potato around the edges.

'I should hope not!' I laugh. 'No, no. It's mostly boxsets and books and things like that. All probably totally useless in the age of Netflix and e-readers, but I enjoy getting them.'

'Stephen doesn't even have an e-reader,' James chips in. 'He likes collecting hardbacks, don't you, son? Signed copies. First editions, some of them.'

Stephen nods.

'I do rather love all the Christmas wrapping,' Louise says brightly. 'Especially with a roaring fire and a big box of those praline shells open in front of me while watching a good TV drama or festive film. I've got quite addicted to some shows – I watch episode after episode, even during the day. I keep recommending them to Ernest but he rarely manages to . . .'

Ernest cuts off his wife. 'Well, we can't all be housewives. Some of us have to manage our time with a lot of discipline. When so much stuff is competing for one's attention, one has to be quite brutal in one's choices.'

Louise looks hurt and starts spooning food into her mouth a little too quickly.

'Which brings me,' Ally says, cutting in, probably pre-empting a barbed retort from me to counteract Ernest's dig at stay-at-home moms, 'to my previous question, Julianne, which you never answered: have you started watching the second season of *The Man in the High Castle*?'

I shake my head. 'No, sadly I haven't found the time.'

Ernest sniffs a little, which in itself feels like a comment, and I feel my eyes flaring. This really isn't a good time for him to test my patience.

'Well, it is *so* good. You really must catch up. Now that's something my oh-so-busy brother does manage to watch, don't you?'

'I put it on my iPad and watch it in the car sometimes on the way to the Commons. I should probably be reading over my notes for the day but it's hard to resist. Once you've clicked play, you're in. Best not tell the P.M.' He laughs loudly.

'Probably explains the state the country's in,' says James with a smirk.

'Cut it mild, dear chap,' Ernest says, winking at him. 'You're the one who left the party floundering so you could go and spy on people's Facebook pages and harvest their innermost secrets for profit.'

'You were a fan of the book, weren't you?' I turn to James, hoping to steer the conversation away from James's job and the kind of content he might encounter as a result of it. '*The Man in the High Castle*. Philip K. Dick, isn't it?'

He smiles. 'Yes, it's brilliant. I'm a big fan of all his work.'

'Love a bit of Dick, don't you, James?' Ernest says while his wife chokes on her wine. 'Philip K., of course.' Another wink from him, this time at me. I stare back at him blankly and he gives up and looks away. 'Remember that Christmas when we read through his entire oeuvre when we were at school?'

'Very well,' James nods. 'I loved our Christmas read-athons. Binge-reading, they'd probably call it now.'

'Oh God, I remember those,' says Ally, rolling her eyes. 'We used to go to Hatchards at the start of every Christmas and you'd spend a few grand on a load of books and devour them through the whole of December while everyone else was busy organising Christmas around you.'

'It wasn't a few grand,' he says. 'But yes, quite a bit. And then we had to do it at Blackwells, when we were at Oxford. That's when you started joining in, wasn't it, Julianne?'

'Mmm,' I murmur, 'I wouldn't call it joining in. I met you there a couple of times while you piled up books on tables and people kept mistaking you for booksellers. I don't think I was much help.'

'Probably shagging James in the sci-fi section,' Ernest said.

'Ernest!' Louise gasps, but Ally guffaws with laughter.

The thought of James and I being intimate sends a flash of alarm through me and reminds me again of the sex we had two nights ago. I was just a body to him. Just something to push into, to pound away at, to fuck like he didn't care. Was it like that back then? Back when we were still just about teenagers and everything felt new?

'Probably right,' James says. His slightly wicked grin – the one I usually find quietly alluring – now looks smug and self-satisfied. 'Though I don't think it was sci-fi'.

Their voices are steadily growing fainter, as if I'm sinking slowly under water. I can't do this. I can't sit here and be the happy host, giving her guests a merry Christmas dinner party. I lay down my cutlery and put my hands on my knees, trying to stop my racing heart, forcing myself to calm down. Slow breaths. I pull my hands up towards me along my legs and my fingers feel the small, solid mass in my right pocket. I snatch them away as if it's burnt me.

'I need to go upstairs,' I say, standing suddenly. 'I have a migraine.'

James stares at me. 'But . . . you don't get migraines.'

'There's a first time for everything. I'm sorry, everyone, do please carry on. I'll be all right. I just need twenty minutes in a darkened room.'

'We can turn out the lights here!' Ally says, as if excited by the prospect. 'I'm sure we can still finish our food in the dark.' Everyone's looking around, clearly aware something is wrong and I'm not telling the full truth. Everyone apart from Stephen. His eyes are on his plate, is if he's not really there at all.

I attempt a sound I hope resembles a laugh, not bothering to counteract Ally's semi-joke with anything worth saying, and leave the room, a pang of guilt reverberating through me at leaving Stephen with them. They'll want to talk about me, about how my behaviour is becoming stranger and stranger as the evening goes on, but I think they'll resist with him and James there. Louise and Ernest will politely refocus the conversation onto something completely different and James will do his best to stay merry and play the good host, wondering all the while why I'm acting as if I've lost my marbles.

In the bedroom, I lie down immediately, burying my face in the sheets, and smell the same scent of washing powder and air freshener as when James and I had sex the other night. What used to be a nice, homely scent now seems sickly and fake. I pull myself away and sit up properly, my hand going to my pocket again. In that moment, part of me wishes Stephen had never told me. Never come to me and said the word 'Mum' in that terrible way that had made my heart start to disintegrate. Never showed me what he'd found on his iPad. Never sent me spiralling into the vacuum of panic that's steadily suffocating me. It's a horrible thought – that my son shouldn't have told his mother what was worrying him. But I can't lie to myself: ignorance really can be bliss. Again, I feel my conscience stab at me through my thoughts. Calling it ignorance is a cop-out. Denial is the right word. Denial is bliss. And this gives me the kick I need.

I stand up, take the USB stick out of my pocket and walk over to the wardrobe to find an old Windows tablet I rarely use any more, preferring the interface of my newer, flashier iPad. I plug it into its charger and the home screen comes into view, bringing with it an image of my husband, smiling before my eyes. He's standing topless on a beach, one hand raised, waving at the camera. In the other he's holding Stephen's hand, stooping to hold on to the little boy. He must have been about five or six. I stare at the image for a few seconds, then insert the USB.

The files that greet me show that heart-sinkingly familiar set of long numbers. I check the first one. It is indeed Ashley Brooks, the file identical to the one I read before. I skip a few and tap on one of the later ones. I'm taken aback to see a young man's face come into view. In fact, it's not a young man. It's a teenager. I read the details:

Name: Dave Bolton
Date of Birth: 20 December 2000
Occupation: Officially unemployed, previously earnt money from stolen goods
Area: Grays, Essex

Aside from his gender and much younger age, it's similar to the other records. The same lifestyle, the same sorts of problems, the same sense of desperation. He's been in and out of care homes all his life. Absconding from a lot of them. A life ruined or wasted. A person in need of help or support.

I don't spend too much time on Dave Bolton. I scroll all the way down to the end and see there's a subfolder with the title HIGH COST INVESTMENTS. And another document. A different file type to the other PDFs. And the name spells it out simply. CALENDAR 2020. I tap it and the month of January 2020 appears in front of me. It's completely bare, apart from one word, on the twenty-third of the month. *Daffodil.*

My pulse quickens at the sight of it. Then I flick to February. Again, there's one day, the twenty-first, with one word. *Daisy.*

I stare at the word for what feels like a long, long time. Then exit the calendar and go back to the previous run of documents. And that subfolder. HIGH COST INVESTMENTS. I touch its name. Another list of files unfurls, looking the same as the last. The top one has a different title to the others – words instead of seemingly random numbers: BEST PRACTICE GUIDELINES. I tap on it and immediately start to read the document that comes up.

BEST PRACTICE –
REVISED GUIDELINES
AS OF NOVEMBER 2019

- It is strongly advised participants use a condom for all vaginal and anal penetration of subjects.

- The use of a condom is also generally advisable for forced oral sex. Please be aware that a small number of members have sustained injuries while receiving oral sex when the subject has used their teeth in attempts to withdraw from sessions. If oral sex is a preference, we strongly suggest allowing one of our armed customer-assistance members to remain present in the same room for the full duration of the session in case their intervention is necessary.

- To provide the highest protection from facial recognition, all participants are advised (though not required) to wear a form of face-covering material. Garments can be supplied upon request.

- Although we do not require participants to remain completely silent, sessions carried out 'on location' require a degree of sensitivity in respect to their surroundings (which are frequently densely populated areas) so as to avoid complications. If you would prefer not to be restricted by this, arrangements for off-site sessions can be made with select subjects.

- All sessions with minors are off-site and will be monitored by one of our staff members throughout.

- Although all subjects are tested for sexually transmitted diseases, including HIV and hepatitis B, we strongly advise participants to undergo regular STD screenings. This is a service we can provide upon request if necessary.

- A large proportion of our subjects are from 'high-risk groups' for HIV infection. These include intravenous drug users, men who have sex with men and people originally from sub-Saharan Africa. Although, as previously stated, subjects are tested for HIV prior to going live in our catalogue, we cannot guarantee they are free from infection. We can provide a course of post-exposure prophylaxis (PEP) for participants who feel they have had an instance of high-risk exposure. We can also provide pre-exposure prophylaxis (PrEP) for partici-

pants who regularly wish to take part in sessions without a condom.

- **While it is understood that there may be a level of violence during sessions with subjects, participants are prohibited from a) causing deliberate bone breakages or bleeding that would require immediate medical attention, b) causing substantial bruising to the face of a subject, c) bringing weapons such as knives or firearms to sessions without prior discussion and clear consent from one of our personnel.**

I am stunned. Sickened. Appalled. All my worst suspicions are coming true. I now know what this is. And I can hardly bear it. Jabbing hard at the screen, I come out of the BEST PRACTICE GUIDELINES quickly and look back at the rest of the files. I'm pretty sure of what I'm going to find in there. A number of references in the previous document have given me a rather clear idea. My hand hovers over the first of the long-numbered PDF documents, as if there's a small voice screaming at me, telling me to stop. That as soon as I find out for sure what's in here, I won't be able to continue, to go on pretending, to stay sane. I think about putting everything away, flushing the USB down the toilet and spending my life trying not to think about what else might have been on it. But I know this isn't possible. I tap on the first file.

★

Minutes later, I'm in tears. It's as if I've pushed my face down on broken glass and rubbed it until my eyes are bleeding. I hold tight to the pillows and pull them up to me so I can cry into them; screaming, sobbing. I don't care if they hear me down in the dining room. I don't care about anything. I only know I will never be able to rid my mind of what I have just seen or look at my husband the same way again. I want to go down there and drag him up to the room right now and push the device in his face. Beg him for an explanation. Make him tell me why he would own something so vile. I reach for the wastepaper basket under the bedside table and vomit into it, bringing up my undigested dinner in a poisonous rush. I hold on to the sides of the bed, steadying myself as if I'm on a ship in a storm. I can feel the mattress moving, as if it's swaying beneath me, and details, sick little details, float into my mind: *Amelia Cousins. Date of birth: 6 July 2011. Fleet Ward Care Home, Surrey. Jimmy North. Date of Birth: 10 January 2013. Fleet Ward Care Home, Surrey. Alisha Jindal. Date of Birth: 2 August 2017. Fleet Ward Care Home, Surrey.*

These details go round and round in my head. I can't stop them. I make a small humming noise in my throat. Not an actual tune, just a low hum. It's a mechanism I learnt when I was young, when my parents used to have blazing rows. I'd hide myself in the smallest place I could find in the house and focus on making that quiet but uninterrupted noise. It calmed me, gave me something to do, some place to fix my attention while the torment outside gradually ebbed away. With relief, I find that it's working now in the same way it did back then. It takes some effort, but eventually I am able to pull myself back up onto the bed in a sitting position. If I sit still, the nausea isn't too strong.

I stay in this position for what may be an hour, or may be just five minutes. I can't tell. Time seemed to stop the moment I arrived in this room and opened my tablet. I can't even begin to assemble my memories of the past few minutes – I don't really want to. I'd prefer to forget everything.

'Julianne.' The voice at the door almost stops my heart. And then the handle turns.

Thank God I locked it, I think to myself.

I hear James shuffle closer. He must be trying to hear if I'm awake. A gentle knock follows seconds later. The thought of letting him in makes me think I'm going to be sick again, so I just sit as still as I can, looking at the door. The strip of light on the cream carpet at its base shifts and dances subtly as his shape moves across it. Then there's a soft, rubbing noise. He must have leant against the door.

'Julianne, I'm here. Please talk to me. I'm here and listening. There's obviously something wrong. You don't have a migraine, do you?'

I don't move, even though my neck is now starting to ache. I just want him to go away.

'Please. We've never been like this. We're always able to talk. I know I maybe didn't express myself the best I could have . . . the other day . . . when we were . . . that thing about the sex. I didn't know you didn't like what I was doing. That was my fault. I really should have allowed there to be . . . a more open dialogue.'

I wince at his phrasing. *A more open dialogue.*

'Well, I just wanted to come and say that.' I hear him shift his weight a bit and wonder if he's going.

I feel like I am now dealing with two different people: the version of my husband I have known for twenty-nine years and the version I am getting to know now. The version that talks through locked doors at me while I refuse to let him in.

'Julianne . . . can you hear me?'

Slowly, I get up off the bed. I have no real plan, but I let my feet carry me to the door. I don't open it – I'm not even sure I could if I wanted to. I just slump against it and talk, softly.

'James, I've got a migraine. I'm going to go to sleep.'

I hear his intake of breath. Slow, deep, clearly trying to decide if I'm lying or if I really am unwell. Then the door handle moves again.

'Why have you locked the door?' He doesn't sound confrontational. In fact, he sounds genuinely concerned and ever so slightly hurt.

'I . . . I don't know. I did it automatically.'

A beat's silence. 'But you never lock the door.'

He's right, but trying to come up with a reasonable excuse right now is beyond me so I don't even try. 'I'm going to sleep for a bit. Please tell Ally, Ernest, Louise, all of them, that I'm sorry. I'll be down in a little while if I feel up to it. If not, I'll see you in the morning.'

With that I walk away from the door and back to

the bed. I get in properly, the duvet engulfing me amidst its soft folds. I don't bother taking any of my clothes off. I just burrow down and let my mind close up, hoping the man outside my door will eventually walk away.

I don't sleep properly. It's like I start to souse in my own thoughts, with every bad thing in my head infecting the rest of me, seeping into my blood so I'm coated in a nauseating layer of dread and despair. I drift in and out of full lucidity and a strange, dreamlike hinterland. One moment I'm determined to pull myself together, go back downstairs, apologise to our guests and try to pretend none of this has happened. The next, I'm convinced James is in the room with me, telling me I'm stupid, that I'm sick, that I'm terrible for even thinking he would be involved in the procuring of children for sex and the very thought of it repulses him; that I'm an embarrassment to him, myself and all our guests. Eventually, I force myself to rise, slowly at first and then all at once. It's a monumental effort, with so much of my body crying out in the process. It's like I've run a marathon, both physically and mentally. After what feels like years, I'm standing in front of the large mirror opposite the bed. I'm alarmed at what I see. The thin layer of make-up I'd put on earlier in the afternoon seems to have vanished. Instead of a forty-seven-year-old woman ready to host a Christmas dinner party, the reflection that greets me bears a closer resemblance to that of a much older, troubled woman, perhaps on the verge of a nervous breakdown. Maybe I am. Maybe this is what it feels like before you tip over the edge and surrender to the ravages of one's own mind.

I pull the arms of my sweater down to cover my elbows and flatten out the creases in my grey pants. James would prefer me to wear a dress, but I've never liked them. When I was young, I used to pretend I did, that I was one of those girls who would turn heads when they arrived at a party. When I reached thirty, I faced up to the fact that I was a lot more conservative at heart. And now I do as I please – never too scruffy or casual to cause James to openly protest, but occasionally I see him raise an eyebrow.

I take a couple of minutes to get myself together. Employing a hairbrush to calm the red-brown waves that would add to my on-the-edge appearance, I manage to make myself look a little closer to normal. I glance at my watch. I've already been away for over an hour. As I put myself back together, I find myself getting stronger and realise I have chosen a path from the crossroads that has faced me ever since I opened that first document. I am going to go back downstairs, smile at the guests, be a dutiful host. Then, once everyone's gone home, I'll bring James upstairs and lay out everything before him. Including my plan of action. It has occurred to me to flee the house without speaking to anyone, but with a certain degree of shame I have to admit to myself that I don't really have anywhere to go. There is always my mother, of course, but she's never exactly been a great comfort in even minor crises. And I'm not sure I can face trying to articulate my current concerns to her. Then there is the question of Stephen. I can't just leave him here, faced with the situation.

As I think of him, the memory of his haunted face floats to the surface of my mind. And he's down there now, trying to pretend everything is fine; something I'm going to attempt to do for the next few hours.

It's on the landing, just before the stairwell, that I have my first wobble. I reach forward and grab on to the banister, letting myself fall to my knees on the soft cream carpet. I think I may have made a thud, but nobody comes. James must be back downstairs with the others. Swivelling slightly, I look back to my bedroom, the door slightly ajar. I haven't bothered to close it. Thinking about going back there makes me feel nauseous again. But I can't go back downstairs. Try as I might, I can't pretend everything is fine and just carry on with dinner. I look down the hallway, towards Stephen's room and James's study. Neither of them appeals to me as a place of shelter. I just need somewhere to go. To hide. To bide my time, away from the bin full of vomit in my bedroom and that terrible sliver of plastic and metal I'm still carrying in my pocket. I'm about to pull myself up, hoping a standing position will make the decision as to where to go a bit easier, when I hear a voice.

'Julianne? Are you okay?'

Louise is standing there, halfway up the stairs, on the little semi-landing in the middle. I pray she hasn't been there for ages, watching me, and attempt a smile.

'Louise. Hi. I'm . . . I'm just looking for an earring.'

I cringe inwardly at the lie and realise with a pang of embarrassment that both my earrings are still intact and hanging from my ears. Louise smiles and walks slowly up the last half of the stairs, the warm light from the landing giving a flattering glow to her brown, short-cut hair and kind face.

'Julianne. Are you . . . are you unhappy?'

This takes me completely by surprise. I'd expected Louise to gloss over my weird behaviour, pretend she was on her way to the bathroom. At most, I thought she might ask how my migraine was. But this is probing. And I'm not sure I can take probing right now.

'I'm . . . I'm very happy. It's Christmas.' I attempt a bright and cheerful grin but feel my face contort awkwardly, my muscles refusing to do what I ask of them.

Louise sits on the top step in front of me. 'I've had problems. You'd be surprised how many people do. It was when both the boys left home. One off gadding around the world, the other now boarding and only coming back for the holidays. I'm not trying to downplay your anxiety, Julianne, but please know you're not alone. There was one year I couldn't stomach even the most calm gathering with a bunch of old school chums. I walked out of the Starbucks in tears and I didn't even know why. That was when I realised I needed some help. I went to a doctor on Harley Street – a Dr Rhodes – and he really did help me see things a bit better. Gave me some perspective. It's just an adjustment period all women go through – all parents, really, in their own way. My mistake was that I didn't trust my husband. I couldn't look at the bigger picture, only a small part of it. Dr Rhodes made it possible for me to step back and see the whole canvas and, when one does that, some things just pale into insignificance. They fall away.'

I'm not quite sure what she's going on about and am about to excuse myself, but she presses on, speaking earnestly, with a quiver in her voice. 'I think it comes from this myth that everything needs to be so out in the open. When really, the best course of action is just to let sleeping dogs lie. Don't feel you have to examine every feeling, every action, Julianne. Changes of all kinds can be a challenge to us, big or small, scary or seemingly trivial. And I know it will feel strange when Stephen goes off to university and you and James have different things to concern yourselves with, but you'll find another rhythm. That's all I'm saying. But if you feel you need help, I could put you in touch with Dr Rhodes, if you like. He's got a waiting list, but I'm sure I could do something about that.'

Her misreading of the situation irritates me slightly and I straighten up.

'No. Thank you, but no. I have a migraine, Louise. Not depression.'

Her eyes widen in alarm. 'Oh no, sorry, I didn't mean to presume . . . And I'm aware it's not as simple as depression. I wouldn't say I was depressed. Just stretched too thinly, if you know what I mean. It's just important to know that nobody has to feel like that these days. Nobody is obliged to feel lost or hopeless or upset. There are drugs that can make it all so much easier. Honestly, I was a sceptic myself at first, but then I tried these SSRIs Dr Rhodes prescribed, fluoxetine and then Seroxat, and they worked wonders.'

I don't say anything. I can't be bothered to tell her again.

'I just wanted you to know you're not the only one. James need never know.'

The mention of James's name makes me start. 'What do you mean?'

Louise glances down at the stairs as if worried about being overheard and lowers her already quiet voice. 'I mean that all marriages have difficult patches. If you're in one now, just hold on tight and sail through it. It will pass. You just need to know that you don't have to be holding on tight alone. There is help, you know. Ernest and I . . . well, we had a bad patch. A very bad patch a couple of years ago. I really thought it was all over. I think you learn a lot about yourself during times like that. What sort of person you are. How strong you can be. That sort of thing. I was naïve – I see that now. Naïve to think marriage is all just chocolates and roses. But with time I've found it's important to remember that whatever dark clouds crowd your horizon, you still have your horizon, Julianne. The horizon will still be there.'

On other days, I would have found it hard not to roll my eyes. I have a pretty low tolerance level for corny mantras and inspirational quotes at the best of times – something Stephen has always said is very 'un-American' of me. I consider telling Louise that whatever dark clouds she's had to deal with – probably something about Ernest leaving his coffee mugs out or spending too much money on his extensive collection of Savile Row suits – they are nothing compared to mine. Her face, however, makes that impossible. Sweet, good-natured concern stares back at me, mingled with a little too much understanding. She

274

enjoys being the caregiver, the mother hen, the one to provide help and comfort. She is good at it. I can't criticise her for that. I take a tissue out of my pocket and blow my nose, giving me a few seconds' thinking time.

'I think . . . I think we should go downstairs,' I say slowly. 'I should probably get back . . . the food . . .'

'You don't have to. Honestly, Julianne, nobody minds at all. The food is delicious as always and Cassie has it all under control. Do you want me to help you back to your bedroom?' She puts out her hand to touch my arm, but I pull it away.

'No. No, thank you. I just think we should go back downstairs. I don't want to go back in there. Hate being cooped up. I'm probably just hungry.'

Louise nods. 'Okay then. Shall we go down now? Or do you want to sit for a bit?'

I hold on to the banister and rise to my feet. 'I'm fine. Let's just go down. Honestly, you don't need to worry.'

We walk down the stairs in silence, Louise a couple of steps behind me. The hum of voices, and Ally's raucous laugh, get me as I arrive in the hallway.

'Once more into the fray,' says Louise, giving my shoulder a squeeze of encouragement. 'Don't worry, we won't stay late. And if you need to go back upstairs at any time, just do it, Julianne. You don't owe us a thing.'

I give a small murmur as a response and then slowly walk through the doorway into the dining room.

Chapter 20

Holly

Wickford, Essex, 1991

My conversation with Julianne, lying in my bed, my body a mass of aches and pains as she held my hand, was the last I ever had with a student at the university. After she had left, I managed to sit myself up and take a few tester steps over to my chest of drawers. I could walk, but it didn't feel like the type of walking I was used to. I tried to avoid looking at my reflection in the mirror as I pulled on some clothes and put some others into a bag. It was 7.30 a.m. when I reached the train station. I didn't know what time I'd left, but I imagined it had taken me double the usual amount of time to walk there, wincing and crying and at one point pausing to throw up in a bin. If anyone saw me, they didn't bother to stop. Probably just another drunk student, they thought.

At the station I bought a one-way ticket to Wickford and sat next to a family on the train. They had travel bags and suitcases, obviously on their way to London and then onwards, perhaps to an airport, the children clearly excited. One of them, the little girl, looked over at me at one point and beamed and I smiled back. She looked slightly scared, as if my smile was an unnatural contortion. As if I was a creature she didn't quite know how to deal with.

When I finally reached Wickford a few hours later, my bag was hurting my shoulders and my lower back was driving me crazy with the pain. Without even thinking much about it, I threw my bag into a hedge near my local off-licence. I couldn't face carrying it any longer, not even for another ten minutes. What did it matter, anyway? At the front door I almost started crying again as I realised I'd left my keys in my desk drawer, but it opened a few seconds later and I was greeted by the sight of my father in a dressing gown holding a mug of something. He stared at me, clearly shocked, first, by seeing another human facing him and then by the realisation that it was his daughter. When the power of speech returned he said, 'Blimey, love, what you doing here?'

I fell on him and he caught me, hugging me close to him. I sobbed and sobbed and he rocked me gently in his arms just as he'd done when I was a child. I heard noises on the stairs and Mum's voice, telling Dad to close the door as he was letting all the cold air in. When she saw me she stopped talking. I looked up from his shoulder and murmured, 'Hi, Mum.'

She looked as shocked as Dad had, then went into the full-on level of questioning I had expected. 'What on earth are you doing here? Why aren't you at uni? Why's your face all blotchy? What are you crying for?'

Eventually they got me into the lounge and settled me on the sofa. A hot drink and slice of toast were offered to me and I took them gratefully, realising I was dehydrated and feeling vaguely hungry. They kept asking me what was wrong – I could hear the kindness, the concern, in their voices, and then, when I kept shaking my head, an edge of slight impatience in my mother's tone. 'Well, if you can't tell us what it is, Holly, maybe you should go and have a shower and get yourself sorted, then maybe you'll feel more up to talking properly.'

I did what she suggested, dully aware I was probably doing the worst thing: ridding myself of any evidence that still clung to my body. I knew I was making it harder for myself, limiting my options, but as I washed and gently caressed myself clean with shower gel, I realised I knew something emphatically: I wasn't going to go to the police. I wasn't going to tell anyone. I couldn't tell anyone. This was so plain to me I couldn't face entertaining any thoughts to the contrary. It would be hard, I knew that. But the other option would be harder. The option of intrusive examinations, photographs, interviews, statements, questions. Then, since it had occurred at the most famous university in the world, the inevitable media attention, made all the more sensational by the fact that one of the accused was the son of a member of parliament. I thought of the newspaper headlines, the column inches devoted to what I had been through. The neighbours in my street would look at me differently. I would be 'the raped girl'. And then there would be the doubters. The people who would say I'd brought it on myself. I was drinking. I had consensual sex with the others watching. I'd happily performed sex acts as part of a game with a young man who had a girlfriend. I'd be a loose woman. A whore. A slut. A slag. The problem with young women today. I'd be the poster girl for those who felt women should be shamed for their sex lives while the boys went scot-free. All of this, of course – every last miserable minute of it – would be nothing compared to the way I'd be treated when called to give evidence in court. I'd recount my experience and I'd be ripped to shreds by one of the best and most highly paid defence lawyers in the country. Strings would be pulled. People would be bought off, I was fairly certain of that. Something would be done and the boys would almost definitely walk from the courtroom and back into their lives, allowing the cushion of privilege to catch them as they fell. They would dust themselves off and carry on. Perhaps they would have wounded reputations. Perhaps girls would think twice before dating them or marrying them. But they would get there eventually. I, on the other hand, would be damaged goods. And branded a liar for life. You'd think you couldn't have it both ways – surely a girl who made up a rape couldn't also be damaged by one – but I had a feeling others wouldn't see it that way.

I'd be both repulsive victim and conniving bitch. And it would linger about me until I died.

With all this swimming around my head, I stepped out of the shower and looked at myself in the bathroom mirror. There were bruises on my shoulders and arms and, when I looked down, I could see some around my thighs, too. My stomach and torso were free from any marks. I'd been putting off looking at my stomach for some weeks now, terrified I'd see it growing at an impossible rate. Although it still felt relatively flat to my touch, there'd been a change. Slight, but it was there.

I avoided putting any pressure on my bruises with the towel as I dried myself. I would need to get some more long-sleeved tops. That shouldn't be a problem. There were enough bargain-basement stores in Wickford high street and it was still chilly outside. By the time the sun arrived and spring blossomed, the bruises would have gone. The thought of time passing like that made me dizzy and I sat on the toilet seat while I pulled on my jeans, t-shirt and jumper, then went back downstairs.

'Here she is,' my mum said as I arrived back in the lounge. She was sitting on the sofa, the *Radio Times* on her lap, right where I'd had sex with George two months previously. The stain was still there. Right near where her left leg rested on the edge of the cushion.

'Do you want to tell us what's upset you?' she said. She had her reading glasses on and they'd fallen to the end of her nose. Like a librarian, I thought, then felt a stab of pain in my head as I was reminded of Oxford and the libraries I would never visit again.

'I had sex with a boy who has a girlfriend.' I said the words bluntly, standing in the middle of the lounge while both my parents stared at me. Dad made a small coughing sound and Mum looked down at the magazine in her hands.

'Right. Well, I suppose that kind of thing goes on at university.'

Dad went to get up, then let himself slump back down again into the sofa. He kept looking over at my mum on the other side of the room, then at me, then at the floor. A triangle of embarrassment separated us.

'I was upset because I loved him. But I don't any more.'

I was taking care not to say anything that wasn't true. I didn't really know why that mattered so much to me in that moment – it could have been my fear of one day being called a liar – but regardless, I chose my words sparingly and made sure they could realistically be considered the truth, even if I was technically lying by omission.

'I'm not going back to Oxford.'

Neither made a sound straight away. Then a small crunch came from my left. It was Dad. He'd bitten into a HobNob. Mum set the *Radio Times* down next to her on the sofa and took off her glasses. 'Wouldn't that be a bit of a waste?' She looked concerned, but also faintly frustrated, as if I were a foreigner who didn't speak good English. 'I thought you liked it there?' She made it sound like a restaurant we were thinking of visiting for dinner, not the place where I'd spent nearly four months in total trying to carve out something of a new life for myself.

'I did, but I was wrong. I'm sorry to be a pain, but I need one of you to go and get my things. They're in my room there.'

Dad spoke then, probably grateful the conversation had touched on a subject he felt confident in contributing to. 'Well, I suppose we could go up there in the car next weekend?'

'I'm not going. It will be just you. Or both of you if Mum wants to help. But I'll be staying here.'

They exchanged a look at this. 'Why?' Mum was looking thoroughly baffled. 'Has this boy upset you that badly? Did he lie to you about his girlfriend? I know that's not a very nice thing, love, but I think you could risk bumping into him in the corridor while you get your things. If you ask me, I think throwing in a whole degree for the sake of some lad is preposterous enough . . .'

'There won't be any risk of me bumping into him in the corridor because I won't be going back.' I said the words with force now. Not shouting, but I didn't stop the anger coming through.

'Well, I don't see why your father and I should have to go lugging back boxes of your stuff – no doubt most of it books I bought you – just because you've been a bit free with your favours where the boys are concerned.'

That was the final straw for me. I was done. 'Okay, don't do it then. If it's that much trouble, we'll let it all stay there. Don't trouble yourself. Go on another fucking cruise or something.'

I walked out after that. I didn't know what else I might say if I stayed. I went up to my bedroom, got into bed, ignoring the fact that one of the pillows didn't have a cover, and lay there until I fell asleep. I had no more energy left to fight with.

Chapter 21

Julianne
Knightsbridge, 2019

'I can't stand her,' Ally says after swallowing a large mouthful of apple pie. 'I think she's atrocious.'

Ernest grins at his sister from the other end of the table and rolls his eyes. 'You're just saying that because she's a woman and you think it makes you sound interesting, being dead set against a fellow female.'

'A fellow female!' Ally lets out a laugh of contempt, but her expression is playful. She and her brother do this often. I sometimes join in, but not today. 'I don't remember ever accusing you of being deliberately critical of our previous PM simply because he was a man.' She hiccups loudly and then helps herself to another spoonful of pie.

I wonder how many glasses of wine have passed her lips since I was last sitting here.

'I simply disagreed with him on certain social stances in the manifesto. His gender had nothing to do with it.'

'My dislike of the Ice Queen has nothing to do with her gender . . .'

'And I certainly didn't resort to using names like that,' Ernest cuts in. 'A tad tacky, don't you think?' He rounds on Ally's boyfriend now. 'What would your website make of our prime minister?'

'Oh, don't give me that,' she says before the embarrassed-looking young man next to her can utter a word. 'Julianne, do you have any thoughts?'

For the second time this evening, Ally seems to expect me to rally to her defence. I just want her to go. I want them all to go. I am regretting my decision to come back downstairs with Louise. Couldn't my migraine have just exempted me for the rest of the night? Why on earth had I felt compelled to put up with this? I try my best to focus my gaze on Ally.

'I think I might be out of my depth here. I'm not British.' It's rare for me to use my nationality to back out of a debate, but it's the best I can come up with.

'You'd be the perfect commentator for that very reason!' Ally takes another sip of wine, swallows, then turns to Stephen. He's been sitting looking morose and haunted the whole time I've been there. He must be in quiet anguish about what I've been doing upstairs, all the while trapped with a drunken Ally and the rest for company. I want to tell him everything's going to be okay – that I'm on his side. That I haven't let him down. I take a look at my husband's face, staring at me across the table, full of concern and kindness. A kindness I can no longer accept.

'Stephen, tell me,' Ally slurs, 'what do you think of our current PM? And before you answer, bear in mind she voted against an equal age of consent and gay adoption.'

I feel a jolt of surprise pulse through me. Although I've never regarded my son's sexuality as taboo or even much of a talking point, this sudden reference disconcerts me. I tell myself she doesn't mean anything bad by it. She's just a bit tipsy and keen to get a heated debate going. But Stephen's face doesn't make me relax. He looks like a rabbit in the headlights.

'That's unfair,' Ernest says. 'You're just quoting bite-size snippets you've read from some left-wing broadsheet.'

'Oh, shut up, Ernest. It's not you I'm talking to.' She hits the table with her palm. 'Come on, Stephen, fight for your people!'

Stephen looks hopelessly bewildered by her behaviour and then I see his eyes, glistening, threatening to over-spill.

'Stephen, honey?' I say quietly, and go to reach out a hand to him, but he gets up and walks quickly out of the room.

'Look what you've done now,' Ernest says, looking smugly at his sister. 'You've upset the delicate little flower.'

His words snag on me like barbed wire. I feel my eyelids fly open as I turn to stare at him.

'What did you say?' My voice is slightly raspy and I need to clear my throat, but I stay very still and quiet and stare at Ernest's belligerent, smirking face. Slowly, his expression changes to surprise mingled with irritation.

'Sorry?' he says, as if he had simply misheard me.

'I asked you to repeat what you just said about my son.' I say the words firmly and clearly. There is an ear-ringing silence. Then James says quietly, 'Julianne . . .'

'I want him to explain what he said.'

'I don't think I have to explain it,' Ernest says. The flicker of a smile is twitching his lips.

'Ern,' Louise says now, putting a hand on his arm.

'Get off me,' he snaps, pulling his arm away. 'You're always pawing at me.'

'Delicate little flower.' I almost spit the words at him. I don't want them to get lost in whatever marital spat he might be about to have. 'Could you explain your choice of words to me, Ernest?'

'Oh, for God's sake, Julianne. You're not thick. Your boy's got no backbone. I know it. James knows it. You know it. Just a weak-willed little queer boy with no drive, no focus, no direction.'

Louise gasps at her husband's words and Ally knocks over her wineglass. I hear its stem snap as it catches her plate and see the flash of red staining the cream tablecloth. I ignore it. Instead, I look over at James. He has his eyes lowered to the table in front of him.

'Wow, some friend you have here,' I say to him. 'Are you going to let him talk about your son that way?'

Everyone watches as James raises his head and looks me in the eye. 'I think we should all calm down,' he says slowly.

'I don't feel very calm,' I say, staring resolutely back. 'I'm fucking furious.'

'I think we better go,' Louise now says, moving to get up.

'Stay where you are.' Ernest puts a hand out to hold her still.

Even though everything is motionless, it feels to me as if the whole room is starting to tremble, like there's some unstoppable force awakening within the walls. It's been caged for far too long.

Louise sits down, rubbing her arm. She looks a little dazed, as if her mind is trying to protect her from what's happening. I look over at her, watching her trying not to cry as she stares down at her half-eaten apple pie.

'Is that how a guy with backbone acts?' I say with venom. 'Manhandling women? Treating them like they're his property? If that's your idea of having "drive", I thank God my son's nothing like you.'

James stirs again. 'Julianne, please stop.'

I feel something crack within me, a space between him and me getting wider. I slam my fist on the table and it makes everyone jump. 'Stop? Did you not hear what he called your son? A "weak-willed little queer boy". Is that the kind of language you're going to tolerate? Are you really that pathetic? Does that fucking asshole mean so much to you that you won't even defend your own kid?'

James doesn't speak and for a moment I think I'm

going to have to endure another bout of silence. Then, to my surprise, Ally turns to her brother and says: 'You're a cunt, Ernest.'

That word always shocks me a little and apparently I'm not the only one, as both Louise and Cameron look aghast.

'It's true. That's not the first time he's said stuff like that about Stephen. You should hear what he's like behind closed doors. It would be sickening if it weren't all so fucking hypocritical.'

Ernest stands up and for a second I think he's going to fly at his sister. Then he stops jerkily and sits back down. In a quiet, dangerous voice he says, 'I think you've had too much wine, Aphrodite.'

'Don't call me that. You're afraid, big bro. Aren't you? You're scared the secrets of Ernest Kelman MP will be leaked to the *Daily Mail*.' Her eyes turn back to me. 'I'm sure this has crossed my brother's mind quite a bit.' She reaches for her wineglass then, realising it's broken, grabs her boyfriend's and drinks the last drops from that.

Ernest is now grinding his nails into the tablecloth, looking at Ally as if he'd like nothing better than to murder her. 'You really don't know what you're talking about.'

'Don't I? Shall I start by recalling a few choice occasions with you and Rupert Ashton when we were teenagers? Or how about someone a bit closer to home?' She smirks and looks over obviously at James and then back to Ernest. 'Maybe I should ask James about that?'

The trembling I'm feeling underneath me is now rising

in turbulence. I feel my hands shaking so I scrunch them up tight and force myself to speak without shouting. 'What on earth are you both talking about?'

Ally gives a fake laugh. 'Oh, come on, Julianne, you must know. Granted, I've left off making quite so many digs at Ernest about it over the years, but it's surely pretty obvious. Ernest used to fuck your husband. I don't think he still does, don't worry. No affair has been had. He wouldn't dare in case the press got wind of it. No, they were just bed-buddies at Eton and I suspect at Oxford, too.' She's looking at Ernest instead of me as she says all this, but now turns to James. His face has gone extremely red and he's still looking at the table. He couldn't look more guilty. 'Come on, James. Don't play dumb. We all knew you guys liked to screw around. There's nothing wrong with it. At least, there wasn't until *he* –' she jabs a finger at her brother '– starts spouting his anti-gay bullshit about a boy who's worth ten of him. And you, his father, just sit there and let him. Stephen is your son, for fuck's sake. Have you really not got the courage to stand up for him, or is precious Ernest worth more to you than your own flesh and blood?'

I hold on to the table to keep myself steady. For a second I think I might faint, but manage to keep upright. 'Is this true, James?' Everyone is looking at him now, but he won't move. I have half a mind to throw a plate at him, anything to get a reaction. I am furious. The anger I thought had subsided earlier is coursing through me with such strength I want to scream. 'James! Answer me. Is it true? What Ally's saying?'

291

He doesn't say anything and Ernest starts speaking. 'This is all ancient history . . .'

'Shut up!' I scream at him, then turn back to my husband. 'So what does it mean? Are you gay? Bisexual? Are there any other secrets I'm going to find out today? Because, please, we're on a fucking roll here.'

That gets a reaction. He looks at me now and in his face is a combination of panic and anger. 'Stop talking, Julianne.'

I stare right back at him. 'Don't you fucking dare tell me what to do. Is this where you tell me everything's fine and it's all a mistake? Is this where you try to comfort me and pull the wool over my eyes?' I'm going somewhere I'm terrified of, but it's within me and I know it needs to come out. I can't hide it any longer. It's not good enough. All my demons are here right next to me – all the insecurities and doubts and fears of the past few hours are rushing to the surface like bile and I can't stop. I have to keep going. 'Because men wouldn't be the only thing you're into, would it?' I see his eyes dart around him, like a trapped animal.

'Julianne, for God's sake, calm down,' Ernest says. I'm in the process of standing up, jolting the table as I do so.

'Calm down? I don't know what weird shit is going on between you, but I'm sick of it. You're all the same. You just care about yourselves. You close in and protect the pack. All of you, you've always been like that. I've always been the outsider, never part of the little club. You act like you're all goddamn invincible.'

292

Ernest just looks at me and shakes his head, as if he's mildly repulsed at what he's seeing. 'This kind of hysteria might work in America, Julianne, but here it's rather tedious. I think it would be better if my wife and I went on our way.'

Louise nods enthusiastically. 'Yes, I think that's best.'

'Sit the fuck down.' I say it with such emphasis they both obey instantly. 'You think you're all so special? Think James here is the best thing since sliced fucking bread? You just wait.'

I run from the room, leaving them gaping at me, and take the stairs two at a time. Stephen comes out of his room on the landing and I'm surprised to find Cassie following behind him. 'Mum, what's going on?'

Cassie looks shocked and concerned. 'I found him crying on the stairs, then I heard shouting. Are you okay, Julianne? Is there anything I can do?'

'No. I mean yes. Help Stephen pack a bag and get some clothes together. We're going away for a bit.'

She looks taken aback, and I can't blame her, but I don't want to pause to explain.

'Oh, okay, and James . . .'

'Is staying here,' I say as I walk past them. I stop and look back at Cassie. 'I'm so sorry to ask, but is there any chance you could take Stephen to my mother's?' She's taken aback, I can see it in her eyes, but I don't wait for her to respond. 'I wouldn't ask if it wasn't important. You can call for a car from the place my mother often uses and put it on her account. Please. I just don't want Stephen here for . . . for a bit.' I half-expect him to start talking now, to say he doesn't need to be sheltered, but he doesn't. He just stands there.

'Of course,' Cassie says. 'Anything I can do, I'm here.' She turns to Stephen. 'Come on, let's get some overnight things sorted.' It's like he's a child and she's getting ready for him to go on holiday. For a second I think about going over to hug him, but instead I continue towards my room, flinging the door open so it bangs against the wall. I want to show them. I want to fucking show them and watch them implode – their circle of trust will disintegrate when they realise what their precious James is really like. I can't believe I ever swallowed his preposterous lies. I almost laugh to myself at how easy I am to win over. Grabbing my tablet, I run past Stephen and Cassie, who are still standing and staring. 'Don't come down,' I say. 'I'll come up and get you in a sec.'

I run back downstairs, down the corridor, tapping at the home screen, shoving in the USB, awkwardly clutching it tightly in my left hand, and go back into the lounge. Ernest and Louise are standing again, as if about to flee. 'I told you to fucking sit!' I snap at them.

'We aren't used to being treated like this,' Ernest says pompously.

'Julianne, please, just sit down. I think you're just having a bad day.' Louise has her kind voice back on, but it's tinged with panic.

I laugh, probably sounding slightly hysterical. 'You want to see a bad day? You wait.' I drop the device roughly beside the plates, wedging it up against a dish of half-eaten apple pie, and lean across it, zooming in on the girl's face, her name, her details. Part of me expects James to stop me, but he's still sitting and I can see him shaking, as if trembling from the cold.

'This is a young woman named Ashley Brooks and I believe, in four weeks' time, my husband – your precious James – is going to rape her.' I flick through the files. 'And this is Carly Gale. She's booked in for February. These are drug addicts, by the way. Prostitutes. People on benefits. People with mental health issues. People with no support, no family to help them, no friends, no job. And children. Children from care homes. Children without parents. Children who have probably known nothing but abuse and trauma. This is what he does. He subscribes to some sick company who procure these people for him. This is the type of man he is.'

I see Louise's face has drained of colour as she falls back down into her chair. Ernest shows no sign of emotion, but after a few moments he walks past me calmly and clicks the lock button on the side of the tablet.

'Enough,' he says simply. He then sits back down next to his wife so it's only me left standing. I feel slightly disarmed and exposed and so, at a loss as to what else to do, I sit down, too.

'What is the point of all this?' Ernest says, still talking quietly and calmly. 'What do you expect to get from it? To shame your husband? To see him prosecuted? To get back at me? If so, I have to say, going to the police would be a pretty strange move from you of all people.'

His words confuse me, but I latch on to one of them.

Police. Yes, that's it. I think I always knew it would come to that, deep down, but only now am I really thinking about how it would work.

'Julianne, can you hear me?'

I nod. 'Yes, I can. And yes, I will be going to the police. I don't know what good it will do, but I know it's the right thing.'

He looks pensive as he nods. 'I see. And how much will you tell them?'

I take a deep breath. 'Everything. Every single bit of it. Every single sick little secret. I mean it,' I say.

I see a flash of something in Ernest's eyes after I say this and it scares me slightly, shaking my resolve, so I look away. James, who is still trembling, his face now in his hands, looks like a wreck of a man. Someone I don't know. A complete stranger.

Ernest's voice takes my gaze away from my husband.

'Julianne, please listen to me.' His tone is low and commanding and he fixes upon me with an intense, hard gaze. 'It won't make a difference.'

I look at him in consternation. What is he talking about? I try to ask this out loud, but my jaw is aching from all my shouting and I just manage a 'Whha' sound.

'I'm telling you, Julianne. This is bigger than your husband banging a few worthless drug addicts. Do you understand what I'm telling you?'

I don't understand. Either that, or I don't want to. 'I don't care how big it is. The police won't turn me away. They'll confiscate his stuff, trace the files, arrest him.' I nod my head in the direction of James, unable to say his name. 'Hopefully arrest whatever sick fuck sent them to him, too.'

'Julianne, please stop.' He is still talking maddeningly slowly, still looking me in the eye. It is as if he's trying to tell me something without actually saying it out loud. 'The police won't turn you away, but they won't get very far.'

I make a sound of disbelief. 'Sure they will. They can do all kinds of things with computer forensics . . .' I know I'm out of my depth here, but I'm also not prepared to believe what he's saying.

Ernest sighs. 'Do I have to spell it out for you? The police investigation will fail. They will be polite, say they will look into it, perhaps launch an official investigation, but if they do it will either be for show or it will fail at the first hurdle. No arrests will be made. No names will be released to the public.'

I glance over at Louise, but she's looking away. Ally has her eyes fixed on her brother, but isn't saying anything. Cameron, meanwhile, is staring around, apparently unsure whether to be excited or appalled by what is happening.

'There is a market for this sort of thing, Julianne,' Ernest continues, 'and I'm not talking about your husband indulging himself every month or so. Acting out his fantasies. Having other people pick up the pieces, sort out his mess. I'm talking about a market worth billions, where people will pay a premium to do whatever they want and the circles in which they move will protect them. Always.'

His words aren't hitting home. I look over at James, hoping Ernest's little speech will get some kind of reaction from him, but he still just sits there, his hands pressed into his face, apparently in a great deal of distress, like a scared child. 'What circles?' I ask. 'Do you mean you and your gang of privileged jerks? Lawmakers are not above the law. This is England.'

'Spoken like a true American.' Ernest's smug tone is threatening to return. 'Julianne, you're not naive. You've seen the news stories. There have been investigations, very high-profile ones, in the past about similar things. Things of a rather niche nature. Things it is within the public interest to keep swept under the carpet. Nobody wants to live in a nation run by paedophiles, sadists and perverts. Such words, after all, are part of a discourse put forward by those who don't truly understand. Wouldn't it be better if we just allowed the best people to reach the top without having their sexual preferences judged by those who have no right to judge? Look at your son, for example. Wouldn't it be a tragedy for him if his tastes became the subject of an inquiry? They would have been, you know, not too long ago. But society moved on. And it will again.'

It's not confusion that grips my words now. It's anger. 'It's not the same,' I hiss, my gritted teeth slightly obscuring the words. 'It is *not* the same.'

Ernest smiles the winning *vote-for-me, I'm just like you* smile he uses on the public when approaching election day. 'You keep telling yourself that, Julianne.'

I look at him with disgust. 'You're vile. James is going to prison. And if you're involved in this, so will you.'

He just sits there and laughs. 'I'm sorry to say it, but you are being blind. You have been manipulated by your government, your press and your husband. Although two out of these three are of course not technically "yours". Your adopted government, I should say.'

'People do get found out. People do have to answer for stuff like this. Just look at the news. It happens all the time.'

He rolls his eyes. 'That's because the media thrives on sex, gossip and middle-class outrage. It's just a question of where you shine a light and how much you give them. Why do you think it's only been film producers, TV presenters and film stars who have been the main focus? Have you ever stopped to wonder why everyone gets so hot and bothered about them but conveniently forget about the real people in power? These public outings have been a smokescreen. Everyone thought they were going to open up the floodgates – flush out the perverts and bring us forward into a more transparent time. But their purpose was the opposite. Give the public just enough to satisfy their appetite for a revolution but not enough to bring the walls crumbling down.'

This is all too much for me to handle. I let my head sink into my hands, mirroring my husband.

'He's right, you know,' Ally says softly, causing me to look back up and meet her eyes; her usually expressive face blank, her expression now cold, not giving anything away. The drunken, loose-cannon vibe she was giving off earlier is now extinguished.

'What?' I snap at her, feeling the anger rising again.

'You're defending this? As a woman, you think it's okay that people – real, living and breathing women, men, girls, boys – can be abused just for the sake of vile individuals getting their fucked-up kicks? Are you seriously telling me, Ally, that the thought of that doesn't make you feel ill?'

Ally doesn't answer, but Ernest does. 'Don't use that phrase,' he says. '*As a woman*. I hate that. It immediately takes away any credibility you might have had.'

'Credibility? That's exactly what it gives me. I know what it's like. What it's like to be a woman confronted constantly by men who persistently try to make you feel weak or stupid or insignificant. The snide comments, the wolf whistles, the offers of sex from random strangers in the street. All of these things exist at the start of a long and disturbing road that ends with the likes of him.' I jab my finger in the direction of my husband.

Ernest raises his eyebrows. 'Goodness, James, it's a wonder your wife doesn't go into politics. With this level of self-righteous hysteria, she could give the PM a run for her money.'

Ally makes a strange noise, as if inhaling breath in short bursts, desperate to take in the oxygen but afraid of the sound. 'Ernest isn't very self-aware,' she says quietly. A small part of the heavy, uneasy feeling I'm experiencing is somehow tied up with Ally. Having spent a large part of my life in the company of this big personality, the larger-than-life posh girl who's never minded saying things like 'oh golly gosh!' in her loud, resonant voice in public, it is weirdly devastating to now hear her speak in little more than a whisper. 'Julianne,' she continues quietly, 'I think you should talk to your husband. We'll all go and leave you both in peace.'

Again, Louise looks up hopefully, and even Cameron stirs, as if ready to make a move, but Ernest once again raises his hand. 'Just one moment. I think we need to get a few things settled first.' He's looking at me as he says this, and there's an edge of venom in his voice, though he, too, is now talking quietly. 'I presume we've put to bed the ludicrous notion of going to the police about this.' He waves his hand at the tablet, still leaning against the dishes, the glossy surface of the screen reflecting the warm lights up above.

'I don't think we have,' I cut in.

'We have, Julianne. You need to understand that. No good will come of it, only anxiety for you and probably the destruction of your marriage.' He glances at James.

'I don't care what you say, I'm not going to stand by . . .'

'However,' Ernest carries on, slightly louder, 'forgive me for being, shall we say, slightly concerned at your mention of our other little delicacy.'

'What delicacy?' I say, confused.

'Don't feign ignorance, Julianne. I think we both know what's underpinning all this.'

At this, I see Ally look up sharply. As if on cue she stands and this time her brother doesn't try to stop her. 'Come on, Cameron.'

Her boyfriend looks slightly shell-shocked as he stands

up and I see him give the tablet in the centre of the table a fearful glance.

I can't let Ally go. Half-tempted to stand in front of her to block her exit, I instead try to make eye contact but she's not looking my way. 'Ally, you'll back me up, won't you?' It sounds desperate and pleading, but it's all I can offer her.

My friend pauses on her way to the dining-room door, Cameron stopping behind her abruptly so as not to bump into her.

'Ally, please. Tell him you'll come with me to the police.' My voice rises and cracks, like someone begging for mercy, but it's my last hope. 'And Cameron. You saw those files. I promise you, this isn't nothing. Please. I need you to . . .'

'I think Ally and Cameron know what's good for them. And my sister's very good at turning a blind eye when it suits her. I think she knows this is one of those moments when her discretion is required.' Ernest speaks now in a dangerous voice that has a real element of threat to it. 'Cameron and I understand each other, too, don't we, Cameron?' I see the young man look over at Ernest. He's out of his depth. *You and me both*, I want to say to him, but it's clear that, unlike me, he's not willing to fight. He nods eventually and Ernest nods and smiles in return.

He and Ally exit the room in silence. She doesn't even look at me as she leaves. I'm astonished. I've always had problems with her, always been slightly irritated by her larger-than-life characteristics and direct way of putting things, but I have genuinely counted her as a friend. But here she is, passing me by in my hour of need, obeying her bullying brother rather than coming to my aid. She's a coward, I think, as she disappears out of sight down the corridor.

'Ernest, let's go, please, let's just go.' Louise sounds almost as desperate as I am now, reaching for her husband's arm then flinching when he pulls himself away from her. 'I don't think . . . I'm really not able . . .'

'Fine, go back to the house,' he says. 'I'm staying here, but you can go. And don't wait up.'

Louise flinches slightly as he spits this final sentence, then scurries out of the room.

Just us three now. Me, Ernest and the silently crying, trembling man I used to proudly and lovingly call my husband. He used to put his hand over mine if I cried. Rub it slightly with his thumbs in a circle. And, very occasionally, when he cried, I would do the same to him. I can't imagine comforting him now. I can't imagine ever touching him again.

Ernest waits until he hears the slam of the front door before starting up again. 'Julianne. I'm waiting for some assurance you're not going to do something stupid. Please don't think you can play me. This isn't the time for digging up the past. You of all people should know that.'

I try to breathe but it's as if my airways are shrinking. 'I don't know what you're implying . . .'

'I'm talking about Holly Rowe.'

The name hits me like a bullet. 'What?' I whisper, staring back at him.

303

'Holly Rowe. And I'm really not in the mood for your faux-ignorance right now.'

Ernest's face is distorting out of proportion. I can't focus on anything. I go to stand up. 'I need you to leave. I'm done.'

'Sit down,' Ernest says.

'Do you know,' I say, struggling to keep the strength in my voice, 'I'm getting so fucking sick of you telling people what to do in my house.'

'Noted. But all the same, I need you to sit.'

I look at the two of them seated there, at one end of the large table, then sink back into my seat. 'I'm not talking about Holly Rowe and I don't know why you're bringing her up now,' I say to my dinner plate. 'I'm really tired, Ernest. James and I have a lot of talking to do. You probably think bringing up Holly now is some easy way to upset me, but—'

'So you do remember her after all? We can stop pretending then?' Ernest says.

This isn't happening. There's nothing to talk about here.

'I told you, I'm not talking about her. Or any of it. James made a mistake. A stupid mistake when he was nineteen. He's never been unfaithful since. It has . . . no relevance.' I can't stop the tears from slipping out now.

'Are you at least fooling yourself? Because you're really not convincing me, Julianne. My patience is being tested.'

'Your patience! Fucking hell, you dare to talk to me like that after you've done God knows what damage to my family.'

'You said,' he carries on, almost shouting, too, 'that you were going to tell the police everything. You said that word, *everything*.'

'Yes, and I am.'

'So I presume you are also talking about Holly Rowe. And if you are, I feel it my responsibility to offer you some advice on the matter.'

I raise my hands to my head, feeling a dull, throbbing pain in my temples. 'I don't know what you're talking about, Ernest.'

'I think you do. I've wondered for years whether one day you'd play your little trump card. Give yourself a moment in the limelight. I looked out for the slightest crack in your marriage, waiting for it to come, but you seemed so intoxicated with James – or, rather, with his money – I didn't really have to worry about that. But now it's come up, forgive me for not being keen to walk out of here without getting a few things absolutely clear. I'm not a big fan of uncertainty – I have enough of it in my professional life.'

I make a move to get up, but feel myself wobble and sit back down. If I didn't feel so disoriented I would hit him, lash out, smash his head into the remnants of his apple pie. 'I don't know what—' I begin to say, but he grabs my arm, tight. Very tight.

'You sat with her, Julianne. You sat with her all night afterwards. You listened to her talk. And then you said we would never speak about it again.'

I feel like I'm breaking. My world is cracking apart at the seams and, if I don't run, I'll be swallowed by the darkness underneath. I want to leave, but he's got me so tight, and James is just sitting there, looking like he's about to be sick, his face stained with tears.

'Fuck you,' I say back through gritted teeth. 'This is a separate issue . . .'

'Are you sure about that? Are you sure you've had quite the perfect married life you've always made out? Are you sure he's never got a bit heavy-handed with you when the urge gets too strong?'

'You're sick. You're fucking sick. I don't know what you're talking about, but I'm not going to stand for it. I don't know what you think a silly little affair James had at uni has to do with any of this. And I am still,' I say, pointing to the tablet, 'taking that to the police tomorrow.'

'And when they learn you helped cover up a rape, Julianne? What then?'

My vision distorts. The whole room tilts suddenly. I can't bear it. 'No . . . I didn't . . .' I gasp. I'm struggling to hold myself upright. My head's made of lead and I'm convinced I'm about to vomit, but nothing comes up.

'You sat there, holding the hand of a girl your boyfriend had just raped, repeatedly, and you did nothing. You forgave him. You told him you would move on. And then you fucking married him. I had my doubts about it at the time. Personally I was hoping you'd fuck off back to America, but James insisted you'd keep quiet. And you did keep quiet, for twenty-nine years.'

I look down at my hands and for a moment think I can see another hand holding on to mine. A young woman's hand. A girl's hand. Fingernails slightly jagged, as if she bites them, and her palm strangely soft. Marks on her arm. Red marks. The beginnings of a bruise.

I start to cry. Long and hard, as if I'll cry for ever.

'I'm glad it's finally hit home,' Ernest says. He might have started to say something more, but his voice floats away. I'm losing my grip on reality. I can't hold on. I let go. Everything is slow, soft darkness.

Chapter 22

Julianne

Oxford, 1991

I somehow knew the event was going to involve some of us taking off our clothes. I also knew she fancied him. I'd noticed a few times the way she looked at him – as if he were some strange, exotic creature she longed to stroke, but kept her distance from because the park ranger had told her he might bite. Foolish though it was, I never really believed he would cheat on me. Never believed he'd be tempted by someone as plain and ordinary as her. I wasn't exactly vain about my appearance, but I was aware of the effect I had on men. Aware they were drawn to me. Aware, when I came to England, how my American accent apparently only added to my natural attractiveness.

Holly, meanwhile, seemed like a nobody. On the few occasions I'd tried to talk with her – at Rupert's party, or even as I'd arrived in Ally's room before we started playing that ridiculous spin the bottle game – she'd come across as dull. There's no other way to really say it. She was boring.

Having watched the effects of alcohol slowly break apart my parents' relationship, I'd often steered clear of drinking excessively. However, that night, I was keen to get drunk. Not to the point of sickness – though that did come, eventually – but just to anaesthetise my feelings after a horrible, horrible day. It had started with James in the morning when he'd snubbed my attempts to have sex. We'd woken up to the sound of rain, a sound I love to hear in the morning when I don't have to get up and do anything. He was lying on top of me, giving me a dead arm, so I gently eased him off and started touching him under the covers. He let me carry on for a moment or two before stopping my hand and getting out of bed. I watched his naked form as he walked across the room, put out that he'd left the warm comfort of the bed. He said he was going for a game of squash with Ernest. 'Cancel,' I said, simply, and let the duvet drop down to reveal my bare chest, hoping it would tempt him back. But no. He pulled on his gym clothes and said he'd be back in a couple of hours.

Later in the day, when he'd come back and showered, he sat on the bed and smiled. He said he was sorry he'd been in a mood earlier and asked if I wanted to get brunch. I was starving, not having bothered to get up to eat, instead choosing to tend my hurt feelings by reading the first chapters of the new Stephen King novel I'd bought earlier in the week. I agreed and he kissed me and I fell back among the covers, the hardback cover of *Four Minutes to Midnight* digging into my thighs. I slipped my hand under his boxer shorts, pulled them down and started to use my mouth on him. He stopped me after less than a minute. 'We need to eat,' he said, and got up, his erection pushing against his underwear as he pulled it back on. I felt puzzled and hurt, unsure why he was avoiding sex with me.

The row occurred when we were paying the bill at the café. I made a joke that he shouldn't keep buying me things – meals, clothes, perfume. He asked why not and I said it made me feel like a whore. I probably should have expressed the sentiment more elegantly, but he got very funny about it and asked what I meant. I told him it didn't matter, but he persisted and I told him to drop it, since my comment made little sense regardless, as I wasn't even able to give sex in return these days. He became angry at that, saying just because he didn't want his cock sucked every minute of the day didn't mean we weren't having sex. I was mortified. I saw the couple next to us look over, eyes widened in shock. Some teenagers nearby laughed. This wasn't my James. His tone was more like the belligerent confidence of Ernest than his normally calm, mild-mannered self.

We made up eventually later that afternoon, but not everything was resolved; at least not by me. I was trying to think back over the previous week and couldn't remember an occasion when he'd instigated sex or completely followed through if I had tried. I was starting to get anxious. Maybe he wasn't into me any more. Maybe he felt we'd run our course and was now keen to look elsewhere. But if I'd had to pick a girl I thought he would cheat with, it wouldn't have been Ally's mousy, unremarkable friend. Perhaps he found her attraction to him too hard to resist. Or maybe he was just horny and she was awake and eager and I was passed out down the hall. Regardless, that evening became so horrible, so tainted by his actions, that I would do my best to forget it for the rest of my life.

I knew something wasn't right the moment I woke up and tasted vomit. Nobody had come to get me. I could feel I'd been there for hours by how stiff my legs were, and my back clicked when I pulled myself up, hanging on to the toilet seat as I slowly got into a sitting position. I'd been sick over the toilet, managing to get only a portion inside the bowl, with the rest speckling the bathroom floor. Though I was more than a little put out nobody had bothered to come and find out where I was, I was grateful they hadn't seen me like this. It wasn't my style. I rather pathetically tried to dab at the small splashes of vomit with a bit of tissue before abandoning my attempts and stumbling out of the stall, feeling bad for the cleaners who'd have to scrub up what I'd left behind me. As I walked the short distance back down the corridor to Ally's bedroom I thought I heard someone laugh. Or maybe it was a cry. I couldn't be sure. I reckoned they were all still in the swing of the game. Maybe Ernest was doing something outrageous or Ally had cracked one of her inappropriate jokes. But when I got to the room, I found it empty, apart from Ally, fast asleep, leaning against her chest of drawers, some saliva escaping from the corner of her mouth, her thick waves of blonde hair covering half her face. Then I heard the creaking. The sound of the bed in the room next door, rhythmically groaning under the weight of someone. More than just someone.

There are times in life when your brain plays tricks on you. When you're told one thing but you see another and you have to wrestle with yourself over which one's real and which is an illusion. Like the feeling you get if you unwrap a present that so obviously isn't for you, or step on a stationary escalator, expecting it to be moving, or mishear someone and think they've said something rude or embarrassing. It disconcerts you. And then you fill in the blanks. You suppose. You reason. You choose the likely version of the truth that fits best in that moment. When James opened that door to me – the door of Holly's room – there was something that didn't feel right. I knew it, but couldn't put my finger on it. Something about the way she lay there, entirely still as he spoke to me. As he pleaded with me. As he said how sorry he was and that he had just lost himself in the moment. How she had begged him to have sex with her; said she was a virgin and wanted him to be the one to do it while the others were asleep. How she'd got a bit upset because it hurt and she'd started to bleed a little. All this information came crashing down on me in a rush as he tried to confess his crime. Confess he'd had sex with another girl and how he would never, ever do it again. He didn't want to let

313

me into the room, but I pushed past him and went over to her, stepping over the sleeping figures of Ernest and Peter on the floor.

Losing my virginity was a pretty horrendous experience. It was with a boy named Mark Cohen in the backseat of a car in Jacksonville, Florida, in the parking lot of a Home Depot store. I was on holiday with my parents, had met a boy at the hotel and ended up getting laid. Though I tried to convince myself at the time that I was into it, I knew as soon as he started kissing me that it was probably a mistake. I wanted him to do it, to be free of my V card, but as soon as he started entering me I couldn't help crying out in pain. It hurt, and continued to hurt, even when I told him it was fine and he could carry on. I just gritted my teeth and tried not to cry. He kept stopping and asking if I was okay, but I told him to just get it over with. And then the regret. The mounting sense of regret I felt when I walked gingerly back to my hotel, crying quietly, hoping my parents would be too drunk or busy arguing to notice what a state I was in. And so when I walked into that bedroom and saw Holly's tears rolling silently down her face, I did the only thing that came naturally to me in that moment. I held her hand. I told her it was all going to be okay. I wanted to hit her. I wanted to scream in her face and tell her she was a fucking bitch. But more than that, I wanted to give her the comfort and support I'd never received two years previously when I had to come to terms with my own mistake.

She drifted off to sleep soon after, but I stayed with

her for over an hour, not really seeing her, lost in my thoughts. I barely noticed when Ernest and Peter came to and exited the room without saying anything to me. When I finally left her around dawn and walked back to James's dorm room to find him crying on his bed, I had already formulated what I was going to say. I told him that under no circumstances were we going to talk about this incident ever again. We would never allude to it or mention it. That was the only way I felt I could carry on with him and not have it all implode around me. A complete redaction of it from our history. I would sponge it away, write it off as a catastrophic error of judgement on his part. We'd had a row that day, he was stressed about exam work and the pressure he was being put under by his father, and I had probably been unfair with him. We were both to blame. He had been angry and probably hadn't read the situation as well as he could have. Things like this happened. Mistakes happened. We all floated into grey areas from time to time where the boundaries were blurred. That's what I told myself. And he accepted it. He promised me he would love me for ever and devote every second of every day to making sure he never put me in this position again.

I discovered about a week later from Ally that her friend Holly had decided to drop out of university altogether. 'Just wasn't for her, I don't think,' she said, as she bit into a large burger in the pub where we were eating. I nodded and agreed that the experience wasn't for everyone. She didn't pursue the subject and I was pleased to move on and talk about something else – the weather, the impending exams, the book I was reading, how I was going to stay with James and his parents over the spring holiday. All of it seemed so much more important than the subject of Holly Rowe. She was a nobody. She always would be.

Chapter 23

Holly

Wickford, Essex, 1991

It took a while for me to face up to the changes my body was going through. As one part of me healed, the superficial bruises and sore parts of my legs, thighs and wrists steadily fading, another side of me was going through a change. A change that had been going on for weeks, in spite of my attempts to ignore it. To carry on. To battle through.

Sometime late in the season snow had settled on my small corner of Essex, causing my parents to moan even more than usual. Grumpy references to how much nicer it was in the Caribbean started to become frequent, and there was a distinctly more ratty tone to the way they spoke to each other. I did my best to keep away, avoiding joining in with their conversations, the rough ball of anger within me always in danger of spilling out whenever I spoke.

One day – the fourth of our early spring snowfall – I journeyed down from my bedroom, my usual place of sanctuary, for a breath of fresh air outside in the garden. The fine, dusty coating on the patio crunched under the soles of my trainers and as I looked up, the afternoon light starting to dwindle, I got a snowflake in my eye. I tried to rub it out and my arm brushed against my left breast, causing me to wince. It was tender. So was the other. Two days later, after some nights of feeling hot and cold, I woke up to a sensation of low-level nausea which increased in intensity the moment I tried to walk normally to the bathroom.

I was going through an evolution, one that was competing with the emotional warfare I was already saddled with. One I couldn't ignore any longer.

I went to my local GP one day when both my parents were out. My dad wanted to pick up an old dressing table he was sure he could sell on and Mum intended to drift around a nearby branch of Laura Ashley, looking at throws and floral frocks she couldn't afford. I made an appointment over the phone with the receptionist then walked the short distance to the practice surgery, an awkward, ugly-looking building that had probably looked very modern in the 1960s. The conversation with the doctor didn't take long, although one of his questions did cause me to wobble a little, the tears that were never far away threatening to arrive in front of him: 'What's your support network like? Are you here with your parents?'

I told him I wasn't. And that was that. He gave me some leaflets, some advice on my next steps, on antenatal groups and some stuff about scans. Then I left and walked back to the house, nervous, scared, but with a growing resolve within me, a steadily strengthening refusal to be beaten, one I would carry with me and, years later, still hold to me like a trophy I had crafted all by myself. It was still there. My ability to cope. To deal with the situation. To survive.

Three weeks after the snow had gone, I woke up one morning to find my mother standing over me. 'Ah, you're awake,' she said and sat on my bed. I noticed she'd drawn the curtains and had that expression on her face that said very plainly she was about to start a discussion she would rather not face.

'I was wondering . . . well . . . your dad and I were wondering what the plan was?'

I pulled myself up from my bed, feeling a ripple of nausea run through me, and reached for the bottle of water I kept near the alarm clock I hadn't bothered setting for the past month.

'What plan?' I said, confused.

'Your plan. What, er . . . what happens now? Now the Oxford dream is dead and you apparently won't even take part in a conversation about why you left in such a hurry.'

'I've told you why.'

'Yes, I know, your little crush. Are you sure you didn't embarrass yourself in some way? You can tell me, dear.'

I looked away towards the open window, unable to look her in the eye – if I did, I wouldn't be able to keep the tears at bay.

'I don't want to talk about it.'

She sighed and I think I saw the flicker of an eye-roll. 'Why must you be so proud? This superior silence you've always kept. Do you think your father and I are stupid? We know there's more to all this than you've told us.'

I took a deep breath and then said, 'I don't think you really want to hear the truth.'

She didn't say anything, just stared at the wardrobe, waiting for me to elaborate. Finally I said the words I'd been practising in my head. 'I'm pregnant,' I said.

I heard a quick intake of breath and she put her hand to her mouth. 'Oh God,' she whimpered. She sat there, rocking slightly, her head dipped so I couldn't see her face clearly. 'I suspected this. I just hoped it wasn't true.'

'You suspected it?' I said, gulping down some more water.

'A mother knows,' she said, now rubbing the tops of her knees. She always did this when she was upset about something. 'And your sudden wardrobe change hasn't gone unnoticed. These big chunky jumpers and baggy t-shirts. I've heard you being sick, too. Stomach flu doesn't last this long, you know. When were you going to tell us?'

'I'm telling you now,' I said, then added, 'I've only known myself for a few weeks. Well, longer than that, if I'm honest, but I didn't really want to believe it.'

Some deep breaths. My mother swayed slightly. 'Of course you must be expecting my next question.'

I nodded. 'Yes. The father is George Treadway.'

That made her stop with her knee rubbing. She turned around, a look of shock on her face. 'My God, you don't mean . . . that rough-looking boy you went to school with?'

Now it was my turn to roll my eyes. 'He isn't "rough". He's perfectly nice.'

'I thought you'd been made pregnant at Oxford?' she said, sounding almost disappointed.

'Well, I'm sorry your first grandchild won't be the illegitimate son of an earl or something,' I snapped. 'Is that what you would have preferred?'

She stood up and walked away from me, towards the door. 'Your father's out. When he's home we'll tell him this together. God, I knew it was something like this. I knew there was some reason you'd turned up suddenly here out of the blue. This is all such a mess.'

'Are you worried you won't be able to go on any more cruises?'

Instead of walking out of the door, she slammed it shut and turned back to me. It was strange to see her lose her temper. She usually just bottled things up and went silent, but in this case she apparently wanted to have it out with me.

'You're in no position to use that high and mighty tone with me, sitting there with some random youth's child inside you!' She hissed this, then threw a look towards the window, as if the neighbours might have overheard. We stared at each other for a few seconds, then I finally said it, the thing I'd been terrified of saying out loud, more than the pregnancy, more than about George Treadway, more than anything in my whole life.

'Mum,' I said, and I started crying. 'I was attacked.'

The colour drained from her face and she looked at me with an expression I would never forget. 'Oh dear lord,' she whispered. 'That boy raped you. That Treadway boy . . . he . . . he forced himself on you?' She came over to the bed now and picked up my hand. 'We need to go to the police. I can't believe you didn't tell me this sooner.'

'Mum, I—'

'Jesus Christ, I knew there was something strange about him. I knew it. I'm not going to let him get away with it. I won't.'

She started muttering away to herself about the kind of vengeance she'd wreak on George Treadway, clearly more concerned about being victorious in the pursuit of punishment than the wellbeing of her daughter. 'Mum,' I said quietly. 'Please, Mum, stop. It wasn't him.'

She looked at me, clearly baffled. 'What do you mean, it wasn't him? You just said he was the father.'

I shook my head. 'Mum, George and I had . . . we had sex. Consensual sex. At Christmas when you and Dad left me here. He's harmless.'

'Then who . . . ?'

I stared at my hands for almost a full minute, then started to speak. I told her everything. I described the whole evening to her. How we'd started playing a drinking game, how I'd been a bit tipsy and gone a bit overboard. How I'd followed the three boys back to my room and it had got out of control. They had taken advantage of me and attacked me. Once I'd finished I finally lifted my gaze from my fingernails and looked her in the face. I couldn't quite see it at first, since she was turned towards the wardrobe, not looking at me. Then she finally leant in my direction.

'You say one of them's the son of Clive Kelman?' She spoke evenly with barely any emotion, quite differently to when she'd been fantasising about George's incarceration.

'Yes. His name is Ernest Kelman.'

She didn't say anything for a bit, then asked another question. 'Do you get drunk like that regularly?'

A steady sense of dread started to creep down my shoulders. 'No . . . but, what's that—'

'And do you regularly have sex with . . . with multiple participants of an evening?'

Her strange and archaic turn of phrase would have made me laugh under different circumstances, but the full horror of what she was saying was sinking in. 'I've never had sex with more than one "participant". As if that really matters.'

'Of course it matters,' she said scathingly. 'The thought of my little girl off cavorting, playing sex games and having drunken orgies, not to mention dropping her knickers for any random lout that comes knocking.'

I cried into the top of my duvet and she let me. She didn't offer a hand to comfort me. She didn't even look at me. 'Please, Mum, I'm telling the truth.'

I saw that she, too, was crying, but silently, without sobs, the tears just running down. Slowly, she shook her head. 'You stupid, stupid girl. Do you know what they'll say? If we take this to the police and accuse an MP's son and his mates of improper behaviour? Do you know how it makes you look?'

'It doesn't matter,' I said firmly. 'It was rape. It was assault. Doesn't that bother you?'

She stood up now. 'If every woman who did something regrettable after getting drunk cried rape . . . God, the thought of you taking those three men back to your room. I thought I'd raised you to respect yourself.'

'Christ, you'll have to give me a rundown sometime as to how you did that, because I can't really remember you raising me at all! And so what if I had taken them back to my room to have sex with them. With all of them. Me and all those boys, in a bed together, fucking the night away!' She flinched visibly at the word 'fucking', but I didn't stop. 'If we were all happy about it, there would be nothing wrong at all. But I *wasn't* happy with it. They carried on and I didn't want them to. And that's never acceptable.'

She stood up and again started walking away, only this time I doubted she'd be back. 'I don't know where you've got these ideas from, Holly, or who's put all this stuff into your head, but the world doesn't work that way. Actions have consequences.'

I felt hatred towards her in that moment. Pure, full-blooded hatred. 'Are you saying I asked for it? That I deserved it?'

She looked back at me as if I were some strange, vaguely disgusting animal who had wandered uninvited into her clinically clean house. 'Get dressed,' she said coldly. 'We need to tell your father about the baby. Just the baby. Nothing more.' With that, she left the room.

'Wait,' I say, wiping my nose on my hand. 'We haven't discussed the other option. I could have an abortion.'

I really did think then that she was going to faint, but she held on tight to the door to steady herself. Her biting words came seconds later.

'I really don't think we need to add that to your list of sins.' Then she left.

Ten minutes later, on my way back from the bathroom after giving in to my morning sickness, I heard her crying properly, too, in her bedroom. I didn't feel pity towards her, just a strained sense of numbness, like my emotions had been overworked to the point of losing feeling.

The conversation with Dad was one of the most awkward of my life, but on the whole he handled it a bit better than Mum did. He just stayed silent through most of the explanation, then afterwards simply said: 'It's a shame we sold your old cot and pushchair when we realised we couldn't have any more. We'll have to see about getting some new stuff for you.' My love for him increased a little when he said that, but I wasn't in a position to show it. We weren't really a hugging family, so I just sat there on the sofa while Mum tried not to cry, eventually walking away to clatter about in the kitchen, making an early lunch that nobody wanted.

The thing I really found hard to deal with as I made my way back to my bedroom, ready to sink myself into the Ruth Rendell novel I was in the middle of, was the thought of the endless years stretching ahead of me. Would this be it now? Me, them and a baby who would grow up shaped by the same cold, colourless existence? I got back into bed and opened my book. No, I thought to myself. I wouldn't let it be so. I didn't know how I was going to do it, but I was convinced I wouldn't let this situation beat me. I wasn't going to be 'the victim', 'the teenage mum', 'the Oxford drop-out' for the rest of my life. I didn't know at that point exactly what course of action I'd choose, but the small seed of determination sown within me became like a life-raft to cling to in the years to come. It was a reminder that I could decide what defined me, not other people, my parents, my circumstances. It gave me hope that there was more than this.

Chapter 24

Julianne

Knightsbridge, 2019

The Christmas tree lights are blurry, as if viewed through water. As my vision clears, I realise my eyes are filled with tears. I reach up to rub them and feel my hands brush against the soft cotton of a cushion. I'm on the sofa, stretched out, as if I've been sleeping. Have I been asleep? What time is it? I try to look over at the clock on the mantelpiece but I see Ernest first. He's standing there, in front of the fire. It's burning in its grate. Someone must have lit it while I was out.

'Nice of you to return, Julianne.'

Ernest is talking at me in that infuriatingly superior voice, while standing in my lounge as if he owns the place.

If I didn't feel so nauseous I'd throw something at him. 'Jesus,' I moan, while trying to sit up, but then feel sick again and lie back down.

'He isn't in attendance, I'm afraid. Your husband is, however.'

I look over at the single-seat sofa near the TV. James is sitting there, his demeanour more or less identical to when he was at the table; hunched over and looking like he's been drained of blood.

'Where's Stephen?' I ask. The voice feels thick, my mouth dry and leathery.

'Your housekeeper has taken him in a car to your mother's. She said you'd asked her to. He was rather upset.'

'Right,' I say, briefly wondering what Stephen will say to my mom. 'Is this where you both kill me or something?'

'Hilarious, Julianne,' Ernest says, sounding rather irritable. 'But this isn't a Lifetime movie.'

I manage to pull myself up into a sitting position, breathing slowly. 'You watch many Lifetime movies, Ernest? Wouldn't have thought they were your style.'

He gives a low chuckle. 'It's sometimes better if I don't object to Louise's viewing choices. I can't bear the fuss.'

'I bet you're a hoot on a Sunday night,' I say, rubbing my face. 'So what happens now? I'm still going to the police, you know. To be honest, I'm just waiting for you to leave my house.'

'I'm going home in a moment. I just want to make certain of a few things before I do.' He walks over to James and sits next to him. 'My silent friend here has been

328

reduced to this trembling mess because he knows what could happen if things get too . . . hot, shall we say.'

'He raped Holly Rowe. I know that now. He's pathetic. He's going to prison.'

'You've known it for a long time, Julianne.'

I feel a jolt inside me when he says this. I tell myself to calm down and shake my head slowly. 'No. It wasn't like that. It isn't like that . . .'

'You've kept quiet for over twenty years because you didn't want your chance at the high life to end in ruins.'

'No,' I say forcefully. 'You covered it up and you're trying to pin it on me.'

'How did I cover it up, Julianne?'

'I don't know. You must have threatened her or something.'

'You're grasping at thin air.'

He is right, but at the same time I'm not put off. He is taunting me and I am desperate to get back in control. Get the information I need. With great effort, I try to remember that night, that room, that awful feeling of dread I had as I saw her lying there. Did I know what I was seeing then? What was it about that room that really didn't sit right? A detail I've pushed right to the back of my mind where it can't hurt me? I look at Ernest and narrow my eyes. His leg brushes against James's, causing him to flinch a little, as if from a loud noise. Then it drops in. The image just falls into my mind, as if it has been as clear as day all along.

'You weren't wearing any trousers.'

His expression remains impassive. 'What?'

'You were sleeping there, in the room. You and Peter.'

'I know, Julianne. And we woke up to find you sitting, holding Holly's hand.'

'Yes, and you weren't wearing any pants. No trousers or underwear. I remember now. You had your shirt on, but nothing else. And Peter was naked, I think.'

'Are you saying this like it's some kind of eureka revelation? What do you think it's proving?'

I sink back into the sofa. I am trembling now and feel like I'm going to pass out again as the full horror of the situation comes into focus. But there is another part of me that feels strengthened by the terrible, terrible realisation, because at last the true evil of the situation is becoming plain.

'You gang-raped her. All three of you. Didn't you?'

Ernest is watching me closely, then looks over at James. He shakes his head. 'Good lord, James. I do believe your wife is actually as stupid as you suggested.'

To my surprise, my husband finally speaks. 'Please, can you just stop and . . . can you not . . . I really don't think it's necessary . . . I think it would be better if . . .'

Even in my state of distress, I find watching him embarrassing. This is so much the complete opposite of his character; it's like I'm watching a performing animal doing something weird, something unnatural, something against their innermost instincts. He's spouting stock phrases, the kind he would have used to defuse the odd spat between Stephen and I or if we'd had a minor row.

Ernest doesn't seem very impressed either. Smirking, he turns back to me. 'Ask your husband, Julianne, what he said when he came running to me, saying you'd woken up too early. Ask him.'

I shake my head. 'I'm not fucking speaking to him. I'll never speak to him again.'

'That isn't very helpful now, is it?' Ernest sighs. 'When I came to and found you sitting there with the girl, I needed to assess the situation quickly. I didn't want to discuss the situation with you before I'd had the chance to talk to James. I found him sobbing in his bed, under the sheets. He said you'd woken up too early and he'd tried to feed you some bullshit about it being consensual. Apparently he had convinced you. I questioned at first how likely this was, but I was fairly certain I had the measure of you by that point. All those expensive clothes he'd bought for you. All those gifts. It's amazing what sins a woman can excuse when you give her a taste of luxury . . .'

'If you think for one second I would have—'

'I did think exactly that. I knew you and your mother had been living on something of a shoestring ever since coming over to the UK. And I knew James was your chance to escape the poverty your family was sinking into. But it seems I was wrong. It seems you were actually even more stupid than I expected.'

I look at James. I had been half-convinced never looking at or speaking to him again would be the best course of action, but I find I can't keep it up. 'I was in love with you. So much,' I say, tears slipping from my eyes. 'I believed you. I . . .' I break off, at a loss for words. James takes one look at me, his eyes red and raw and full of pain, then stares back at the floor.

Ernest clears his throat. I am growing tired of listening to him, acting as if he is my husband's spokesperson or defence lawyer, but I don't seem to have much choice. It is as if James's power of speech has left him completely. 'James and I have a slight . . . quirk. Our appetites are different to most men's. We desire something stronger. Normal sex isn't enough to satisfy us. Ally's right – we did dabble in homosexuality, and the taboo nature of it at the time satisfied us to an extent. But it wasn't enough.'

His words remind me of what he said about Stephen earlier and I wince. 'There's nothing taboo about gay sex,' I say firmly.

Ernest rolls his eyes. 'Oh, don't start on that. It's abnormal, an inversion. I'm tired of the overly polite rhetoric surrounding it.'

'Bit rich from someone who confesses to fucking his male best friend,' I spit at him, my fury returning.

'Yes, but don't you see? That was precisely the point. We were doing something abnormal. Something that went against the natural order of things. Two heterosexual men aren't naturally supposed to do that to each other, so for us it had the allure of the forbidden I think we both craved. James, I think, invested slightly more emotion in it than I did. Eventually, however, it stalled. It wasn't enough. We both knew it, and talked extensively about what we wanted to do – what we would truly want to do, if there were nothing stopping us, nothing in our way.'

James twitches at this. 'Don't tell her any more.'

His words startle me, as if he has spoken a foreign language. He's said it to the ground, clearly unwilling to look either of us in the eye.

'My dear fellow, don't you think Julianne's heard too much already? Do you really think it's going to do any real damage her hearing the rest of it? She won't tell a soul. I can guarantee that.'

I shake my head. 'You can't guarantee that. Because I'm going to tell everyone.'

Ernest smirks. 'So you keep saying. I promise you, if you're still in any doubt about remaining silent by the time I'm finished, we will address your concerns in full.'

'Address my concerns?' I almost shout it, but Ernest holds up a hand to stop me.

'As I was saying, before I was interrupted – we had come to the end of our little liaison, James and I. Peter was actually the one who suggested Holly Rowe as our first . . . er . . . conquest.'

Conquest. The word sickens me. I want to interrupt, but he sweeps on.

'He was never quite as daring as James and I. Liked to watch more than take part, I think. But I was impressed at his choice and, as it turned out, Holly worked out rather beautifully. That is, of course, until you woke up earlier than planned.'

I look at him quickly. 'Than planned?' I repeat, realising what he is suggesting.

'You were drugged, Julianne. I know you're a bit of a lightweight when it comes to drink, but you hadn't drunk *that* much. It worked to a point. You and my sister were completely out of it when we took Holly back to her room.'

I shake my head. 'I think I'm going to be sick.'

Ernest just shrugs. 'It's your carpet,' he says simply. He pauses to fiddle with one of the ornaments on the Christmas tree, looping its string round so it is stuck tighter to the branch. I wait for him to speak, but my mind quickly flashes to my time on Oxford Street yesterday. The desperate face that confronted me. The pleading voice, begging me to talk to her. The years and years of suffering she must have endured, contending with memories nobody should have to face.

'What happened to Holly Rowe?'

When I mention Holly's name, Ernest's expression changes for a second. He looks troubled. He comes away from the Christmas tree and instead runs his hand along the mantelpiece, as if checking for dust. 'She's under observation.'

'Observation?'

'Yes. I check up on her now and again. She works at a domestic-violence refuge in Northern Ireland. Don't worry, she's not like one of those destitute, drug-addled prostitutes you seem to care so much about. I set up an account with an anonymous standing order twenty years ago and sent her the details, but she's never touched the money. There's over three hundred thousand pounds in that account now and not a penny of it has been withdrawn. I'm sure you'll probably work that into some kind of feminist victory.'

He pauses, as if waiting for me to retort, but I just wait for him to continue.

334

'She has a child. A girl. A woman now, of course. She, too, works at the refuge.' He sees my expression change and raises a hand. 'Keep calm. She's not James's child, or mine. She was born a little too early for that. She discovered she was pregnant shortly after leaving Oxford. It seems she'd had unprotected sex a bit before we . . . had our little bit of night-time fun.'

Night-time fun. The phrase disgusts me and I look away.

Almost a minute's silence follows before he says his next sentence. When he speaks, my stomach constricts.

'And now we must get to James's little mistake.'

Just as he says it, I notice the tablet. It's on the coffee table, propped up against two big Taschen books on Monet I keep there. I can't believe I didn't see it before now. Ernest is looking at it, too.

'I'm afraid we've both been rather slipshod when it comes to our wives,' he says, glancing at me, then at James, then resting his gaze on the blank screen once again.

'What do you mean?' I ask, apprehensive as to what he's going to reveal now.

'You aren't the first to discover our, er, little hobby.'

Something clicks into place in my mind and I gasp. 'Louise. She knows. That's why she didn't look surprised.'

Ernest nods. 'I'm afraid she came back from her trip to Paris two days earlier than planned a little while ago. I thought I was completely alone in the house. She overheard a rather important phone conversation. It wasn't a pleasant discussion. It took some time to put things in perspective. In the end, she needed to get some professional help. And it did help, in its way. She has to take medication, but most of the time she sees the world the right way up.'

'*Mad, Bad and Sad*,' I say under my breath.

'What?'

'It's a book by Lisa Appignanesi. About the history of women and mental health.'

'Right,' he says, as if wholly uninterested in Ms Appignanesi and whatever book she might have written. 'It seems James now finds himself in a similar situation to me with his little . . . er . . . faux pas. To be honest, I'm astounded he didn't protect his picks from the recent catalogue of options more carefully. But we all live stressful lives, I suppose. It's so easy to transfer highly sensitive documents into very public places. Human error. The downfall of many.'

'He tried to tell me they were for MI5,' I say.

Ernest laughs. 'Yes, I think he's always fancied himself as a spy. I gather his aim was to either frighten or impress you into silence. I think he's been watching too much *Homeland*.'

He looks at James again, who continues to avoid eye contact.

'He was warned about this, when he begged me some years ago to be let in on my little hobby and join the club I'd founded. You see, the thing is, it takes rather a lot of money to keep this type of thing working smoothly, and for that you need a certain kind of investor. And our investors – or, rather, my business partners, I should say – are not the types to take breaches of security lightly. We're supposed to keep these things on entirely separate devices, not general home computers, email addresses or shared accounts anyone could pick up. No automatic sign-ins, no 'remember password', no insecure Cloud accounts. But middle age is when the memory starts to fade, even in the best of us.'

James has started crying again, and is now looking at me pleadingly, as if silently begging me to come to his rescue.

'And it's through ignoring protocol like this that we find ourselves in the kind of situation we have here.'

I don't want to look at either of the two men. My eyes settle on the presents under the tree: gift bags, unopened cards, beautifully wrapped boxes. My mind travels to the box delivered from Apple. It now feels like a lifetime ago. 'What's his new MacBook for? The one that arrived the other day? Next season's *catalogue*?' The word repulses me as I say it, my nausea rising once again.

Ernest raises an eyebrow. 'Not exactly the height of subtlety, your James. We used to think his quiet, brooding nature was a sign of the depths of his intelligence. I think we all overestimated him a bit. His potentially calamitous behaviour in this instance really does test my faith in him.'

'Maybe he wanted to be found out. Helped. Given treatment.' The words sound false as I say them aloud, like wishful thinking or cod-psychology. Ernest seems to think so, too, and scoffs disbelievingly.

'I'd be surprised if that were the case,' he says, getting up off the sofa and walking over to me. I feel myself drawing away from him automatically, back into the sofa, as if he's about to attack. This seems to amuse him, but he doesn't touch me. Instead, he reaches forward to the coffee table, picks up the tablet and turns it on. 'I seriously doubt he would want to risk something so precious to him.' He's holding it out, the screen facing me, and again I see that familiar, terrible list of numbered files. 'Tap the first one, Julianne.'

I shake my head. 'I've read it. More than once already. I know what it says.'

He raises his eyebrows. 'Oh, you haven't read this one, Julianne. This document is brand-new. Or rather, it's been kept safe for a while. As insurance. Just in case anything went wrong.'

He gently places the tablet into my hands. I take it.

'Just have a read of this,' he says. And taps the first file.

I can't speak. Words fail me completely. The screen is a blurry mess. I can barely see through my tears. But I know what's there. I recognise the photo as soon as it comes on-screen. And the key details at the start of the page are ones I'll be able to recite until my dying day.

Name: Stephen Knight
Date of Birth: 1 June 2002
Occupation: School student
Area: Knightsbridge, West London

Tears fall from my eyes silently. 'No,' I say, shaking my head. 'This can't be real. You've done this just now . . . you're trying to upset me . . .' I look over at James. He's got his face buried in the sofa now. I can't think because of a horrible noise filling my ears, and then I realise it's him. He's crying, howling, as if someone is tearing him apart.

'Shut up!' Ernest shouts at him.

'Please, just stop this,' I say, my vision clouding through my tears, dropping the tablet. 'I can't take any more.'

'You don't want to go on, Julianne? You don't want to read the finer points of what your son's got to offer? Many people will want to know, Julianne. Of course, no trial runs have taken place yet, but they will be arranged. Very swiftly, I assure you.'

I wipe my nose and eyes. 'I can't . . . I can't . . .'

'Stop crying. Both of you,' he barks. He is standing in the centre of the room now and for a fleeting moment I'm reminded what a good politician he is. How he can command the House with just his tone of voice and the movement of his hand. People revere him. Some are intimidated by him. I fucking hate him.

'I apologise to you both that we had to do this, but it was necessary.' His voice is strong, hard and confident and I can't help but listen to his every word. 'Necessary for you to understand exactly what we are dealing with here, and necessary for me to get some assurance that this is where it all stays. Inside this room. As I'm sure you remember, what I alluded to earlier isn't just a joke or a tabloid theory. I am being deadly serious. If you choose to act on what you've seen here tonight – Julianne, I'm talking to you – things will get extremely uncomfortable.'

I stare at him through torn-up eyes, tears and lashes smearing the sides so he looks like he's floating in front of the Christmas tree. 'And this isn't uncomfortable?' I sob at him.

'This is reality. I don't want to get melodramatic, Julianne, but if you go to the police, or your husband over there gets a crisis of conscience, you really don't want to know where that will lead. In the end, it all comes down to how much you love your son.'

I feel myself tremble as he comes towards me and puts his hand on my leg. He pats it, as if comforting me, then, with a single finger, turns my head so I'm facing him. 'Things can so easily go awry, Julianne,' he says quietly, almost in a whisper. 'It would be such a shame if your son were to be unsuccessful in his attempts to get a place at a good university. Of course, when one fails at such an important hurdle in life, it can be hard to live with the setback. Even the strongest of people might start to lose their grip on sanity at that point. Depression is rife among teenagers. And then, who knows, his health might start to suffer. Or he might get hurt.'

I pull my leg closer to me, away from his hand, but he holds on tight. Like he did to Holly. Like he's no doubt done to hundreds of women. 'You don't want to know what would happen if this document were to go live. If his profile was circulated. If people who are particularly interested in a beautiful young lad like him were to receive an update to their current catalogues. A late addition. Higher risk than most, maybe, but still a relatively sound investment.'

His face is now calm, his voice low and slow. He could be reading me a bedtime story. And worst of all, I can tell he's enjoying this.

'Perhaps he might end up somewhere unsafe. Wander into the wrong part of London and find himself with people who are dangerous. Or maybe things won't really get interesting until he gets into university. Not Oxford, of course, but some lesser institution where children are sent by their disappointed parents to coast along with all the other lightweights. What if someone were to slip into his dorm room at night? Or put something in his drink at a bar? Lead him away to somewhere less busy. Somewhere lonely. It's a real risk, Julianne. And James knows this already. We had a little chat while you were out for the count, so to speak.'

I feel bile rising in my throat. I'm paralysed. Can hardly breathe.

'I hear you get all types hanging around abandoned warehouses or factories.' He comes in close, his face near mine as he continues in that terrible half-whisper. 'They'd rape him, Julianne. Violently and without a condom. He'd be shared around, passed from one man to another. They'd make him do things. Terrible things. I can't guarantee they'd always be careful with him. I hear the number of HIV infections is on the rise among young gay men in the UK. It would be so awful if he became one of the thousands a year who contract it. Or hepatitis B. Or maybe an addiction. Bad men carry needles. It only takes a little bit of heroin for him to want more, and more and more. All these things are real issues, Julianne. I'm just concerned for the boy's safety. I'd hate for it to all end in tears. For him to overdose. And his fine young dead body to be, er . . . interfered with.'

I throw up. I can't stop myself. The hot vomit rises quickly and arrives on my lap and on his hand, splashing onto the tablet on the floor.

'Christ,' he mutters as he pulls his hand back, wiping it on the side of the sofa. I stand up as soon as he relinquishes his grip and walk out of the room. I need to get out. I can't stay here. I don't want to set foot in my home ever again. It's not my home. It's a house of horrors – a place where I've been made to imagine the worst things imaginable. And I've had enough. The world spins as I enter the entrance hall.

'Julianne!' I hear one of them shout – I think it's Ernest but I can't be sure.

I don't respond or slow down. I'm running now. Grabbing my keys as I pull open the front door. It's started to snow since I last looked outside and a fine coating greets me on the pavement under my feet. I get in the car and start the ignition, but the windscreen has frozen. I turn on the de-icer then climb out, brushing the excess snow from the car with my bare hands. I barely even feel it sting.

'Julianne!' It's James's voice. I can tell the sound of his voice instantly now. He runs out of the front door and over to me. 'I'm sorry! Please. Please. I've always tried . . . I've always loved . . .'

'Get the fuck away from me!' I scream at him. I hear a front door across the street open. We're causing a scene. People are watching and I don't care. Let them watch.

'Please, I need to talk. I need to explain.'

'Explain! I've just had to listen to your cunt of a best

friend explain what you are. Explain what you've done. And you said nothing. Nothing to defend yourself, nothing to defend your son, nothing to comfort me. You didn't even bother trying.'

He's shaking his head, brushing tears off his cheeks as he sobs. 'I couldn't. I was so scared—'

'Well, join the fucking club,' I snap as I get back into the car and slam the door. The window is still coated with large patches of ice but I don't stop. I reverse out of the tight parking space with a screech and, from the corner of my eye, see him jump out of the way as the car comes close to him. Part of me wishes I'd hit him – run over his feet, broken some bones – but I see him run off.

The car pulls out behind me almost immediately. His car. James is following me. I speed up, turning down a side street, desperate to get away from him. I don't really know where I'm going. The snow is getting heavier and I can barely see through the sparse patches of clear glass that have defrosted. I'm going to my mother's. Away from all of this. Away from the horror my life has become. Although I'm slightly ashamed to admit it, I've never driven from Knightsbridge to Richmond, especially not in conditions like this. I need to use the inbuilt satnav and for that I need my mother's postcode. I swerve round a corner, narrowly missing a lamppost, and feel in my pocket for my phone. By some miracle it's still in my cardigan pocket and I pull it out. This is madness and I know it. I'm barely in control of the car as it is, and then, within a second, the steering wheel is spinning and I can't slow down. With a horrible screeching sound I hit the brakes. The car comes to a stop, but only after I've scraped up against the side of a vehicle parked alongside the pavement. I'm breathing heavily. I should go and check out the damage, but I need a second to get my head straight.

And that's when I hear the bang. A horrendous crash mingled with a crunching, splintering sound. It's happened just behind me.

I get out of the car immediately and turn to face the wreckage. I'm standing in a residential square, mere walking distance from my house, my car parked at the side, houses similar to my own all around me. I see lights come on in windows. Then I see James's car. It's collided with a tree at the side of the snow-laden expanse of grass in the centre. The tree looks broken, its branches arranged strangely, as if it shouldn't be standing upright, with its scraggly arms pressed down onto the car's roof. I don't think about it – I just run automatically, skidding on the icy road as I cross over to the grass and run towards the car.

'Don't go over to it!' A woman's voice from the other side of the square, from one of the houses, shouts over to me. 'It might blow up.'

'It's my husband!' I shout as I reach the front passenger door.

'I've called an ambulance,' the voice shouts back.

I stop dead still, trying to work out what I'm seeing. The windscreen is smashed. Half of it has come away completely from the body of the car. It still has a thick coating of ice and snow. James hadn't had time to defrost it before he'd pulled out. And there he is. Sitting in the driver's seat, a splintered and severed branch of the tree pinning him there. Part of me expects to feel sick again, but I don't. I feel strangely calm. I open the car door and get in, and I see, through the darkness and the snow, which is starting to come in and settle on the dashboard, that the spikes of wood have torn into his neck and chest and part of his stomach. His yellow Oxford shirt is starting to change colour from all the blood, large stains of it growing and spreading. I think he's dead, then suddenly he takes in a loud, rattling gasp of air. It makes me jump.

'Juli . . . .anne . . .' He croaks my name, weakly raising his left hand off the steering wheel. I just stare at it. He's dying. I know it. With an immense effort, I turn to look him in the eye and find that it's right, what they say in books and films and poetry – you really can see the life leaving them.

'Please . . .' he says, managing to get his hand a few inches closer to mine. He wants me to take it. He wants me to hold his hand as he leaves this world. As he leaves me. And I lift my hand, too, and for a second both are suspended in mid-air, none of the fingers touching, both reaching out for the other. And then I pull mine away, and leave his raised in the darkness without anything to take hold of.

'I . . . love . . .' He starts to say the words, but can't finish them. I see the last tear leave his eyes. I look down at his wounds and I can literally see the blood trickling out of him. 'You.'

I don't respond. I wait until the last glimmer of life leaves his face. The orange lamplight makes his skin glow strangely, as if lit from within. Then I brush the snow off my sleeve and get out of the car, closing the door behind me.

EPILOGUE

The car draws up at the house and she gets out of the front seat. She's still beautiful. I hadn't really noticed it when I spoke to her briefly in London last year. Her red-brown hair is still strong in colour, her figure still slim. It's only when she comes closer and taps on the front door that I notice the lines in her face. Age, sure, but I get the sense there's something else there, too. I can tell she's experienced something.

I leave the sitting-room window seat and walk round to let her in. She smiles when she sees me. A nice smile – warm and genuine – and I try to return it, though I'm conscious my expression is stiff and unconvincing. I look quickly at the ground, feeling awkward.

'Hello, Holly,' she says. 'It's good to see you.'

'Hello,' I say, forcing myself to look up and meet her eyes. 'Thanks for coming all this way.'

'I wanted to.' Then, after a few seconds, she says, 'So, can I come in?'

I laugh and she laughs, and the awkwardness, if not entirely gone, is diluted a little while I take her coat and she follows me into the kitchen. She comments what a nice house it is and how she's always rather fancied moving out to the countryside. 'I envy the amazing view you have,' she says, looking out of the kitchen window, over the vast expanse of hills with only the odd white smudge of a building speckling the landscape.

'Have you been to Northern Ireland before?' I ask.

'Never. Nor the Republic. Nor Scotland or Wales. Three decades spent living in the UK, and I've only seen one tiny corner of it. It's mad, I know.'

It takes us a while to get on to the subject that has brought her here. We chat a little about the Irish weather and how she's tired of London and is thinking of moving. Then she finally broaches the subject. 'Stephen, my son. He's in America now. At university. Brown.' I nod, knowing she's not bragging. She's looking serious now and I understand what she's saying.

'Ernest threatened him, didn't he?' I say. 'Is that why you finally decided?'

I see Julianne's eyes start to shine a little. She nods. 'I wanted him out of the country. I don't know how safe

348

he'll be out there. I don't really know what I'm dealing with. I just knew I wanted him away from everything that was going on.' She takes a sip of her tea, looking as if she is trying to choose her words carefully. 'When James died in the car accident last year, Stephen was in the middle of trying to get into Oxford. After all that happened, both he and I decided something different would be best. And I knew I'd want him to be at a distance if I was going to do what . . . what we're doing now.'

I nod. I'd had the same thought, too, when Julianne first made contact and laid out her plan.

'Does your daughter know?' She asks this quietly, mindful of the fact I've skirted around the subject in our emails.

'Yes,' I say, nodding slowly. 'It was . . . it was a difficult conversation. Of course, she's a bit older than your son. I said to her that the last thing I wanted was to put her in danger. She just said if anyone tried to hurt her she'd show them how tough Irish women can be.'

Julianne looks serious. 'And what did you say to that?'

I laugh. 'Well, first and foremost, I reminded her she's technically English. But I also said I'd be more comfortable if she went into hiding. Mind you, then I thought it's probably no use anyway. If they want to find her, they'll find her. Tell you the truth, I've been having mixed thoughts about the whole thing as each day goes by. On some days I've got nerves of steel. I'm determined to beat them. But on the other hand, I don't want to put my little girl in harm's way.

'And her father? Are you still in touch?'

'Yes, he moved over here to be with me and Abigail. Not as a couple. We're not together. Never have been, really. But he's been a bit of a dream, to be honest. He sells ice cream in a little shop in the nearby town. It's not much, but he owns the business and it does well. I think he's just happy to be close to his daughter.'

'He doesn't know? About the rest of it?'

I falter slightly before I speak again. 'I've told him bits. But never the complete story. I've made it quite clear I'd rather not speak of it. It's not possible to forget it, but at the same time I don't think he needs to know all the details. But I suppose I'll have to rethink that position if . . . well, if what we're going to do pays off. I told most of the story of Oxford to Abigail, though. Once I'd made up my mind. She told me if I didn't come forward, she'd go to the press herself. I'm not sure if they'd listen, but she was so determined. She said I needed to do it, not just for myself, but for every woman those men have harmed since that . . . that terrible night.'

Julianne nods, and blows on her tea, allowing me a moment to dab at my eyes with a tissue. Then she says, 'They could be empty threats, you know. Ernest likes to talk about himself in such a grand way. He may be exaggerating.'

I agree with her, but we both know we're playing with fire. Gambling the lives of our most loved, most precious children for the sake of justice. But that's what I think has united us, above everything else. The horror, the shame, the feeling of being wronged: it's reached such an apex now, in both our lives, that we can't continue being victims of the damage it's doing to us. To the damage it's doing to men, women and children across the country, maybe even across the globe.

A minute passes in silence before Julianne speaks again. 'When my nerve wavers – and it does, sometimes – I think to myself, what if it were my son or daughter or sister or someone close to me being offered up to those monsters? And someone had known and done nothing about it? I don't know what I'd do. But I do know I don't want to be that person. The person who does nothing.'

I feel a tear slide down my cheek. I can't help it, though I've tried to fight the compulsion to cry since she stepped through the door. I don't brush it aside. I just let it fall. 'Myanna's good,' I say. 'She really is. I thought, when she had to put the project on pause to work on her ISIS documentary, that my chance had gone and she wouldn't get back in touch. But she kept her promise. And she really knows her stuff.'

I pick up my phone and tap on the web browser icon. Once I've found the page I'm after I pass it to Julianne. 'I wasn't sure if you'd heard of the programme, *Insight*? I expect you googled her before you came.'

'I haven't watched it, but I know of it. It's terrible of me, but I've never watched many current affairs programmes or exposé documentaries.'

She looks down at my phone and scrolls through Myanna's profile on the production company's website.

'It's like a competitor to *Panorama*,' I say. 'Myanna is one of their lead researchers. There's a list on there of the investigations she's covered. She's convinced we've got something. She understands what we're dealing with and thinks we've both got what's needed to bring it out into the open.'

After a few seconds, Julianne passes the phone back to me. I glance at the long list of projects, news stories and incidents Myanna's worked on. I must have read the page a hundred times, but each time I do, the feeling of confidence inside me grows a little more.

Expenses scandal, 2008

News of the World phone-hacking scandal, 2011

Midwives undercover – child deaths at Cherringford Hospital, 2011

East London slaves – unlawful slavery operations in Barking and Dagenham, 2012

'The list is extensive,' Julianne says, sounding impressed. 'And she broke all these stories?'

I shake my head. 'Not all of them. Some she followed up after they'd already gone large. Others she reignited after everyone thought there wasn't anything more to find. I knew she was the right person. There are hundreds of other people like her I could have picked, but for some reason I immediately felt I could trust her. After I'd spoken to her the first time, I knew I didn't want anyone else. I felt she'd have the bravery and strength needed. The courage to fight.'

Julianne's face looks sombre as she nods towards the phone in my hand. 'It was the 2013 one that caught my eye.'

I look down, even though I already know which one she's referring to.

Operation Yewtree.

I look up at Julianne and meet her eye. 'As you can see, she knows what she's dealing with here. She's on our side. And what's more, she knows this is going on. Now I come to think of it, I must have sat through a dozen news reports describing the very thing we're talking about. It's all going to come out at some point. They must know that. And they — the people who have been hurt, the lives that have been destroyed by them — need our help to make that happen.'

She holds my gaze for a few seconds, then smiles. 'Thank you.'

It takes me aback. 'For what?'

'For being so strong. For being brave. For trying to convince me to meet Myanna again. For not letting sleeping dogs lie. That would have been the easy option.'

Something in her phrasing makes me pause before I reply. And then I ask her the question I've been wanting to voice for nearly thirty years. 'Did you know?' I say quietly.

Although I've spoken softly, I can see I've alarmed her. 'About what?'

'What they did to me. That night you held my hand. Did you know what had happened?'

She gets up and goes over to stand by the window. The sunlight starts to stream into the kitchen, turning everything a shining shade of yellow.

'Please,' I say. 'Just tell me. Yes or no.'

She raises a hand to her cheek, perhaps to dab away a tear. 'I'm sorry. I wish I could give you an answer. You deserve one. But it isn't that simple.'

I feel the heat of the sun on my hand as it starts to warm my skin. Some of the tension I've been holding within me since Julianne's first email arrived in my inbox, maybe even since that night in Oxford in 1991, seems to finally be subsiding. Floating away slowly, turning into air before my eyes. Eventually, I look up and see that Julianne has returned to the table. She reaches across and puts her hand over mine.

'Okay,' she says, looking straight at me. I see the resolve in her eyes. 'I'll talk to her. Properly, this time.' She gives me a little nod. 'I'm ready.'

Acknowledgements

Writing this book has been such a rollercoaster and made possible by so many people it's hard to know where to begin. It makes sense to start with my family. After I finished university, my parents generously gave me the space and time to try to pursue writing and have been with me every step of the way. Their continued support has been the best thing in the whole world. Thanks to my sisters, Molly and Amy, for our many fun-filled Siblings Book Club meetings. A total joy.

I'd like to say a massive thank you to my wonderful agent Joanna Swainson at Hardman & Swainson who saw potential in an early draft of my novel and has been amazing through its journey to publication. Huge thanks to my utterly brilliant editor Phoebe Morgan – her tremendous help and support has made the whole process a dream come true. A big thankyou to everyone in the Avon HarperCollins team for welcoming me into such a great family.

I would also like to thank all of the Faber Academy class of Autumn 2016 and author/tutor extraordinaire Rowan Coleman. I don't think I could have done this without her kindness and encouragement. A big thankyou also to all the other authors and people in the world of books who have given me invaluable advice along the way and the courage to keep going, especially Tig Wallace, Ruth Ware, Clare Mackintosh, A.J. Finn, Hannah Bright, Jojo Moyes, Isabelle Broom, David Nicholls, Tineke Mollemans, Erin Kelly, Joseph Knox, Cathy Rentzenbrink and Leigh Bardugo.

A huge thankyou to my dear friend and dream of a 'first tester reader' Rebecca Bedding. One of the very best people in the world. Massive thankyous must go to all first-readers and friends who have been a consistent source of support. Special thanks to Lucy Clayton, Emma Ruttley, Meg Wallace, Thomas Bedding, Corinne Gurr, Alice Johnston, Rachael Bull, George Doel and Timothy Blore.

I would like to thank Will Rycroft and all my colleagues at Waterstones for their support and generous enthusiasm. I will be eternally grateful to them for making it possible for me to juggle being a full time social media person and pursue a writing career.

Last, but not least, I'm always keen to promote the importance of teachers – a group that seems to do one of the toughest jobs for the least amount of praise. I'd like to give thanks to every teacher and educational professional throughout my life who has encouraged creativity and perseverance, especially the staff of the Film Studies department of the University of Southampton, and the English department of The Billericay School.

If you loved
A Version of the Truth,
you will love this . . .

The new thriller
from bestselling author
Claire Allan.

There's a kidnapper
on the loose . . .

The gripping new thriller
from M.J. Ford